The
LONG
DARK
TEA-TIME
OF THE SOUL

DOUGLAS ADAMS

◆

Simon and Schuster

NEW YORK   LONDON   TORONTO   SYDNEY   TOKYO

SIMON AND SCHUSTER
SIMON & SCHUSTER BUILDING
ROCKEFELLER CENTER
1230 AVENUE OF THE AMERICAS
NEW YORK, NEW YORK 10020

ORIGINALLY PUBLISHED IN GREAT BRITAIN BY WILLIAM HEINEMANN
LTD.

SIMON AND SCHUSTER AND COLOPHON ARE REGISTERED TRADE-
MARKS OF SIMON & SCHUSTER INC.
DESIGNED BY MARYBETH KILKELLY/LEVAVI & LEVAVI
MANUFACTURED IN THE UNITED STATES OF AMERICA

1   3   5   7   9   10   8   6   4   2

ISBN 0-671-62583-7

FOR JANE

This book was written and typeset on an Apple Macintosh II and an Apple LaserWriter II NTX. The word-processing software was FullWrite Professional from Ashton Tate. The final proofing and photosetting was done by the Last Word, London SW6.

I would like to say an enormous thank you to my amazing and wonderful editor, Sue Freestone.

Her help, support, criticism, encouragement, enthusiasm and sandwiches have been beyond measure. I also owe thanks and apologies to Sophie, James and Vivian, who saw so little of her during the final weeks of work.

The
LONG
DARK
TEA-TIME
OF THE SOUL

DOUGLAS
ADAMS

•

1

◆

It can hardly be a coincidence that no language on earth
has ever produced the expression "As pretty as an airport."

Airports are ugly. Some are very ugly. Some attain a
degree of ugliness that can only be the result of a special
effort. This ugliness arises because airports are full of
people who are tired, cross, and have just discovered that
their luggage has landed in Murmansk (Murmansk airport
is the only known exception to this otherwise infallible

rule), and architects have on the whole tried to reflect this in their designs.

They have sought to highlight the tiredness and crossness motif with brutal shapes and nerve-jangling colors, to make effortless the business of separating the traveler forever from his or her luggage or loved ones, to confuse the traveler with arrows that appear to point at the windows, distant tie racks, or the current position of Ursa Minor in the night sky, and wherever possible to expose the plumbing on the grounds that it is functional, and conceal the location of the departure gates, presumably on the grounds that they are not.

Caught in the middle of a sea of hazy light and a sea of hazy noise, Kate Schechter stood and doubted.

All the way out of London to Heathrow she had suffered from doubt. She was not a superstitious person, or even a religious person, she was simply someone who was not at all sure she should be flying to Norway. But she was finding it increasingly easy to believe that God, if there was a God, and if it was remotely possible that any godlike being who could order the disposition of particles at the creation of the Universe would also be interested in directing traffic on the M4, did not want her to fly to Norway either. All the trouble with the tickets, finding a next-door neighbor to look after the cat, then finding the cat so it could be looked after by the next-door neighbor, the sudden leak in the roof, the missing wallet, the weather, the unexpected death of the next-door neighbor, the pregnancy of the cat—it all had the semblance of an orchestrated campaign of obstruction which had begun to assume godlike proportions.

Even the taxi driver—when she had eventually found a taxi—had said, "Norway? What you want to go there for?" And when she hadn't instantly said, "The aurora borealis!" or "Fjords!" but had looked doubtful for a moment and bitten her lip, he had said, "I know, I bet it's some bloke dragging you out there. Tell you what, tell him to stuff it. Go to Tenerife."

There was an idea.

Tenerife.

Or even, she dared to think for a fleeting second, home.

She had stared dumbly out of the taxi window at the angry tangles of traffic and thought that however cold and miserable the weather was here, that was nothing to what it would be like in Norway.

Or, indeed, at home. Home would be about as icebound as Norway right now. Icebound, and punctuated with geysers of steam bursting out of the ground, catching in the frigid air and dissipating between the glacial cliff faces of Sixth Avenue.

A quick glance at the itinerary Kate had pursued in the course of her thirty years would reveal her without any doubt to be a New Yorker. For though she had lived in the city very little, most of her life had been spent at a constant distance from it: Los Angeles, San Francisco, Europe, and a period of distracted wandering around South America five years ago following the loss of her newly married husband, Luke, in a New York taxi-hailing accident.

She enjoyed the notion that New York was home, and that she missed it, but in fact the only thing she really missed was pizza. And not just any old pizza, but the sort of pizza they brought to your door if you phoned them up and asked them. That was the only real pizza. Pizza that you had to go out and sit at a table staring at red paper napkins for wasn't real pizza however much extra pepperoni and anchovy they put on it.

London was the place she liked living in most, apart, of

course, from the pizza problem, which drove her crazy. Why would no one deliver pizza? Why did no one understand that it was fundamental to the whole nature of pizza that it arrived at your front door in a hot cardboard box? That you slithered it out of greaseproof paper and ate it in folded slices in front of the TV? What was the fundamental flaw in the stupid, stuck-up, sluggardly English that they couldn't grasp this simple principle? For some odd reason it was the one frustration she could never learn simply to live with and accept, and about once a month or so she would get very depressed, phone a pizza restaurant, order the biggest, most lavish pizza she could describe—pizza with an extra pizza on it, essentially—and then, sweetly, ask them to deliver it.

"To what?"

"Deliver. Let me give you the address—"

"I don't understand. Aren't you going to come and pick it up?"

"No. Aren't you going to deliver? My address—"

"Er, we don't do that, miss."

"Don't do what?"

"Er, deliver."

"You *don't deliver?* Am I *hearing* you correctly?"

The exchange would quickly degenerate into an ugly slanging match which would leave her feeling drained and shaky, but much, much better the following morning. In all other respects she was one of the most sweet-natured people you could hope to meet.

But today was testing her to the limit.

There had been terrible traffic jams on the motorway, and when the distant flash of blue lights made it clear that the cause was an accident somewhere ahead of them Kate had become more tense and had stared fixedly out of the other window as eventually they had crawled past it.

The taxi driver had been bad-tempered when at last he had dropped her off because she didn't have the right money, and there was a lot of disgruntled hunting through tight trouser pockets before he was eventually able to find change for her. The atmosphere was heavy and thundery, and now, standing in the middle of the main check-in concourse at Terminal Two, Heathrow Airport, she could not find the check-in desk for her flight to Oslo.

She stood very still for a moment, breathing calmly and deeply and trying not to think of Jean-Philippe.

Jean-Philippe was, as the taxi driver had correctly guessed, the reason why she was going to Norway, but was also the reason why she was convinced that Norway was not at all a good place for her to go. Thinking of him therefore made her head oscillate and it seemed best not to think about him at all but simply to go to Norway as if that was where she happened to be going anyway. She would then be terribly surprised to bump into him at whatever hotel it was he had written on the card that was tucked into the side pocket of her handbag.

In fact she would be surprised to find him there anyway. What she would be much more likely to find was a message from him saying that he had been unexpectedly called away to Guatemala, Seoul or Tenerife and that he would call her from there. Jean-Philippe was the most continually absent person she had ever met. In this he was the culmination of a series. Since she had lost Luke to the great yellow Chevrolet she had been oddly dependent on the rather vacant emotions that a succession of self-absorbed men had inspired in her.

She tried to shut all this out of her mind, and even shut her eyes for a second. She wished that when she opened them again there would be a sign in front of her saying, "This way for Norway," which she could simply follow without needing to think about it or anything else ever again. This, she reflected, in a continuation of her earlier train of thought, was presumably how religions got started, and must be the reason why so many sects hang around airports looking for converts. They know that people there are at their most vulnerable and perplexed, and ready to accept any kind of guidance.

Kate opened her eyes again and was, of course, disappointed. But then a second or two later there was a momentary parting in a long surging wave of cross Germans in inexplicable yellow polo shirts, and through it she had a brief glimpse of the check-in desk for Oslo. Lugging her garment bag onto her shoulder, she made her way toward it.

There was just one other person before her in the line at the desk and he, it turned out, was having trouble or perhaps making it.

He was a large man, impressively large and well-built —even expertly built—but he was also definitely odd-looking in a way that Kate couldn't quite deal with. She couldn't even say what it was that was odd about him, only that she was immediately inclined not to include him on her list of things to think about at the moment. She remembered reading an article which had explained that the central processing unit of the human brain had only seven memory registers, which meant that if you had seven things in your mind at the same time and then thought of something else, one of the other seven would instantly drop out.

In quick succession she thought about whether or not she was likely to catch the plane, about whether it was just her imagination that the day was a particularly bloody one, about airline staff who smile charmingly and are breathtakingly rude, about duty-free shops which are able to charge much lower prices than ordinary shops but —mysteriously—don't, about whether or not she felt a magazine article about airports coming on which might help pay for the trip, about whether her garment bag would hurt less on her other shoulder, and finally, in spite of all her intentions to the contrary, about Jean-Philippe, who was another set of at least seven subtopics all to himself.

The man standing arguing in front of her popped right out of her mind.

It was only the announcement on the airport loud-speaker of the last call for her flight to Oslo which forced her attention back to the situation in front of her.

The large man was making trouble about the fact that he hadn't been given a first class seat reservation. It had just transpired that the reason for this was that he didn't in fact have a first class ticket.

Kate's spirits sank to the very bottom of her being and began to prowl around there making a low growling noise.

It now transpired that the man in front of her didn't actually have a ticket at all, and the argument then began to range freely and angrily over such topics as the physical appearance of the airline check-in girl, her qualities as a person, theories about her ancestors, speculations as to what surprises the future might have in store for her and the airline for which she worked, and finally lit by chance on the happy subject of the man's credit card.

He didn't have one.

Further discussions ensued, having to do with checks and why the airline did not accept them.

Kate took a long, slow, murderous look at her watch.

"Excuse me," she said, interrupting the transactions. "Is this going to take long? I have to catch the Oslo flight."

"I'm just dealing with this gentleman," said the girl. "I'll be with you in just one second."

Kate nodded, and politely allowed just one second to go by.

"It's just that the flight's about to leave," she said then. "I have one bag, I have my ticket, I have a reservation. It'll take about thirty seconds. I hate to interrupt, but I'd hate even more to miss my flight for the sake of thirty seconds. That's thirty actual seconds, not thirty 'just one' seconds, which could keep us here all night."

The check-in girl turned the full glare of her lip gloss on to Kate, but before she could speak, the large blond man looked around, and the effect of his face was a little disconcerting.

"I, too," he said in a slow, angry Nordic voice, "wish to fly to Oslo."

Kate stared at him. He looked thoroughly out of place in an airport, or rather, the airport looked thoroughly out of place around him.

"Well," she said, "the way we're stacked up at the moment it looks like neither of us is going to make it. Can we just sort this one out? What's the holdup?"

The check-in girl smiled her charming, dead smile and said, "The airline does not accept checks, as a matter of company policy."

"Well, I do," said Kate, slapping down her own credit card. "Charge the gentleman's ticket to this, and I'll take a check from him.

"OK?" she added to the big man, who was looking at her with slow surprise. His eyes were large and blue and conveyed the impression that they had looked at a lot of glaciers in their time. They were extraordinarily arrogant and also muddled.

"OK?" she repeated briskly. "My name is Kate Schechter. Two 'c's, two 'h's, two 'e's and also a 't,' an 'r' and an 's.' Provided they're all there, the bank won't be fussy about the order they come in. They never seem to know themselves."

The man very slowly inclined his head a little toward her in a rough bow of acknowledgement. He thanked her for her kindness, courtesy and some Norwegian word that was lost on her, said that it was a long while since he had encountered anything of the kind, that she was a woman of spirit and some other Norwegian word, and that he was indebted to her. He also added, as an after-thought, that he had no checkbook.

"Right!" said Kate, determined not to be deflected from her course. She fished in her handbag for a piece of paper, took a pen from the check-in counter, scribbled on the paper and thrust it at him.

"That's my address," she said. "Send me the money. Hock your fur coat if you have to. Just send it to me. OK? I'm taking a flyer on trusting you."

The big man took the scrap of paper, read the few words on it with immense slowness, then folded it with elaborate care and put it into the pocket of his coat. Again he bowed to her very slightly.

Kate suddenly realized that the check-in girl was silently waiting for her pen back to fill in the credit-card form. She pushed it back at her in annoyance, handed over her own ticket and imposed on herself an icy calm.

The airport loudspeaker announced the departure of their flight.

"May I see your passports, please?" said the girl unhurriedly.

Kate handed hers over, but the big man didn't have one.

"You *what?*" exclaimed Kate. The airline girl simply

stopped moving at all and stared quietly at a random point on her desk waiting for someone else to make a move. It wasn't her problem.

The man repeated angrily that he didn't have a passport. He shouted it and banged his fist on the counter so hard that it was slightly dented by the force of the blow.

Kate picked up her ticket, her passport and her credit card and hoisted her garment bag back onto her shoulder.

"This is where I get off," she said, and simply walked away. She felt that she had made every effort a human being could possibly be expected to make to catch her plane, but that it was not to be. She would send a message to Jean-Philippe saying that she could not be there, and it would probably sit in a slot next to his message to her saying why he could not be there either. For once they would be equally absent.

For the time being she would go and cool off. She set off in search of first a newspaper and then some coffee, and by dint of following the appropriate signs was unable to locate either. She was then unable to find a working phone from which to send a message, and decided to give up on the airport altogether. Just get out, she told herself, find a taxi, and go back home.

She threaded her way back across the check-in concourse, and had almost made it to the exit when she happened to glance back at the check-in desk that had defeated her, and was just in time to see it shoot up through the roof engulfed in a ball of orange flame.

As she lay beneath a pile of rubble, in pain, darkness, and choking dust, trying to find sensation in her limbs, she was at least relieved to be able to think that she hadn't merely been imagining that this was a bad day. So thinking, she passed out.

2

♦

The usual people tried to claim responsibility.

First the IRA, then the PLO and the Gas Board. Even British Nuclear Fuels rushed out a statement to the effect that the situation was completely under control, that it was a one in a million chance, that there was hardly any radioactive leakage at all, and that the site of the explosion would make a nice location for a day out with the kids and a picnic, before finally having to admit that it wasn't actually anything to do with them at all.

No cause could be found for the explosion.

It seemed to have happened spontaneously and of its own free will. Explanations were advanced, but most of these were simply phrases which restated the problem in different words, along the same principles which had given the world "metal fatigue." In fact, a very similar phrase was invented to account for the sudden transition of wood, metal, plastic and concrete into an explosive condition, which was "nonlinear, catastrophic structural exasperation," or to put it another way—as a junior cabinet minister did on television the following night in a phrase which was to haunt the rest of his career—the check-in desk had just got "fundamentally fed up with being where it was."

As in all such disastrous events, estimates of the casualties varied wildly. They started at forty-seven dead, eighty-nine seriously injured, went up to sixty-three dead, a hundred and thirty injured, and rose as high as one hundred and seventeen dead before the figures started to be revised downward once more. The final figures revealed that once all the people who could be accounted for had been accounted for, in fact no one had been killed at all. A small number of people were in hospital suffering from cuts and bruises and varying degrees of traumatized shock, but that, unless anyone had any information about anybody actually being missing, was that.

This was yet another inexplicable aspect to the whole affair. The force of the explosion had been enough to reduce a large part of the front of Terminal Two to rubble, and yet everyone inside the building had somehow either fallen very luckily or been shielded from one piece of falling masonry by another, or had the shock of the explosion absorbed by their luggage. All in all, very little luggage had survived at all. There were questions asked in Parliament about this, but not very interesting ones.

It was a couple of days before Kate Schechter became aware of any of these things, or indeed of anything at all in the outside world.

She passed the time quietly in a world of her own in which she was surrounded as far as the eye could see with old cabin trunks full of past memories in which she rummaged with great curiosity, and sometimes bewilderment. Or, at least, about a tenth of the cabin trunks were full of vivid and often painful or uncomfortable memories of her past life; the other nine tenths were full of penguins, which surprised her. Insofar as she recognized at all that she was dreaming, she realized that she must be exploring her own subconscious mind. She had heard it said that humans are supposed only to use about a tenth of their brains, and that no one was very clear what the other nine tenths were for, but she had certainly never heard it suggested that they were used for storing penguins.

Gradually the trunks, the memories and the penguins began to grow indistinct, to become all white and swimmy, then to become like walls that were all white and swimmy, and finally to become walls that were merely white, or rather a yellowish, greenish kind of off-white, and to enclose her in a small room.

The room was in semi-darkness. A bedside light was on but turned down low, and the light from a streetlamp found its way between the gray curtains and threw sodium patterns on the opposite wall. She became dimly aware of the shadowed shape of her own body lying under the white, turned-down sheet and the pale, neat blankets. She stared at it for a nervous while, checking that it looked right before she tried, tentatively, to move any part of it. She tried her right hand, and that seemed to be fine. A little stiff and aching, but the fingers all responded, and all seemed to be of the right length and thickness, and to bend in the right places and in the right directions.

She panicked briefly when she couldn't immediately locate her left hand, but then she found it lying across her stomach and nagging at her in some odd way. It took her a second or two of concentration to put together a number of rather disturbing feelings and to realize that there was a needle bandaged into her arm. This shook her quite badly. From the needle there snaked a long thin transparent pipe that glistened yellowly in the light from the streetlamp and hung in a gentle curl from a thick plastic bag suspended from a tall metal stand. An array of horrors briefly assailed her in respect of this apparatus, but she peered dimly at the bag and saw the words "Dextro-Saline." She made herself calm down again and lay quietly for a few moments before continuing her exploration.

Her rib cage seemed undamaged—bruised and tender, but there was no sharper pain anywhere to suggest that anything was broken. Her hips and thighs ached and were stiff, but revealed no serious hurt. She flexed the muscles down her right leg and then her left. She rather fancied that her left ankle was sprained.

In other words, she told herself, she was perfectly all right. So what was she doing here in what she could tell from the septic color of the paint was clearly a hospital?

She sat up impatiently, and immediately rejoined the penguins for an entertaining few minutes.

The next time she came around she treated herself with a little more care and lay quietly, feeling gently nauseous.

She poked gingerly at her memory of what had happened. It was dark and blotchy and came at her in sick, greasy waves like the North Sea. Lumpy things jumbled themselves out of it and slowly arranged themselves into a heaving airport. The airport was sour and ached in her head, and in the middle of it, pulsing like a migraine, was the memory of a moment's whirling splurge of light.

It became suddenly very clear to her that the check-in concourse of Terminal Two at Heathrow Airport had been hit by a meteorite. Silhouetted in the flare was the fur-coated figure of a big man who must have caught the full force of it and been reduced instantly to a cloud of atoms that were free to go as they pleased. The thought caused a deep and horrid shudder to go through her. He had been infuriating and arrogant, but she had liked him in an odd way. There had been something oddly noble in his per-verse bloody-mindedness. Or maybe, she realized, she liked to think that such perverse bloody-mindedness was noble because it reminded her of herself trying to order pizza to be delivered in an alien, hostile and non-pizza-delivering world. Nobleness was one word for making a fuss about the trivial inevitabilities of life, but there were others.

She felt a sudden surge of fear and loneliness, but it quickly ebbed away and left her feeling much more com-posed, relaxed, and wanting to go to the lavatory.

According to her watch it was shortly after three o'clock, and according to everything else it was nighttime. She should probably call a nurse and let the world know she had come around. There was a window in the side wall of the room through which she could see a dim corri-dor in which stood a stretcher trolley and a tall black oxygen bottle, but which was otherwise empty. Things were very quiet out there.

Peering around her in the small room she saw a white-painted plywood cupboard, a couple of tubular steel-and-vinyl chairs lurking quietly in the shadows, and a white-painted plywood bedside cabinet which supported a small bowl with a single banana in it. On the other side of the bed stood her drip stand. Set into the wall on that side of the bed was a metal plate with a couple of black knobs and a set of old Bakelite headphones hanging from it, and wound around the tubular side pillar of the bed head was a cable with a bell push attached to it, which she fingered, and then decided not to push.

She was fine. She could find her own way about.

Slowly, a little woozily, she pushed herself up on to her elbows, and slid her legs out from under the sheets and onto the floor, which was cold to her feet. She could tell almost immediately that she shouldn't be doing this because every part of her feet was sending back streams of messages telling her exactly what every tiniest bit of the floor that they touched felt like, as if it was a strange and worrying thing the like of which they had never encountered before. Nevertheless she sat on the edge of the bed and made her feet accept the floor as something they were just going to have to get used to.

The hospital had put her into a large, baggy, striped thing. It wasn't merely baggy, she decided on examining it more closely, it actually was a bag. A bag of loose blue and white striped cotton. It opened up the back and let in chilly night draughts. Perfunctory sleeves flopped half-way down her arms. She moved her arms around in the light, examining the skin, rubbing it and pinching it, especially around the bandage which held her drip needle in place. Normally her arms were lithe and the skin was firm and supple. Tonight, however, they looked like bits of chickens. Briefly she smoothed each forearm with her other hand, and then looked up again, purposefully.

She reached out and gripped the drip stand and, because it wobbled slightly less than she did, she was able to use it to pull herself slowly to her feet. She stood there, her tall, slim figure trembling, and after a few seconds she held the drip stand away at a bent arm's length, like a shepherd holding a crook.

She had not made it to Norway, but she was at least standing up.

The drip stand rolled on four small and independently perverse wheels which behaved like four screaming children in a supermarket, but nevertheless Kate was able to propel it to the door ahead of her. Walking increased her sense of wooziness, but also increased her resolve not to give in to it. She reached the door, opened it, and, pushing the drip stand out ahead of her, looked out into the corridor.

To her left the corridor ended in a couple of swing doors with circular porthole windows, which seemed to lead into a larger area, an open ward perhaps. To her right a number of smaller doors opened off the corridor as it continued on for a short distance before turning a sharp corner. One of those doors would probably be the lavatory. The others? Well, she would find out as she looked for the lavatory.

The first two were cupboards. The third was slightly bigger and had a chair in it and therefore probably counted as a room, since most people don't like to sit in cupboards, even nurses, who have to do a lot of things that most people wouldn't like to. It also had a stack of Styrofoam beakers, a lot of semi-congealed coffee creamer and an elderly coffee maker, all sitting on top of a small table together and seeping grimly over a copy of the *Evening Standard*.

Kate picked up the dark, damp paper and tried to reconstruct some of her missing days from it. However, what with her own wobbly condition making it difficult to read, and the droopily stuck-together condition of the newspaper, she was able to glean little more than the fact that no one could really say for certain what had happened. It seemed that no one had been seriously hurt, but that an employee of one of the airlines was still unaccounted for. The incident had now been officially classified as an "Act of God."

"Nice one, God," thought Kate. She put down the remains of the paper and closed the door behind her.

The next door she tried was another small side ward like her own. There was a bedside table and a single banana in the fruit bowl.

The bed was clearly occupied. She pulled the door to quickly, but she did not pull it quickly enough. Unfortunately, something odd had caught her attention, but although she had noticed it, she could not immediately say what it was. She stood there with the door half closed, staring at the floor, knowing that she should not look again, and knowing that she would.

Carefully she eased the door back open again.

The room was darkly shadowed and chilly. The chilliness did not give her a good feeling about the occupant of the bed. She listened. The silence didn't sound too good either. It wasn't the silence of healthy deep sleep, it was the silence of nothing but a little distant traffic noise.

She hesitated for a long while, silhouetted in the doorway, looking and listening. She wondered about the sheer bulk of the occupant of the bed and how cold he was with just a thin blanket pulled over him. Next to the bed was a small tubular-legged vinyl bucket chair which was rather overwhelmed by the huge and heavy fur coat draped over it, and Kate thought that the coat should more properly be draped over the bed and its cold occupant.

At last, walking as softly and cautiously as she could, she moved into the room and over to the bed. She stood looking down at the face of the big Nordic man. Though cold, and though his eyes were shut, his face was frowning slightly as if he was still rather worried about something. This struck Kate as being almost infinitely sad. In life the man had had the air of someone who was beset by huge, if somewhat puzzling, difficulties, and the appearance that he had almost immediately found things beyond this life that were a bother to him as well was miserable to contemplate.

She was astonished that he appeared to be so unscathed. His skin was totally unmarked. It was rugged and healthy—or rather had been healthy until very recently. Closer inspection showed a network of fine lines which suggested that he was older than the mid-thirties she had originally assumed. He could even have been a very fit and healthy man in his late forties.

Standing against the wall, by the door, was something unexpected. It was a large Coca-Cola vending machine. It didn't look as if it had been installed there: it wasn't plugged in and it had a small neat sticker on it explaining that it was temporarily out of order. It looked as if it had simply been left there inadvertently by someone who was probably even now walking around wondering which room he had left it in. Its large red-and-white wavy panel stared glassily into the room and did not explain itself. The only thing the machine communicated to the outside world was that there was a slot into which coins of a variety of denominations might be inserted, and an aperture to which a variety of different cans would be delivered if the machine was working, which it was not. There was also an old sledgehammer leaning against it, which was, in its own way, odd.

Faintness began to creep over Kate, the room began to develop a slight spin, and there was some restless rustling in the cabin trunks of her mind.

Then she realized that the rustling wasn't simply her imagination. There was a distinct noise in the room—a heavy, beating, scratching noise, a muffled fluttering. The noise rose and fell like the wind, but in her dazed and woozy state, Kate could not at first tell where the noise was coming from. At last her gaze fell on the curtains. She stared at them with the worried frown of a drunk trying to work out why the door is dancing. The sound was coming from the curtains. She walked uncertainly toward them and pulled them apart. A huge eagle with circles tattooed on its wings was clattering and beating against the window, staring in with great yellow eyes and pecking wildly at the glass.

Kate staggered back, turned and tried to heave herself out of the room. At the end of the corridor the porthole doors swung open and two figures came through them. Hands rushed toward her as she became hopelessly entangled in the drip stand and began slowly to spin toward the floor.

She was unconscious as they carefully laid her back in her bed. She was unconscious half an hour later when a disturbingly short figure in a worryingly long white doctor's coat arrived, wheeled the big man away on a stretcher trolley and then returned after a few minutes for the Coca-Cola machine.

She woke a few hours later with a wintry sun seeping through the window. The day looked very quiet and ordinary, but Kate was still shaking.

3

◆

The same sun later broke in through the upper windows of a house in North London and struck the peacefully sleeping figure of a man.

The room in which he slept was large and bedraggled and did not much benefit from the sudden intrusion of light. The sun crept slowly across the bedclothes, as if nervous of what it might find among them, slunk down the side of the bed, moved in a rather startled way across some objects it encountered on the floor, toyed nervously with a couple of motes of dust, lit briefly on a stuffed fruit bat hanging in the corner, and fled.

This was about as big an appearance as the sun ever put in here, and it lasted for about an hour or so, during which time the sleeping figure scarcely stirred.

At eleven o'clock the phone rang, and still the figure did not respond, any more than it had responded when the phone had rung at twenty-five to seven in the morning, again at twenty to seven, again at ten to seven, and again for ten minutes continuously starting at five to seven, after which it had settled into a long and significant silence, disturbed only by the braying of police sirens in a nearby street at around nine o'clock, the delivery of a large eighteenth-century dual manual harpsichord at around nine fifteen, and the collection of same by bailiffs at a little after ten. This was a not uncommon sort of occurrence—the people concerned were accustomed to finding the key under the doormat, and the man in the bed was accustomed to sleeping through it. You would probably not say that he was sleeping the sleep of the just, unless you meant the just asleep, but it was certainly the sleep of someone who was not fooling about when he climbed into bed of a night and turned off the light.

The room was not a room to elevate the soul. Louis XIV, to pick a name at random, would not have liked it, would have found it not sunny enough, and insufficiently full of mirrors. He would have desired someone to pick up the socks, put the records away, and maybe burn the place down. Michelangelo would have been distressed by its proportions, which were neither lofty nor shaped by any noticeable inner harmony or symmetry, other than that all parts of the room were pretty much equally full of old coffee mugs, shoes and brimming ashtrays, most of which were now sharing their tasks with each other. The walls were painted in almost precisely that shade of green which Raffaello Sanzio would have bitten off his own right hand at the wrist rather than use, and Hercules, on seeing the room, would probably have returned half an hour later armed with a navigable river. It was, in short, a dump, and was likely to remain so for as long as it remained in the custody of Mr. Svlad, or "Dirk," Gently, né Cjelli.

At last Gently stirred.

The sheets and blankets were pulled up tightly around his head, but from somewhere halfway down the length of the bed a hand slowly emerged from under the bedclothes and its fingers felt their way in little tapping movements along the floor. Working from experience, they neatly circumvented a bowl of something very nasty that had been sitting there since Michaelmas, and eventually happened upon a half-empty pack of untipped Gauloises and a box of matches. The fingers shook a crumpled white tube free of the pack, seized it and the box of matches, and then started to poke a way through the sheets tangled together at the top of the bed, like a magician prodding at a handkerchief from which he intends to release a flock of doves.

The cigarette was at last inserted into the hole. The cigarette was lit. For a while the bed itself appeared to be smoking the cigarette in great heaving drags. It coughed long, loud and shudderingly and then began at last to breathe in a more measured rhythm. In this way, Dirk Gently achieved consciousness.

He lay there for a while feeling a terrible sense of worry and guilt about something weighing on his shoulders. He wished he could forget about it, and promptly did. He levered himself out of bed and a few minutes later padded downstairs.

The mail on the doormat consisted of the usual things: a rude letter threatening to take away his American Express card, an invitation to apply for an American Express card, and a few bills of the more hysterical and unrealistic type. He couldn't understand why they kept sending them. The cost of the postage seemed merely to be good money thrown after bad. He shook his head in wonderment at the malevolent incompetence of the world, threw the mail away, entered the kitchen and approached the fridge with caution.

It stood in the corner.

The kitchen was large and shrouded in a deep gloom that was not relieved, only turned yellow, by the action of switching on the light. Dirk squatted down in front of the fridge and carefully examined the edge of the door. He found what he was looking for. In fact he found more than he was looking for.

Near the bottom of the door, across the narrow gap that separated the door from the main body of the fridge, which held the strip of gray insulating rubber, lay a single human hair. It was stuck there with dried saliva. That he had expected. He had stuck it there himself three days earlier and had checked it on several occasions since then. What he had not expected to find was a second hair.

He frowned at it in alarm. A *second* hair?

It was stuck across the gap in the same way as the first one, only this hair was near the top of the fridge door, and he had not put it there. He peered at it closely, and even went so far as to go and open the old shutters on the kitchen windows to let some extra light in upon the scene.

The daylight shouldered its way in like a squad of policemen and did a lot of *what's-all-this*ing around the room, which, like the bedroom, would have presented anyone of an aesthetic disposition with difficulties. Like most of the rooms in Dirk's house it was large, looming and utterly disheveled. It simply sneered at anyone's attempts to tidy it, sneered at them and brushed them aside like one of the small pile of dead and disheartened flies that lay beneath the window, on top of a pile of old pizza boxes.

The light revealed the second hair for what it was—gray at the root, the rest dyed a vivid metallic orange. Dirk pursed his lips and thought very deeply. He didn't need to think hard in order to realize who the hair belonged to—there was only one person who regularly entered the kitchen looking as if her head had been used for extracting metal oxides from industrial waste—but he did have seriously to consider the implications of the discovery that she had been plastering her hair across the door of his fridge.

It meant that the silently waged conflict between himself and his cleaning lady had escalated to a new and more frightening level. It was now, Dirk reckoned, fully three months since this fridge door had been opened, and each of them was grimly determined not to be the one to open it first. The fridge no longer merely stood there in the corner of the kitchen, it actually lurked. Dirk could quite clearly remember the day on which the thing had started lurking. It was about a week ago, when Dirk had tried a simple subterfuge to trick Elena—the old bat's name was Elena, pronounced to rhyme with "cleaner," which was an irony that Dirk now no longer relished—into opening the fridge door. The subterfuge had been deftly deflected and had nearly rebounded horribly on Dirk.

He had resorted to the strategy of going to the local

mini-market to buy a few simple groceries. Nothing con-
tentious—a little milk, some eggs, some bacon, a carton
or two of chocolate custard and a simple half-pound of
butter. He had left them, innocently, on top of the fridge
as if to say, "Oh, when you have a moment, perhaps you
could pop these inside . . . "

When he had returned that evening his heart bounded
to see that they were no longer on top of the fridge. They
were gone! They had not been merely moved aside or put
on a shelf, they were nowhere to be seen. She must finally
have capitulated and put them away. In the fridge. And
she would surely have cleaned it out once it was actually
open. For the first and only time his heart swelled with
warmth and gratitude toward her, and he was about to
fling open the door of the thing in relief and triumph when
an eighth sense (at the last count, Dirk reckoned he had
eleven) warned him to be very, very careful, and to consider first where Elena might have put the cleared-out
contents of the fridge.

A nameless doubt gnawed at his mind as he moved
noiselessly toward the garbage bin beneath the sink.
Holding his breath, he opened the lid and looked.

There, nestling in the folds of the fresh black bin liner,
were his eggs, his bacon, his chocolate custard and his
simple half-pound of butter. Two milk bottles stood rinsed
and neatly lined up by the sink into which their contents
had presumably been poured.

She had thrown it away. Rather than open the fridge
door, she had thrown his food away.

He looked around slowly at the grimy, squat white
monolith, and that was the exact moment at which he
realized without a shadow of a doubt that his fridge had
now begun seriously to lurk.

He made himself a stiff black coffee and sat, slightly

trembling. He had not even looked directly at the sink, but he knew that he must unconsciously have noticed the two clean milk bottles there, and some busy part of his mind had been alarmed by them.

The next day he had explained all this away to himself. He was becoming needlessly paranoiac. It had surely been an innocent or careless mistake on Elena's part. She had probably been brooding distractedly on her son's attack of bronchitis, peevishness or homosexuality or whatever it was that regularly prevented her from either turning up or from having a noticeable effect when she did. She was Italian and probably had absentmindedly mistaken his food for garbage.

But the business with the hair changed all that. It established beyond all possible doubt that she knew exactly what she was doing. She was under no circumstances going to open the fridge door until he opened it first, and he was under no circumstances going to open the fridge until she did.

Obviously she had not noticed his hair, otherwise it would have been her most effective course simply to pull it off, thus tricking him into thinking she had opened the fridge. He should presumably now remove her hair in the hope of pulling that same trick on her, but even as he sat there he knew that somehow that wouldn't work, and that they were locked into a tightening spiral of non-fridge-opening that would lead them both to madness or perdition.

He wondered if he could hire someone to come and open the fridge.

No. He was not in a position to hire anybody to do anything. He was not even in a position to pay Elena for the last three weeks. The only reason he didn't ask her to leave was that sacking somebody inevitably involved paying them off, and this he was in no position to do. His secretary had finally left him on her own initiative and gone off to do something reprehensible in the travel business. Dirk had attempted to cast scorn on her preferring monotony of pay over—

"*Regularity* of pay," she had calmly corrected him.

—over job satisfaction.

She had nearly said, "Over *what?*," but at that moment she realized that if she said that she would have to listen to his reply, which would be bound to infuriate her into arguing back. It occurred to her for the first time that the only way of escaping was just not to get drawn into these arguments. If she simply did not respond this time, then she was free to leave. She tried it. She felt a sudden freedom. She left. A week later, in much the same mood, she married an airline cabin steward called Smith.

Dirk had kicked her desk over, and then had to pick it up himself later when she didn't come back.

The detective business was currently as brisk as the tomb. Nobody, it seemed, wished to have anything detected. He had recently, to make ends meet, taken up doing palmistry in drag on Thursday evenings, but he wasn't comfortable with it. He could have withstood it— the hateful, abject humiliation of it all was something to which he had, in different ways, now become accustomed, and he was quite anonymous in his little tent in the back garden of the pub—he could have withstood it all if he hadn't been so horribly, excruciatingly good at it. It made him break out in a sweat of self-loathing. He tried by every means to cheat, to fake, to be deliberately and cynically bad, but whatever fakery he tried to introduce always failed, and he invariably ended up being right.

His worst moment had come about as a result of the poor woman from Oxfordshire who had come in to see him one evening. Being in something of a waggish mood, he had suggested that she should keep an eye on her husband, who, judging by her marriage line, looked to be a bit of a flighty type. It transpired that her husband was in fact a fighter pilot, and that his plane had been lost in an exercise over the North Sea only a fortnight earlier.

Dirk had been flustered by this and had soothed meaninglessly at her. He was certain, he said, that her husband would be restored to her in the fullness of time, that all would be well, and that all manner of things would be well and so on. The woman said that she thought this was not very likely, seeing as the world record for staying alive in the North Sea was rather less than an hour, and since no trace of her husband had been found in two weeks it seemed fanciful to imagine that he was anything other than stone dead, and she was trying to get used to the idea, thank you very much. She said it rather tartly.

Dirk lost all control at this point and started to babble.

He said that it was very clear from reading her hands that the great sum of money she had coming to her would be no consolation to her for the loss of her dear, dear husband, but that at least it might comfort her to know that he had gone on to that great something or other in the sky, that he was floating on the fleeciest of white clouds, looking very handsome in his new set of wings, and that he was terribly sorry to be talking such appalling drivel but she had caught him rather by surprise. Would she care for some tea, or some vodka, or some soup?

The woman demurred. She said she had only wandered into the tent by accident, she had been looking for the lavatories, and what was that about the money?

"Complete gibberish," Dirk had explained. He was in great difficulties, what with having the falsetto to keep up. "I was making it up as I went along," he said. "Please allow me to tender my most profound apologies for intruding so clumsily on your private grief, and to escort you to, er, or rather, direct you to the, well, what I can only in the circumstances call the lavatory, which is out of the tent and on the left."

Dirk had been cast down by this encounter, but was then utterly horrified a few days later when he discovered that the very following morning the unfortunate woman had learned that she had won £250,000 on the Premium Bonds. He spent several hours that night standing on the roof of his house, shaking his fist at the dark sky and shouting, "Stop it!" until a neighbor complained to the police that he couldn't sleep. The police had come round in a screaming squad car and woken up the rest of the neighborhood as well.

Today, this morning, Dirk sat in his kitchen and stared dejectedly at his fridge. The bloody-minded ebullience which he usually relied on to carry him through the day had been knocked out of him in its very opening moments by the business with the fridge. His will sat imprisoned in it, locked up by a single hair.

What he needed, he thought, was a client. Please, God, he thought, if there is a god, any god, bring me a client. Just a simple client, the simpler the better. Credulous and rich. Someone like that chap yesterday. He tapped his fingers on the table.

The problem was that the more credulous the client, the more Dirk fell foul at the end of his own better nature, which was constantly rearing up and embarrassing him at the most inopportune moments. Dirk frequently threatened to hurl his better nature to the ground and kneel on its windpipe, but it usually managed to get the better of him by dressing itself up as guilt and self-loathing, in which guise it could throw him right out of the ring.

Credulous and rich. Just so that he could pay off some, perhaps even just one, of the more prominent and sensational bills. He lit a cigarette. The smoke curled upward in the morning light and attached itself to the ceiling.

Like that chap yesterday . . .

He paused.

The chap yesterday . . .

The world held its breath.

Quietly and gently there settled on him the knowledge that something, somewhere, was ghastly. Something was terribly wrong.

There was a disaster hanging silently in the air around him waiting for him to notice it. His knees tingled.

What he needed, he had been thinking, was a client. He had been thinking that as a matter of habit. It was what he always thought at this time of the morning. What he had forgotten was that he had one.

He stared wildly at his watch. Nearly eleven-thirty. He shook his head to try and clear the silent ringing between his ears, then made a hysterical lunge for his hat and his great leather coat that hung behind the door.

Fifteen seconds later he left the house, five hours late but moving fast.

4

◆

Aminute or two later Dirk paused to consider his best strategy. Rather than arriving five hours late and flustered, it would be better all around if he were to arrive five hours and a few extra minutes late, but triumphantly in command.

"Pray God I am not too soon!" would be a good opening line as he swept in, but it needed a good follow-through as well, and he wasn't sure what it should be.

Perhaps it would save time if he went back to get his car, but then again it was only a short distance, and he

had a tremendous propensity for getting lost when driving. This was largely because of his "Zen" method of navigation, which was simply to find any car that looked as if
it knew where it was going and follow it. The results were
more often surprising than successful, but he felt it was
worth it for the sake of the few occasions when it was
both.

Furthermore he was not at all certain that his car was
working.

It was an elderly Jaguar, built at that very special time
in the company's history when they were making cars
which had to stop for repairs more often than they needed
to stop for petrol, and frequently needed to rest for
months between outings. He was, however, certain, now
that he came to think about it, that the car didn't have
any petrol, and furthermore he did not have any cash or
valid plastic to enable him to fill it up.

He abandoned that line of thought as wholly fruitless.

He stopped to buy a newspaper while he thought things
over. The clock in the newsagent's said eleven thirty-five.
Damn, damn, damn. He toyed with the idea of simply
dropping the case. Just walking away and forgetting
about it. Having some lunch. The whole thing was fraught
with difficulties in any event. Or rather it was fraught
with one particular difficulty, which was that of keeping a
straight face. The whole thing was complete and utter
nonsense. The client was clearly loopy, and Dirk would
not have considered taking the case except for one very
important thing.

Three hundred pounds a day plus expenses.

The client had agreed to it just like that. And when
Dirk had started his usual speech to the effect that his
methods, involving as they did the fundamental interconnectedness of all things, often led to expenses that might

appear to the untutored eye to be somewhat tangential to the matter in hand, the client had simply waved the matter aside as trifling. Dirk liked that in a client.

The only thing the client had insisted upon in the midst of this almost superhuman fit of reasonableness was that Dirk had to be there, absolutely had, had, had to be there, ready, functioning and alert, without fail, without even the merest smidgen of an inkling of failure, at six-thirty in the morning. Absolutely.

Well, he was just going to have to see reason about that as well. Six-thirty was clearly a preposterous time, and he, the client, obviously hadn't meant it seriously. A civilized six-thirty for twelve noon was almost certainly what he had in mind, and if he wanted to cut up rough about it, Dirk would have no option but to start handing out some serious statistics. Nobody got murdered before lunch. But nobody. People weren't up to it. You needed a good lunch to get both the blood-sugar and blood-lust levels up. Dirk had the figures to prove it.

Did he, Anstey (the client's name was Anstey—he was an odd, intense man in his mid-thirties with staring eyes, a narrow yellow tie and one of the big houses in Lupton Road; Dirk hadn't actually liked him very much and thought he looked as if he were trying to swallow a fish), did he know that 67 percent of all known murderers who expressed a preference had had liver and bacon for lunch? And that another 22 percent had been torn between a prawn biryani and an omelet? That dispensed with 89 percent of the threat at a stroke, and by the time you had further discounted the salad eaters and the turkey and ham sandwich munchers and started to look at the number of people who would contemplate such a course of action without any lunch at all, then you were well into the realms of negligibility and bordering on fantasy.

After two-thirty, but nearer to three o'clock, was when you had to start being on your guard. Seriously. Even on good days. Even when you weren't receiving death threats from strange gigantic men with green eyes, you had to watch people like a hawk after the lunch hour. The really dangerous time was after four o'clockish, when the streets began to fill up with marauding packs of publishers and agents, maddened with fettuccine and kir and baying for cabs. Those were the times that tested men's souls. Six-thirty in the morning? Forget it. Dirk had.

With his resolve well stiffened, Dirk stepped back out of the newsagent's into the nippy air of the street and strode off.

"Ah, I expect you'll be wanting to pay for that paper, then, won't you, Mr. Dirk, sir?" said the newsagent, trotting gently after him.

"Ah, Bates," said Dirk loftily, "you and your expectations. Always expecting this and expecting that. May I recommend serenity to you? A life that is burdened with expectations is a heavy life. Its fruit is sorrow and disappointment. Learn to be one with the joy of the moment."

"I think it's twenty pence, that one, sir," said Bates tranquilly.

"Tell you what I'll do, Bates, seeing as it's you. Do you have a pen on you at all? A simple ballpoint will suffice."

Bates produced one from an inner pocket and handed it to Dirk, who then tore off the corner of the paper on which the price was printed and scribbled "IOU" above it. He handed the scrap of paper to the newsagent.

"Shall I put this with the others, then, sir?"

"Put it wherever it will give you the greatest joy, dear Bates, I would want you to put it nowhere less. For now, dear man, farewell."

"I expect you'll be wanting to give me back my pen as well, Mr. Dirk."

"When the times are propitious for such a transaction, my dear Bates," said Dirk, "you may depend upon it. For the moment, higher purposes call it. Joy, Bates, great joy. Bates, please let go of it."

After one last listless tug, the little man shrugged and padded back toward his shop.

"I expect I'll be seeing you later, then, Mr. Dirk," he called out over his shoulder, without enthusiasm.

Dirk gave a gracious bow of his head to the man's retreating back, and then hurried on, opening the newspaper at the horoscope page as he did so.

"Virtually everything you decide today will be wrong," it said bluntly.

Dirk slapped the paper shut with a grunt. He did not for a second hold with the notion that great whirling lumps of rock light years away knew something about your day that you didn't. It just so happened that "The Great Zaganza" was an old friend of his who knew when Dirk's birthday was, and always wrote his column deliberately to wind him up. The paper's circulation had dropped by nearly a twelfth since he had taken over doing the horoscope, and only Dirk and The Great Zaganza knew why.

He hurried on, flapping his way quickly through the rest of the paper. As usual, there was nothing interesting. A lot of stuff about the search for Janice Smith, the missing airline girl from Heathrow, and how she could possibly have disappeared just like that. They printed the latest picture of her, which was on a swing with pigtails, aged six. Her father, a Mr. Jim Pearce, was quoted as saying it was quite a good likeness, but she had grown up a lot now and was usually in better focus. Impatiently, Dirk tucked the paper under his arm and strode onward, his thoughts on a much more interesting topic.

Three hundred pounds a day. Plus expenses.

He wondered how long he could reasonably expect to sustain in Mr. Anstey his strange delusions that he was about to be murdered by a seven foot tall, shaggy-haired creature with huge green eyes and horns, who habitually waved things at him: a contract written in some incomprehensible language and signed with a splash of blood, and also a kind of scythe. The other notable feature of this creature was that no one other than his client had been able to see it, which Mr. Anstey dismissed as a trick of the light.

Three days? Four? Dirk didn't think he'd be able to manage a whole week with a straight face, but he was already looking at something like a grand for his trouble. And he would stick a new fridge down on the list of tangential but non-negotiable expenses. That would be a good one. Getting the old fridge thrown out was definitely part of the interconnectedness of all things.

He began to whistle at the thought of simply getting someone to come round and cart the thing away, turned into Lupton Road and was surprised at all the police cars there. And the ambulance. He didn't like them being there. It didn't feel right. It didn't sit comfortably in his mind alongside his visions of a new fridge.

5

◆

Dirk knew Lupton Road. It was a wide tree-lined affair, with large late-Victorian terraces which stood tall and sturdily and resented police cars. Resented them if they turned up in numbers, that is, and if their lights were flashing. The inhabitants of Lupton Road liked to see a nice, well-turned-out single police car patrolling up and down the street in a cheerful and robust manner—it kept property values cheerful and robust too. But the moment the lights started flashing in that knuckle-whitening blue, they cast their pallor not only on the neatly pointed bricks that they flashed across, but also on the very values those bricks represented.

Anxious faces peered from behind the glass of neighboring windows, and were irradiated by the blue strobes.

There were three of them, three police cars left askew across the road in a way that transcended mere parking. It sent out a massive signal to the world saying that the law was here now taking charge of things, and that anyone who just had normal, good and cheerful business to conduct in Lupton Road could just fuck off.

Dirk hurried up the road, sweat pricking at him beneath his heavy leather coat. A police constable loomed up ahead of him with his arms spread out, playing at being a stop barrier, but Dirk swept him aside in a torrent of words to which the constable was unable to come up with a good response off the top of his head. Dirk sped on to the house.

At the door another policeman stopped him, and Dirk was about to wave an expired Marks and Spencer charge card at him with a deft little flick of the wrist that he had practiced for hours in front of a mirror on those long evenings when nothing much else was on, when the officer suddenly said, "Hey, is your name Gently?"

Dirk blinked at him warily. He made a slight grunting noise that could be either "yes" or "no" depending on the circumstances.

"Because the Chief has been looking for you."

"Has he?" said Dirk.

"I recognized you from his description," said the officer, looking him up and down with a slight smirk.

"In fact," continued the officer, "he's been using your name in a manner that some might find highly offensive. He even sent Big Bob the Finder off in a car to find you. I can tell that he didn't find you from the fact that you're looking reasonably well. Lot of people get found by Big Bob the Finder, they come in a bit wobbly. Just about able to help us with our enquiries but that's about all. You'd better go in. Rather you than me," he added quietly.

Dirk glanced at the house. The stripped-pine shutters were closed across all the windows. Though in all other respects the house seemed well cared for, groomed into a state of clean, well-pointed affluence, the closed shutters seemed to convey an air of sudden devastation.

Oddly, there seemed to be music coming from the basement, or rather, just a single disjointed phrase of thumping music being repeated over and over again. It sounded as if the stylus had got stuck in the groove of a record, and Dirk wondered why no one had turned it off, or at least nudged the stylus along so that the record could continue. The song seemed very vaguely familiar and Dirk guessed that he had probably heard it on the radio recently, though he couldn't place it. The fragment of lyric seemed to be something like:

"Don't pick it up, pick it up, pick i—
"Don't pick it up, pick it up, pick i—
"Don't pick it up, pick it up, pick i—" and so on.

"You'll be wanting to go down to the basement," said the officer impassively, as if that was the last thing that anyone in their right mind would be wanting to do.

Dirk nodded to him curtly and hurried up the steps to the front door, which was standing slightly ajar. He shook his head and clenched his shoulders to try and stop his brain from fluttering.

He went in.

The hallway spoke of prosperity imposed on a taste that

had originally been formed by student living. The floors were stripped boards heavily polyurethaned, the walls white with Greek rugs hung on them, but expensive Greek rugs. Dirk would be prepared to bet (though probably not to pay up) that a thorough search of the house would reveal, among who knew what other dark secrets, five hundred British Telecom shares and a set of Dylan albums that was complete up to "Blood on the Tracks."

Another policeman was standing in the hall. He looked terribly young, and he was leaning very slightly back against the wall, staring at the floor and holding his helmet against his stomach. His face was pale and shiny. He looked at Dirk blankly, and nodded faintly in the direction of the stairs leading down.

Up the stairs came the repeated sound:

"Don't pick it up, pick it up, pick i—
"Don't pick it up, pick it up, pick i—"

Dirk was trembling with a rage that was barging around inside him looking for something to hit or throttle. He wished that he could hotly deny that any of this was his fault, but until anybody tried to assert that it was, he couldn't.

"How long have you been here?" he said curtly.

The young policeman had to gather himself together to answer.

"We arrived about half-hour ago," he replied in a thick voice. "Hell of a morning. Rushing around."

"Don't tell me about rushing around," said Dirk, completely meaninglessly. He launched himself down the stairs.

"Don't pick it up, pick it up, pick i—
"Don't pick it up, pick it up, pick i—"

At the bottom there was a narrow corridor. The main door off it was heavily cracked and hanging off its hinges. It opened into a large double room. Dirk was about to enter when a figure emerged from it and stood barring his way.

"I hate the fact that this case has got you mixed up in it," said the figure, "I hate it very much. Tell me what you've got to do with it so I know exactly what it is I'm hating."

Dirk stared at the neat, thin face in astonishment.

"Gilks?" he said.

"Don't stand there looking like a startled whatsisname, what are those things that aren't seals? Much worse than seals. Big, blubbery things. Dugongs. Don't stand there looking like a startled dugong. Why has that . . ." Gilks pointed into the room behind him—"why has that . . . man in there got your name and telephone number on an envelope full of money?"

"How, m . . ." started Dirk. "How, may I ask, do you come to be here, Gilks? What are you doing so far from the Fens? Surprised you find it dank enough for you here."

"Three hundred pounds," said Gilks. "Why?"

"Perhaps you would allow me to speak to my client," said Dirk.

"Your client, eh?" said Gilks grimly. "Yes. All right. Why don't you speak to him? I'd be interested to hear what you have to say." He stood back stiffly and waved Dirk into the room.

Dirk gathered his thoughts and entered the room in a state of controlled composure which lasted for just over a second.

Most of his client was sitting quietly in a comfortable chair in front of the hi-fi. The chair was placed in the optimal listening position—about twice as far back from the speakers as the distance between them, which is generally considered to be ideal for stereo imaging.

He seemed generally to be casual and relaxed, with his legs crossed and a half-finished cup of coffee on the small table beside him. Distressingly, though, his head was sitting neatly on the middle of the record which was revolving on the hi-fi turntable, with the tone arm snuggling up against the neck and constantly being deflected back into the same groove. As the head revolved it seemed once every 1.8 seconds or so to shoot Dirk a reproachful glance, as if to say, "See what happens when you don't turn up on time like I asked you to," then it would sweep on round to the wall, round, round, and back to the front again with more reproach.

"Don't pick it up, pick it up, pick i—
"Don't pick it up, pick it up, pick i—"

The room swayed a little around Dirk, and he put his hand out against the wall to steady it.

"Was there any particular service you were engaged to provide for your client?" said Gilks behind him, very quietly.

"Oh, er, just a small matter," said Dirk weakly. "Nothing connected with all this. No, he, er, didn't mention any of this kind of thing at all. Well, look, I can see you're busy. I think I'd better just collect my fee and leave. You say he left it out for me?"

Having said this, Dirk sat heavily on a small bentwood chair standing behind him, and broke it.

Gilks hauled him back to his feet again and propped him against the wall. Briefly he left the room, then came back with a small jug of water and a glass on a tray. He poured some water into the glass, took it to Dirk and threw it at him.

"Better?"

"No," spluttered Dirk. "Can't you at least turn the record off?"

"That's Forensic's job. Can't touch anything till the clever dicks have been. Maybe that's them now. Go out on to the patio and get some air. Chain yourself to the railing and beat yourself up a little, I'm pushed for time myself. And try to look less green, will you? It's not your color."

"Don't pick it up, pick it up, pick i—
"Don't pick it up, pick it up, pick i—"

Gilks turned around, looked tired and cross, and was about to go out and up the stairs to meet the newcomers, whose voices could be heard up on the ground floor, when he paused and watched the head revolving patiently on its heavy platter for a few seconds.

"You know," he said at last, "these smart-alec show-off suicides really make me tired. They only do it to annoy."

"Suicide?" said Dirk.

Gilks glanced round at him.

"Windows secured with iron bars half an inch thick," he said. "Door locked from the inside with the key still in the lock. Furniture piled against the inside of the door. French windows to the patio locked with mortise door bolts. No signs of a tunnel. If it was murder, then the murderer must have stopped to do a damn fine job of glazing on the way out. Except that all the putty's old and painted over.

"No. Nobody's left this room, and nobody's broken into it except for us, and I'm pretty sure we didn't do it.

"I haven't time to fiddle around on this one. Obviously

suicide, and just done to be difficult. I've half a mind to do the deceased for wasting police time. Tell you what," he said, glancing at his watch, "you've got ten minutes. If you come up with a plausible explanation of how he did it that I can put in my report, I'll let you keep the evidence in the envelope minus twenty percent compensation to me for the emotional wear and tear involved in not punching you in the mouth."

Dirk wondered for a moment whether or not to mention the visits his client claimed to have received from a strange and violent green-eyed, fur-clad giant who regularly emerged out of nowhere bellowing about contracts and obligations and waving a three-foot glittering-edged scythe, but decided, on balance, no.

"Don't pick it up, pick it up, pick i—
"Don't pick it up, pick it up, pick i—"

He was seething at himself at last. He had not been able to seethe at himself properly over the death of his client because it was too huge and horrific a burden to bear. But now he had been humiliated by Gilks, and he found himself in too wobbly and disturbed a state to fight back, so he was able to seethe at himself about that.

He turned sharply away from his tormentor and let himself out into the patio garden to be alone with his seethings.

The patio was a small, paved, west-facing area at the rear, which was largely deprived of light, cut off as it was by the high back wall of the house and by the high wall of some industrial building that backed onto the rear. In the middle of it stood, for who knew what possible reason, a stone sundial. If any light at all fell on the sundial you would know that it was pretty close to noon, GMT. Other than that, birds perched on it. A few plants sulked in pots.

Dirk jabbed a cigarette in his mouth and burned a lot of the end of it fiercely.

> *"Don't pick it up, pick it up, pick i—*
> *"Don't pick it up, pick it up, pick i—"*

still nagged from inside the house.

Neat garden walls separated the patio on either side from the gardens of neighboring houses. The one to the left was the same size as this one, the one to the right extended a little farther, benefiting from the fact that the industrial building finished flush with the intervening garden wall. There was an air of well-kemptness. Nothing grand, nothing flashy, just a sense that all was well and that upkeep on the houses was no problem. The house to the right, in particular, looked as if it had had its brickwork repointed quite recently, and its windows reglossed.

Dirk took a large gulp of air and stood for a second staring up into what could be seen of the sky, which was gray and hazy. A single dark speck was wheeling against the underside of the clouds. Dirk watched this for a while, glad of any focus for his thoughts other than the horrors of the room he had just left. He was vaguely aware of comings and goings within the room, of a certain amount of tape-measuring happening, of a feeling that photographs were being taken, and that severed-head-removal activities were taking place.

> *"Don't pick it up, pick it up, pick i—*
> *"Don't pick it up, pick it up, pick i—*
> *"Don't pi—"*

Somebody at last picked it up, the nagging repetition was at last hushed, and now the gentle sound of a distant television floated peacefully on the noontime air.

Dirk, however, was having a great deal of difficulty in taking it all in. He was much more aware of taking a succession of huge swimmy whacks to the head, which were the assaults of guilt. It was not the normal background-noise type of guilt that comes from just being alive this far into the twentieth century, and which Dirk was usually fairly adept at dealing with. It was an actual stunning sense of "this specific terrible thing is specifically and terribly my fault." All the normal mental moves wouldn't let him get out of the path of the huge pendulum. *Wham*, it came again, *whizz, wham*, again and again, *wham, wham, wham.*

He tried to remember any of the details of what his late client *(wham, wham)* had said *(wham)* to him *(wham)*, but it was *(wham)* virtually impossible *(wham)* with all this whamming taking place *(wham)*. The man had said *(wham)* that—Dirk took a deep breath—*(wham)* he was being pursued *(wham)* by *(wham)* a large, hairy, green-eyed monster armed with a scythe.

Wham!

Dirk had secretly smiled to himself about this.

Whim, wham, whim, wham, whim, wham!

And had thought, "What a silly man."

Whim, whim, whim, whim, wham!

A scythe *(wham)*, and a contract *(wham)*.

He hadn't known, or even had the faintest idea, what the contract was for.

"Of course," Dirk had thought *(wham)*.

But he had a vague feeling that it might have something to do with a potato. There was a bit of a complicated story attached to that *(whim, whim, whim)*.

Dirk had nodded seriously at this point *(wham)*, and made a reassuring tick *(wham)* on a pad which he kept on

his desk *(wham)* for the express purpose of making reassuring ticks on *(wham, wham, wham)*. He had prided
himself at that moment on having managed to convey the
impression that he had made a tick in a small box marked
"Potatoes."

Wham, wham, wham, wham!

Mr. Anstey had said he would explain further about the
potatoes when Dirk arrived to carry out his task.

And Dirk had promised *(wham)*, easily *(wham)*, casually *(wham)*, with an airy wave of his hand *(wham,
wham, wham)*, to be there at six-thirty in the morning
(wham), because the contract *(wham)* fell due at seven
o'clock.

Dirk remembered having made another tick in a no-
tional "Potato contract falls due at 7:00 a.m." box
(Wh . . .).

He couldn't handle all this whamming any more. He
couldn't blame himself for what had happened. Well, he
could. Of course he could. He did. It was, in fact, his fault
(wham). The point was that he couldn't continue to blame
himself for what had happened and think clearly about it,
which he was going to have to do. He would have to dig
this horrible thing *(wham)* up by the roots, and if he was
going to be fit to do that he had somehow to divest himself
(wham) of this whamming.

A huge wave of anger surged over him as he contem-
plated his predicament and the tangled distress of his life.
He hated this neat patio. He hated all this sundial stuff,
and all these neatly painted windows, all these hideously
trim roofs. He wanted to blame it all on the paintwork
rather than on himself, on the revoltingly tidy patio paving stones, on the sheer disgusting abomination of the
neatly repointed brickwork.

"Excuse me . . ."

"What?" He whirled round, caught unawares by this intrusion into his private raging of a quiet polite voice.

"Are you connected with . . .?" The woman indicated all the unpleasantness and the lower-ground-floorness and the horrible sort of policeness of things next door to her with a little floating movement of her wrist. Her wrist wore a red bracelet which matched the frames of her glasses. She was looking over the garden wall from the house on the right, with an air of slightly anxious distaste.

Dirk glared at her speechlessly. She looked about forty-somethingish and neat, with an instant and unmistakable quality of advertising about her.

She gave a troubled sigh.

"I know it's probably all very terrible and everything," she said, "but do you think it will take long? We only called in the police because the noise of that ghastly record was driving us up the wall. It's all a bit . . ."

She gave him a look of silent appeal, and Dirk decided that it could all be her fault. She could, as far as he was concerned, take the blame for everything while he sorted it out. She deserved it, if only for wearing a bracelet like that.

Without a word, he turned his back on her, and took his fury back inside the house where it began rapidly to freeze into something hard and efficient.

"Gilks!" he said. "Your smart-alec suicide theory. I like it. It works for me. And I think I see how the clever bastard pulled it off. Bring me pen. Bring me paper."

He sat down with a flourish at the cherrywood farmhouse table that occupied the center of the rear portion of the room and deftly sketched out a scheme of events which involved a number of household or kitchen implements, a swinging, weighted light fitting, some very precise timing, and hinged on the vital fact that the record turntable was Japanese.

"That should keep your forensic chaps happy," said Dirk briskly to Gilks. The forensic chaps glanced at it, took in its salient points and liked them. They were simple, implausible, and of exactly that nature which a coroner who liked the same sort of holidays in Marbella that they did would be sure to relish.

"Unless," said Dirk casually, "you are interested in the notion that the deceased had entered into some kind of diabolical contract with a supernatural agency for which payment was now being exacted?"

The forensic chaps glanced at each other and shook their heads. There was a strong sense from them that the morning was wearing on and that this kind of talk was only introducing unnecessary complications into a case which otherwise could be well behind them before lunch.

Dirk gave a satisfied shrug, peeled off his share of the evidence, and, with a final nod to the constabulary, made his way back upstairs.

As he reached the hallway, it suddenly became apparent to him that the gentle sounds of daytime television which he had heard from out in the garden had previously been masked from inside by the insistent sound of the record stuck in its groove.

He was surprised now to realize that they were in fact coming from somewhere upstairs in this house. With a quick look around to see that he was not observed, he stood on the bottom step of the staircase leading to the upstairs floors of the house and glanced up them in surprise.

6

◆

The stairs were carpeted with a tastefully austere matting type of substance. Dirk quietly made his way up them, past some tastefully dried large things in a pot that stood on the first landing, and looked into the rooms on the first floor. They, too, were tasteful and dried.

The larger of the two bedrooms was the only one that showed any signs of current use. It had clearly been designed to allow the morning light to play on delicately arranged flowers and duvets stuffed with something like hay, but there was a feeling that socks and used shaving heads were instead beginning to gather the room into their grip. There was a distinct absence of anything female in the room—the same sort of absence that a missing picture leaves behind it on a wall. There was an air of tension and of sadness and of things needing to be cleaned out from under the bed.

The bathroom, which opened out from it, had a gold disc hung on the wall in front of the lavatory, for sales of five hundred thousand copies of a record called "Hot Potato" by a band called "Pugilism and the Third Autistic Cuckoo." Dirk had a vague recollection of having read part of an interview with the leader of the band (there were only two of them, and one of them was the leader) in a Sunday paper. He had been asked about their name, and he had said that there was an interesting story about it, though it turned out not to be. "It can mean whatever people want it to mean," he had added with a shrug from the sofa of his manager's office somewhere off Oxford Street.

Dirk remembered visualizing the journalist nodding politely and writing this down. A vile knot had formed in Dirk's stomach which he had eventually softened with gin.

"Hot Potato . . ." thought Dirk. It suddenly occurred to him, looking at the gold disc hanging in its red frame, that the record on which the late Mr. Anstey's head had been perched was obviously this one. Hot Potato. Don't pick it up.

What could that mean?

Whatever people wanted it to mean, Dirk thought with bad grace.

The other thing that he remembered now about the interview was that Pain (the leader of Pugilism and the

Third Autistic Cuckoo was called Pain) claimed to have written the lyrics down more or less verbatim from a conversation which he or somebody had overheard in a café or a sauna or an airplane or something like that. Dirk wondered how the originators of the conversation would feel to hear their words being repeated in the circumstances in which he had just heard them.

He peered more closely at the label in the center of the gold record. At the top of the label it said simply, "ARRGH!," while underneath the actual title were the writers' credits—"Paignton, Mulville, Anstey."

Mulville was presumably the member of Pugilism and the Third Autistic Cuckoo who wasn't the leader. And Geoff Anstey's inclusion on the writing credits of a major-selling single was probably what had paid for this house. When Anstey had talked about the contract having something to do with "Potato" he had assumed that Dirk knew what he meant. And he, Dirk, had as easily assumed that Anstey was blithering. It was very easy to assume that someone who was talking about green-eyed monsters with scythes was also blithering when he talked about potatoes.

Dirk sighed to himself with deep uneasiness. He took a dislike to the neat way the trophy was hanging on the wall and adjusted it a little so that it hung at a more humane and untidy angle. Doing this caused an envelope to fall out from behind the frame and flutter toward the floor. Dirk tried unsuccessfully to catch it. With an unfit grunt he bent over and picked the thing up.

It was a largish cream envelope of rich, heavy paper, roughly slit open at one end, and resealed with Sellotape. In fact it looked as if it had been opened and resealed with fresh layers of tape many times, an impression which was borne out by the number of names to which the envelope had in its time been addressed—each successively crossed out and replaced by another.

The last name on it was that of Geoff Anstey. At least Dirk assumed it was the last name because it was the only one that had not been crossed out, and crossed out heavily. Dirk peered at some of the other names, trying to make them out.

Some memory was stirred by a couple of the names which he could just about discern, but he needed to examine the envelope much more closely. He had been meaning to buy himself a magnifying glass ever since he had become a detective, but had never got around to it. He also did not possess a penknife, so reluctantly he decided that the most prudent course was to tuck the envelope away for the moment in one of the deeper recesses of his coat and examine it later in privacy.

He glanced quickly behind the frame of the gold disc to see if any other goodies might emerge but was disappointed, and so he quit the bathroom and resumed his exploration of the house.

The other bedroom was neat and soulless. Unused. A pine bed, a duvet and an old battered chest of drawers that had been revived by being plunged into a vat of acid were its main features. Dirk pulled the door closed behind him, and started to ascend the small, wobbly, white-painted stairway that led up to an attic from which the sounds of Bugs Bunny could be heard.

At the top of the stairs was a minute landing which opened on one side into a bathroom so small that it would best be used by standing outside and sticking into it whichever limb you wanted to wash. The door to it was kept ajar by a length of green hosepipe which trailed from the cold tap of the washbasin, out of the bathroom, across the landing and into the only other room here at the top of the house.

It was an attic room with a severely pitched roof which offered only a few spots where a person of anything approaching average height could stand up.

Dirk stood hunched in the doorway and surveyed its contents, nervous of what he might find among them. There was a general grunginess about the place. The curtains were closed, and little light made it past them into the room, which was otherwise illuminated only by the flickering glow of an animated rabbit. An unmade bed with dank, screwed-up sheets was pushed under a particularly low angle of the ceiling. Part of the walls and the more nearly vertical surfaces of the ceiling were covered with pictures crudely cut out of magazines.

There didn't seem to be any common theme or purpose behind the cuttings. As well as a couple of pictures of flashy German cars and the odd bra advertisement, there were also a badly torn picture of a fruit flan, part of an advertisement for life insurance, and other random fragments which suggested they had been selected and arranged with a dull, bovine indifference to any meaning that any of them might have or effect they might achieve.

The hosepipe curled across the floor and led around the side of an elderly armchair pulled up in front of the television set.

The rabbit rampaged. The glow of his rampagings played on the frayed edges of the armchair. Bugs was wrestling with the controls of an airplane which was plunging to the ground. Suddenly he saw a button marked "Autopilot" and pressed it. A cupboard opened and a robot pilot clambered out, took one look at the situation and bailed out. The plane hurtled on toward the ground but, luckily, ran out of fuel just before reaching it and so the rabbit was saved.

Dirk could also see the top of a head.

The hair on this head was dark, matted and greasy. Dirk watched it for a long, uneasy moment before advancing slowly into the room to see what, if anything, it was attached to. His relief at discovering, as he rounded the armchair, that the head was, after all, attached to a living body was a little marred by the sight of the living body to which it was attached.

Slumped in the armchair was a boy.

He was probably about thirteen or fourteen, and although he didn't look ill in any specific physical way, he was definitely not a well person. His hair sagged on his head, his head sagged on his shoulders, and he lay in the armchair in a sort of limp, crumpled way, as if he'd been hurled there from a passing train. He was dressed merely in a cheap leather jacket and a sleeping bag.

Dirk stared at him.

Who was he? What was a boy doing here watching television in a house where someone had just been decapitated? Did he know what had happened? Did Gilks know about him? Had Gilks even bothered to come up here? It was, after all, several flights of stairs for a busy policeman with a tricky suicide on his hands.

After Dirk had been standing there for twenty seconds or so, the boy's eyes climbed up toward him, failed utterly to acknowledge him in any way at all, and then dropped again and locked back onto the rabbit.

Dirk was unused to making quite such a minuscule impact on anybody. He checked to be sure that he did have his huge leather coat and his absurd red hat on and that he was properly and dramatically silhouetted by the light of the doorway.

He felt momentarily deflated and said, "Er . . ." by way of self-introduction, but it didn't get the boy's attention. He didn't like this. The kid was deliberately and maliciously watching television at him. Dirk frowned. There was a kind of steamy tension building in the room, it seemed to him, a kind of difficult, hissing quality to the whole air of the place which he did not know how to respond to. It rose in intensity and then suddenly ended with an abrupt click that made Dirk start.

The boy unwound himself like a slow, fat snake, leaned sideways over the far side of the armchair and made some elaborate unseen preparations which clearly involved, as Dirk now realized, an electric kettle. When he resumed his earlier splayed posture it was with the addition of a plastic pot clutched in his right hand, from which he forked rubbery strands of steaming gunk into his mouth.

The rabbit brought his affairs to a conclusion and gave way to a jeering comedian who wished the viewers to buy a certain brand of lager on the basis of nothing better than his own hardly disinterested say-so.

Dirk felt that it was time to make a slightly greater impression on the proceedings than he had so far managed to do. He stepped forward directly into the boy's line of sight.

"Kid," Dirk said in a tone that he hoped would sound firm but gentle and not in any way at all patronizing or affected or gauche, "I need to know who—"

He was distracted at that moment by the sight that met him from the new position in which he was standing. On the other side of the armchair there was a large, half-full catering-size box of Pot Noodles, a large, half-full catering-size box of Mars Bars, a half demolished pyramid of cans of soft drink, and the end of the hosepipe. The hose-pipe ended in a plastic tap nozzle, and was obviously used for refilling the kettle.

Dirk had simply been going to ask the boy who he was, but seen from this angle the family resemblance was un-mistakable. He was clearly the son of the lately decapi-tated Geoffrey Anstey. Perhaps this behavior was just his way of dealing with shock. Or perhaps he really didn't know what had happened. Or perhaps he . . .

Dirk hardly liked to think.

In fact, he was finding it hard to think clearly while the television beside him was, on behalf of a toothpaste man-ufacturing company, trying to worry him deeply about some of the things which might be going on in his mouth.

"OK," he said, "I don't like to disturb you at what I know must be a difficult and distressing time for you, but I need to know first of all if you actually realize that this is a difficult and distressing time for you."

Nothing.

All right, thought Dirk, time for a little judicious tough-ness. He leaned back against the wall, stuck his hands in his pockets in an OK-if-that's-the-way-you-want-to-play-it manner, stared moodily at the floor for a few seconds, then swung his head up and let the boy have a hard look right between the eyes.

"I have to tell you, kid," he said tersely, "your father's dead."

This might have worked if it hadn't been for a very popular and long-running commercial which started at that moment. It seemed to Dirk to be a particularly as-tounding example of the genre.

The opening sequence showed the angel Lucifer being hurled from heaven into the pit of hell where he then lay on a burning lake until a passing demon arrived and gave him a can of a fizzy soft drink called *sHades*. Lucifer took it and tried it. He greedily guzzled the whole contents of the can and then turned to camera, slipped on some Porsche design sunglasses, said, "Now we're *really* cookin'!" and lay back basking in the glow of the burning coals being heaped around him.

At that point an impossibly deep and growly American voice, which sounded as if it had itself crawled from the pit of hell, or at least from a Soho basement drinking club to which it was keen to return as soon as possible to marinade itself into shape for the next voice-over, said, "*sHades*. The Drink from Hell . . ." and the can revolved a little to obscure the initial *s*, and thus spell "Hades."

The theology of this seemed a little confused, reflected Dirk, but what was one tiny extra droplet of misinformation in such a raging torrent?

Lucifer then mugged at the camera again and said, "I could really *fall* for this stuff . . ." and just in case the viewer had been rendered completely insensate by all these goings-on, the opening shot of Lucifer being hurled from heaven was briefly replayed in order to emphasize the word "fall."

The boy's attention was entirely captivated by this.

Dirk squatted down in between the boy and the screen.

"Listen to me," he began.

The boy craned his neck round to look past Dirk at the screen. He had to redistribute his limbs in the chair in order to be able to do this and continue to fork Pot Noodle into himself.

"Listen," insisted Dirk.

Dirk felt he was beginning to be in serious danger of losing the upper hand in the situation. It wasn't merely that the boy's attention was on the television; it was that nothing else seemed to have any meaning or independent existence for him at all. Dirk was merely a featureless object in the way of the television. The boy seemed to bear him no malice, he merely wished to see past him.

"Look, can we turn this off for a moment?" Dirk said, and he tried not to make it sound testy.

The boy did not respond. Maybe there was a slight stiffening of the shoulders, maybe it was a shrug. Dirk turned around and was at a loss to find which button to push to turn the television off. The whole control panel seemed to be dedicated to the single purpose of keeping itself turned on—there was no single button marked "on" or "off." Eventually Dirk simply disconnected the set from the power socket on the wall and turned back to the boy, who broke his nose.

Dirk felt his septum crunching from the terrific impact of the boy's forehead as they both toppled heavily backward against the set, but the noise of the bone breaking and the noise of his own cry of pain as it broke were completely obliterated by the howling screams of rage that erupted from the boy's throat. Dirk flailed helplessly to try and protect himself from the fury of the onslaught, but the boy was on top with his elbow in Dirk's eye, his knees pounding first on Dirk's rib cage, then his jaw, and then on Dirk's already traumatized nose, as he scrambled over him to reconnect the power to the television. He then settled back comfortably into the armchair and watched with a moody and unsettled eye as the picture reassembled itself.

"You could at least have waited for the news," he said in a dull voice.

Dirk gaped at him. He sat huddled on the floor, coddling his bleeding nose in his hands, and gaped at the monstrously disinterested creature.

"Whhfff . . . fffmmm . . . nnggh!" he protested, and then gave up for the time being, while he probed his nose for the damage.

There was definitely a wobbly bit that clicked nastily between his fingers, and the whole thing seemed suddenly to be a horribly unfamiliar shape. He fished a handkerchief out of his pocket and held it up to his face. Blood spread easily through it. He staggered to his feet, brushed aside nonexistent offers of help, stomped out of the room and into the tiny bathroom. There, he yanked the hosepipe angrily off the tap, found a towel, soaked it in cold water and held it to his face for a minute or two until the flow of blood gradually slowed to a trickle and stopped. He stared at himself in the mirror. His nose was quite definitely leaning at a slightly rakish angle. He tried bravely to shift it, but not bravely enough. It hurt abominably, so he contented himself with dabbing at it a little more with the wet towel and swearing quietly.

Then he stood there for a second or two longer, leaning against the basin, breathing heavily, and practicing saying "All right!" fiercely into the mirror. It came out as "Aww-bwigh!" and lacked any real authority. When he felt sufficiently braced, or at least as braced as he was likely to feel in the immediate future, he turned and stalked grimly back into the den of the beast.

The beast was sitting quietly absorbing news of some of the exciting and stimulating game shows that the evening held in store for the determined viewer, and did not look up as Dirk re-entered.

Dirk walked briskly over to the window and drew the curtains sharply back, half hoping that the beast might shrivel up shrieking if exposed to daylight, but other than wrinkling up its nose, it did not react. A dark shadow flapped briefly across the window, but the angle was such that Dirk could not see what caused it.

He turned and faced the boy-beast. The midday news bulletin was starting on television, and the boy seemed somehow a little more open, a little more receptive to the world outside the flickering colored rectangle. He glanced up at Dirk with a sour, tired look.

"Whaddayawananyway?" he said.

"I ted you whad I wad," said Dirk, fiercely but hopelessly, "I wad . . . hag od a bobed . . . I gnow thad faith!"

Dirk's attention had switched suddenly to the television screen, where a rather more up-to-date photograph of the missing airline check-in girl was being shown.

"Whadayadoingere?" said the boy.

"Jjchhhhh!" said Dirk, and perched himself down on the arm of the chair, peering intently at the face on the screen. It had been taken about a year ago, before the girl had learned about corporate lipgloss. She had frizzy hair and a frumpy, put-upon look.

"Whoareyou? Wassgoinon?" insisted the boy.

"Loog, chuddub," snapped Dirk, "I'b tryid to wodge dthith!"

The newscaster said that the police professed themselves to be mystified by the fact that there was no trace of Janice Smith at the scene of the incident. They explained that there was a limit to the number of times they could search the same buildings, and appealed for anyone who might have a clue as to her whereabouts to come forward.

"Thadth by segradry! Thadth Mith Pearth!" exclaimed Dirk in astonishment.

The boy was not interested in Dirk's ex-secretary, and gave up trying to attract Dirk's attention. He wriggled out of the sleeping bag and sloped off to the bathroom.

Dirk sat staring at the television, bewildered that he hadn't realized before who the missing girl was. Still, there was no reason why he should have done so, he realized. Marriage had changed her name, and this was the first time they had shown a photograph that actually identified her. So far he had taken no real interest in the strange incident at the airport, but now it demanded his attention.

The explosion was now officially designated an "Act of God."

But, thought Dirk, what god? And why?

What god would be hanging around Terminal Two of Heathrow Airport trying to catch the 15:37 flight to Oslo?

After the miserable lassitude of the last few weeks, he suddenly had a great deal that required his immediate attention. He frowned in deep thought for a few moments, and hardly noticed when the beast-boy snuck back in and snuggled back into his sleeping bag just in time for the advertisements to start. The first one showed how a perfectly ordinary stock cube could form the natural focus of a normal, happy family life.

Dirk leaped to his feet, but even as he was about to start questioning the boy again his heart sank as he looked at him. The beast was far away, sunk back in his dark, flickering lair, and Dirk did not feel inclined to disturb him again at the moment.

He contented himself with barking at the unresponsing child that he would be back, and bustled heavily down the stairs, his big leather coat flapping madly behind him.

In the hallway he encountered the loathed Gilks once more.

"What happened to you?" said the policeman sharply, catching sight of Dirk's bruised and bulging nose.

"Ondly whad you dold me," said Dirk, innocently. "I bead bythelf ub."

Gilks demanded to know what he had been doing, and Dirk generously explained that there was a witness upstairs with some interesting information to impart. He suggested that Gilks go and have a word with him, but that it would be best if he turned off the television first.

Gilks nodded curtly. He started to go up the stairs, but Dirk stopped him.

"Doedth eddydthig dthrike you adth dthraydge aboud dthidth houdth?" he said.

"What did you say?" said Gilks in irritation.

"Subbthig dthraydge," said Dirk.

"Something *what?*"

"Dthraydge!" insisted Dirk.

"Strange?"

"Dthadth right, dthraydge."

Gilks shrugged. "Like what?" he said.

"Id dtheemdth to be cobbleedly dthouledth."

"Completely what?"

"Dthouledth!" He tried again. "Thoul-leth! I dthigg dthadth dverry idderedthigg!"

With that he doffed his hat politely, and swept on out of the house and up the street, where an eagle swooped out of the sky at him and came within a whisker of causing him to fall under a 73 bus on its way south.

For the next twenty minutes, hideous yells and screams emanated from the top floor of the house in Lupton Road, and caused much tension among the neighbors. The ambulance took away the upper and lower remains of Mr. Anstey and also a policeman with a bleeding face. For a short while after this, there was quiet.

Then another police car drew up outside the house. A lot of "Bob's here" type of remarks floated from the house, as an extremely large and burly policeman heaved himself out of the car and bustled up the steps. A few minutes and a great deal of screaming and yelling later he reemerged also clutching his face, and drove off in deep dudgeon, squealing his tires in a violent and unnecessary manner.

Twenty minutes later a van arrived from which emerged another policeman carrying a tiny pocket television set. He entered the house, and reemerged a short while later leading a docile thirteen-year-old boy, who was content with his new toy.

Once all policemen had departed, save for the single squad car which remained parked outside to keep watch on the house, a large, hairy, green-eyed figure emerged from its hiding place behind one of the molecules in the large basement room.

It propped its scythe against one of the hi-fi speakers, dipped a long, gnarled finger in the almost congealed pool of blood that had collected on the deck of the turntable, smeared the finger across the bottom of a sheet of thick, yellowing paper, and then disappeared off into a dark and hidden otherworld whistling a strange and vicious tune and returning only briefly to collect its scythe.

7

◆

A little earlier in the morning, at a comfortable distance from all these events, set at a comfortable distance
from a well-proportioned window through which cool mid-
morning light was streaming, lay an elderly one-eyed man
in a white bed. A newspaper sat like a half-collapsed tent
on the floor, where it had been hurled two minutes before,
at shortly after ten o'clock by the clock on the bedside
table.

The room was not large, but was furnished in exces-
sively bland good taste, as if it were a room in an expen-

sive private hospital or clinic, which is exactly what it was—the Woodshead Hospital, set in its own small but well-kempt grounds on the outskirts of a small but well-kempt village in the Cotswolds.

The man was awake but not glad to be.

His skin was very delicately old, like finely stretched translucent parchment, delicately freckled. His exquisitely frail hands lay slightly curled on the pure white linen sheets and quivered very faintly.

His name was variously given as Mr. Odwin, or Wodin, or Odin. He was—is—a god, and furthermore he was that least good of all gods to be alongside, a cross god. His one eye glinted.

He was cross because of what he had been reading in the newspapers, which was that another god had been cutting loose and making a nuisance of himself. It didn't say that in the papers, of course. It didn't say, "God cuts loose, makes nuisance of himself in airport," it merely described the resulting devastation and was at a loss to draw any meaningful conclusions from it.

The story had been deeply unsatisfactory in all sorts of ways, on account of its perplexing inconclusiveness, its going-nowhereness and the irritating (from the newspapers' point of view) lack of any good solid carnage. There was of course a mystery attached to the lack of carnage, but a newspaper preferred a good whack of carnage to a mere mystery any day of the week.

Odin, however, had no such difficulty in knowing what was going on. The accounts had "Thor" written all over them in letters much too big for anyone other than another god to see. He had thrown this morning's paper aside in irritation, and was now trying to concentrate on his relaxation exercises in order to avoid getting too disturbed about all this. These involved breathing in in a certain way and breathing out in a certain other way and were good for his blood pressure and so on. It was not as if he was about to die or anything—ha!—but there was no doubt that at his time of life—ha!—he preferred to take things easy and look after himself.

Best of all he liked to sleep.

Sleeping was a very important activity for him. He liked to sleep for longish periods, great swaths of time. Merely sleeping overnight was not taking the business seriously. He enjoyed a good night's sleep and wouldn't miss one for the world, but he didn't regard it as anything even half approaching enough. He liked to be asleep by half-past eleven in the morning if possible, and if that could come directly after a nice leisurely lie-in, then so much the better. A little light breakfast and a quick trip to the bathroom while fresh linen was applied to his bed was really all the activity he liked to undertake, and he took care that it didn't jangle the sleepiness out of him and thus disturb his afternoon of napping. Sometimes he was able to spend an entire week asleep, and this he regarded as a good snooze. He had also slept through the whole of 1986 and hadn't missed it.

But he knew to his deep disgruntlement that he would shortly have to arise and undertake a sacred and irritating trust. Sacred, because it was godlike, or at least involved gods, and irritating because of the particular god that it involved.

Sneakily he twitched the curtains at a distance, using nothing but his divine will. He sighed heavily. He needed to think, and, what was more, it was time for his morning visit to the bathroom.

He rang for the orderly.

The orderly arrived promptly in his well-pressed loose green tunic, good-morninged cheerfully, and bustled around locating bedroom slippers and dressing gown. He helped Odin out of bed, which was a little like rolling a stuffed crow out of a box, and escorted him slowly to the bathroom. Odin walked stiffly, like a head hung between two heavy stilts draped in striped Viyella and white toweling. The orderly knew Odin as Mr. Odwin, and didn't realize that he was a god, which was something that Odin tended to keep quiet about, and wished that Thor would too.

Thor was the God of Thunder and, frankly, acted like it. It was inappropriate. He seemed unwilling, or unable, or maybe just too stupid to understand or accept . . . Odin stopped himself. He sensed that he was beginning mentally to rant. He would have to consider calmly what next to do about Thor, and he was on his way to the right place for a good think.

As soon as Odin had completed his stately hobble to the bathroom door, two nurses hurried in and stripped and remade the bed with immense precision, patting down the fresh linen, pulling it taut, turning it and tucking it. One of the nurses, clearly the senior, was plump and matronly, the other younger, darker and more generally birdlike. The newspaper was whisked off the floor and neatly refolded, the floor was briskly Hoovered, the curtains hooked back, the flowers and the untouched fruit replaced with fresh flowers and fresh fruit that would, like every piece of fruit before them, remain untouched.

When after a little while the old god's morning ablutions had been completed and the bathroom door reopened, the room had been transformed. The actual differences were tiny, of course, but the effect was of a subtle but magical transformation into something cool and fresh. Odin nodded in quiet satisfaction to see it. He made a little show of inspecting the bed, like a monarch inspecting a line of soldiers.

"Is it well tucked?" he asked in his old and whispery voice.

"It is very well tucked, Mr. Odwin," said the senior nurse with an obsequious beam.

"Is it neatly turned?" It clearly was. This was merely a ritual.

"Turned very neatly indeed, Mr. Odwin," said the nurse, "I supervised the turning down of the sheets myself."

"I'm glad of that, Sister Bailey, very glad," said Odin. "You have a fine eye for a trimly turned fold. It alarms me to know what I shall do without you."

"Well, I'm not about to go anywhere, Mr. Odwin," said Sister Bailey, oozing happy reassurance.

"But you won't last forever, Sister Bailey," said Odin. It was a remark that puzzled Sister Bailey the times she had heard it, because of its apparent extreme callousness.

"Sure, and none of us lasts forever, Mr. Odwin," she said gently as she and the other nurse between them managed the difficult task of lifting Odin back into bed while keeping his dignity intact.

"You're Irish, aren't you, Sister Bailey?" he asked, once he was properly settled.

"I am indeed so, Mr. Odwin."

"Knew an Irishman once. Finn something. Told me a lot of stuff I didn't need to know. Never told me about the linen. Still, I know now."

He nodded curtly at this memory and lowered his head stiffly back onto the firmly plumped up pillows and ran the back of his finely freckled hand over the folded-back linen sheet. Quite simply he was in love with linen. Clean, lightly starched, white Irish linen, pressed, folded, tucked—the words themselves were almost a litany of desire for him. In centuries nothing had obsessed him or moved him so much as linen now did. He could not for the life of him understand how he could ever have cared for anything else.

Linen.

And sleep. Sleep and linen. Sleep in linen. Sleep.

Sister Bailey regarded him with a sort of proprietary fondness. She did not know that he was a god as such, in fact she thought he was probably an old film producer or a Nazi war criminal. Certainly he had an accent she couldn't quite place, and his careless civility, his natural selfishness and his obsession with personal hygiene spoke of a past that was rich with horrors.

If she could have been transported to where she might see her secretive patient enthroned, warrior father of the warrior gods of Asgard, she would not have been surprised. That is not quite true, in fact. She would have been startled quite out of her wits. But she would at least have recognized that it was consistent with the qualities she perceived in him, once she had recovered from the shock of discovering that virtually everything the human race had ever chosen to believe in was true. Or that it continued to be true long after the human race particularly needed it to be true any more.

Odin dismissed his medical attendants with a gesture, having first asked for his personal assistant to be found and sent to him once more.

This caused Sister Bailey to tighten her lips just a very little. She did not like Mr. Odwin's personal assistant, general factotum, manservant, call him what you will. His eyes were malevolent, he made her jump, and she strongly suspected him of making unspeakable suggestions to her nurses during their tea breaks.

He had what Sister Bailey supposed was what people meant by an olive complexion, in that it was extraordinarily close to being green. Sister Bailey was convinced that it was not right at all.

She was of course the last person to judge somebody by the color of their skin—or if not absolutely the last, she had at least done it as recently as yesterday afternoon when an African diplomat had been brought in to have some gallstones removed and she had conceived an instant resentment of him. She didn't like him. She couldn't say exactly what it was she didn't like about him, because she was a nurse, not a taxi driver, and she wouldn't let her personal feelings show for an instant. She was much too professional, much too good at her job, and treated everyone with a more or less equal efficient and cheerful courtesy, even, she thought—and a profound iciness settled on her at this point—even Mr. Rag.

Mr. Rag was the name of Mr. Odwin's personal assistant. There was nothing she could do about it. It was not her place to criticize Mr. Odwin's personal arrangements. But if it had been her business, which it wasn't, then she would greatly have preferred it, and not just for herself, but for Mr. Odwin's own well-being as well, which was the important thing, if he could have employed someone who didn't give her the absolute heebie-jeebies, that was all.

She thought no more about it, merely went to look for him. She had been relieved to discover when she came on duty this morning that Mr. Rag had left the premises the previous night, but had then, with a keen sense of disappointment, spotted him returning about an hour or so ago.

——— 87 ———

She found him exactly where he was not supposed to be. He was squatting on one of the seats in the visitors' waiting room wearing what looked horribly like a soiled and discarded doctor's gown that was much too big for him. Not only that, but he was playing a thinly unmusical tune on a sort of pipe that he had obviously carved out of a large disposable hypodermic syringe which he absolutely should not have had.

He glanced up at her with his quick, dancing eyes, grinned and continued to tootle and squeak, only significantly louder.

Sister Bailey ran through in her mind all the things that it was completely pointless to say about either the coat or the syringe, or about him being in the visitors' room frightening, or preparing to frighten, the visitors. She knew she wouldn't be able to stand the air of injured innocence with which he would reply, or the preposterous absurdity of his answers. Her only course was simply to let it pass and just get him away from the room and out of the way as quickly as possible.

"Mr. Odwin would like to see you," she said. She tried to jam some of her normal lilting quality into her voice, but it just wouldn't go. She wished his eyes would stop dancing like that. Apart from finding it highly disturbing from both a medical and aesthetic point of view, she also could not help but be piqued by the impression it conveyed that there were at least thirty-seven things in the room more interesting than her.

He gazed at her in this disconcerting manner for a few seconds, then, muttering that there was no peace for the wicked, not even the extremely wicked, he pushed past Sister Bailey and skedaddled up the corridor to receive instructions from his lord and master, quickly, before his lord and master fell asleep.

8

◆

B y the end of the morning Kate had discharged herself from the hospital. There were some initial difficulties involved in this because first the ward sister and then the doctor in charge of Kate's case were adamant that she was in no fit state to leave. She had only just emerged from a minor coma and she needed care, she needed—

"Pizza—" insisted Kate.

—rest, she needed—

"—my own home, and fresh air. The air in here is *horrible*. It smells like a vacuum cleaner's armpit."

—further medication, and should definitely remain under observation for another day or so until they were satisfied that she had made a full recovery.

At least, they were fairly adamant. During the course of the morning Kate demanded and got a telephone and started trying to order pizza to be delivered to her ward. She phoned around all of the least cooperative pizza restaurants she knew in London, harangued them, then made some noisily unsuccessful attempts to muster a motorbike to roam around the West End and try and pick up for her an American Hot with a list of additional peppers and mushrooms and cheeses which the controller of the courier service refused even to attempt to remember, and after an hour or so of this sort of behavior the objections to Kate's discharging herself from the hospital gradually fell away like petals from an autumn rose.

And so, a little after lunchtime, she was standing on a bleak West London street feeling weak and shaky but in charge of herself. She had with her the empty, tattered remains of the garment bag which she had refused to relinquish, and also a small scrap of paper in her purse, which had a single name scribbled on it.

She hailed a taxi and sat in the back with her eyes closed most of the way back to her home in Primrose Hill. She climbed up the stairs and let herself into her top-floor flat. There were ten messages on her answering machine, which she simply erased without listening to them.

She threw open the window in her bedroom and for a moment or two leaned out of it at the rather dangerous and awkward angle which allowed her to see a patch of the park. It was a small corner patch with just a couple of plane trees standing in it. The backs of some of the intervening houses framed it, or rather, just failed totally to obscure it, and made it very personal and private to Kate in the way a vast, sweeping vista would not have been.

On one occasion she had gone to this corner of the park and walked around the invisible perimeter that marked out the limits of what she could see, and had come very close to feeling that this was her own domain. She had even patted the plane trees in a proprietorial sort of way, and had then sat beneath them watching the sun going down over London—over its badly spoiled skyline and its nondelivering pizza restaurants—and had come away with a profound sense of something or other, though she wasn't quite certain what. Still, she had told herself, these days she should feel grateful for a profound sense of anything at all, however unspecific.

She hauled herself in from the window, left it wide open in spite of the chill of the outside air, padded through into the small bathroom and ran the bath. It was a bath of the sprawling Edwardian type which took up a wonderfully disproportionate amount of the space available, and encompassed most of the rest of the room with cream-painted pipes. The taps seethed. As soon as the room was sufficiently full of steam to be warm, Kate undressed and then went and opened the large bathroom cupboard.

She felt faintly embarrassed by the sheer profusion of things she had for putting in baths, but she was for some reason incapable of passing any chemist's or herb shop without going in to be seduced by some glass-stoppered bottle of something blue or green or orange and oily that was supposed to restore the natural balance of some vague substance she didn't even know she was supposed to have in her pores.

She paused, trying to choose.

Something pink? Something with extra Vitamin B? Vitamin B12? B13? Just the number of things with different types of Vitamin B in them was an embarrassment of choice in itself. There were powders as well as oils, tubes of gel, even packets of some kind of pungent-smelling seed that was meant to be good for some obscure part of you in some arcane way.

How about some of the green crystals? One day, she had told herself in the past, she would not even bother trying to choose, but would simply put a bit of everything in. When she really felt in need of it. She rather thought that today was the day, and with a sudden reviving rush of pleasure she set about putting a drop or two of everything in the cupboard into the seething bath until it was confused with mingling, muddying colors and verging on the glutinous to touch.

She turned off the taps, went to her handbag for a moment, then returned and lowered herself into the bath, where she lay with her eyes closed, breathing slowly for fully three minutes before at last turning her attention to the scrap of paper she had brought with her from the hospital.

It had one word on it, and it was a word she had dragged out of an oddly reluctant young nurse who had taken her temperature that morning.

Kate had questioned her about the big man. The big man whom she had encountered at the airport, whose body she had seen in a nearby side ward in the early hours of the night.

"Oh, no," the nurse had said, "he wasn't dead. He was just in some sort of coma."

Could she see him? Kate had asked. What was his name?

She had tried to ask idly, in passing as it were, which was a difficult trick to pull off with a thermometer in her mouth, and she wasn't at all certain she had succeeded. The nurse had said that she couldn't really say, she wasn't really meant to talk about other patients. And anyway, the man wasn't there any more, he had been taken some-where else. They had sent an ambulance to collect him and take him somewhere else.

This had taken Kate considerably by surprise.

Where had they taken him? What was this special place? But the nurse had been unwilling to say anything much more, and a second or two later had been sum-moned away by the Sister. The only word the nurse had said was the one that Kate had then scribbled down on the piece of paper she was now looking at.

The word was "Woodshead."

Now that she was more relaxed she had a feeling that the name was familiar to her in some way, though she could not remember where she had heard it.

The instant she remembered, she could not stay in the bath any longer, but got out and made straight for the telephone, pausing only briefly to shower all the gunk off her.

9

◆

The big man awoke and tried to look up, but could hardly raise his head. He tried to sit up but couldn't do that either. He felt as if he'd been stuck to the floor with superglue and after a few seconds he discovered the most astounding reason for this.

He jerked his head up violently, yanking out great tufts of yellow hair which stayed painfully stuck to the floor, and looked around him. He was in what appeared to be a derelict warehouse, probably an upper floor judging by the wintry sky he could see creeping past the grimy, shattered windows.

The ceilings were high and hung with cobwebs built by spiders who did not seem to mind that most of what they caught was crumbling plaster and dust. They were supported by pillars made from upright steel joists on which the dirty old cream paint was bubbled and flaking, and these in turn stood on a floor of battered old oak onto which he had clearly been glued. Extending for a foot or two in a rough oval all around his naked body the floor glistened darkly and dully. Thin, nostril-cleaning fumes rose from it. He could not believe it. He roared with rage, tried to wriggle and shake himself, but succeeded only in tugging painfully at his skin where it was stuck fast to the oak planks.

This had to be the old man's doing.

He threw his head back hard against the floor in a blow that cracked the boards and made his ears sing. He roared again and took some furious satisfaction in making as much hopeless, stupid noise as he could. He roared until the steel pillars rang and the cracked remains of the windows shattered into finer shards. Then, as he threw his head angrily from one side to the other, he caught sight of his sledgehammer leaning against the wall a few feet from him, heaved it up into the air with a word, and sent it hurtling around the great space, beating and clanging on every pillar until the whole building reverberated like a mad gong.

Another word and the hammer flew back at him, missed his head by a hand's width and punched straight down through the floor, shattering the wood and the plaster below.

In the darker space beneath him the hammer spun and swung around in a slow heavy parabola as bits of plaster fell about it and rattled on the concrete floor below. Then it gathered a violent momentum and hurtled back up through the ceiling, smacking up a stack of startled splinters as it punched through another oak floorboard a hand's width from the soles of the big man's feet.

It soared up into the air, hung there for a moment as if its weight had suddenly vanished, then, deftly flicking its short handle up above its head, it drove hard back down through the floor again—then up again, then down again, punching holes in a splintered ring around its master until, with a long heavy groan, the whole oval section of punctured floor gave way and plunged, twisting, through the air. It shattered itself against the floor below amidst a rain of plaster debris, from which the figure of the big man then emerged, staggering, flapping at the dusty air and coughing. His back, his arms and his legs were still covered with great splintered hunks of oak flooring, but at least he was able to move. He leaned the flat of his hands against the wall and violently coughed some of the dust from his lungs.

As he turned back, his hammer danced out of the air toward him, then suddenly evaded his grasp and skidded joyfully off across the floor striking sparks from the concrete with its great head, flipped up and parked itself against a nearby pillar at a jaunty angle.

In front of him the shape of a large Coca-Cola vending machine loomed through the settling cloud of dust. He regarded it with the gravest suspicion and worry. It stood there with a sort of glazed, blank look to it, and had a note from his father stuck on the front panel saying whatever he was doing, stop it. It was signed "You-know-who," but this had been crossed out and first the word "Odin" and then in larger letters "Your Father" had been substituted. Odin never ceased to make absolutely clear his view of his son's intellectual accomplishments. The big man tore the note off and stared at it in anger. A post-script added darkly, "Remember Wales. You don't want to go through all that again." He screwed the note up and hurled it out of the nearest window, where the wind whipped it up and away. For a moment he thought he heard an odd squeaking noise, but it was probably just the blustering of the wind as it whistled between the nearby derelict buildings.

He turned and walked to the window and stared out of it in a belligerent sulk. Glued to the floor. At his age. What the devil was that supposed to mean? "Keep your head down," was what he guessed. "If you don't keep it down, I'll have to keep it down for you." That was what it meant. "Stick to the ground."

He remembered now the old man saying exactly that to him at the time of all the unpleasantness with the Phantom fighter jet. "Why can't you just stick to the ground?" he had said. He could imagine the old man in his soft-headed benign malice thinking it very funny to make the lesson so literal.

Rage began to rumble menacingly inside him but he pushed it down hard. Very worrying things had recently begun happening when he got angry and he had a bad feeling, looking back at the Coca-Cola vending machine, that another of those very worrying things must have just happened. He stared at it and fretted.

He felt ill.

He had felt ill a lot of late, and he found it impossible to discharge what were left of his godly duties when he felt he was suffering from a sort of continual low-grade flu. He experienced headaches, dizzy spells, guilt and all the sorts of ailments that were featured so often in television advertisements. He even suffered terrifying blackouts whenever the great rage gripped him.

He always used to have such a wonderful time getting angry. Great gusts of marvelous anger would hurl him through life. He felt huge. He felt flooded with power and light and energy. He had always been provided with such wonderful things to get angry about—immense acts of provocation or betrayal, people hiding the Atlantic ocean in his helmet, dropping continents on him or getting drunk and pretending to be trees. Stuff you could really work up a rage about and hit things. In short he had felt good about being a Thunder God. Now suddenly it was headaches, nervous tension, nameless anxieties and guilt. These were new experiences for a god, and not pleasant ones.

"You look ridiculous!"

The voice screeched out and affected Thor like fingernails scratched across a blackboard lodged in the back of his brain. It was a mean voice, a spiteful, jeering voice, a cheap white nylon shirt of a voice, a shiny-trousered pencil moustache of a voice, a voice, in short, which Thor did not like. He reacted very badly to it at the best of times, and was particularly provoked to have to hear it while standing naked in the middle of a decrepit warehouse with large sections of an oak floor still stuck to his back.

He spun around angrily. He wanted to be able to turn around calmly and with crushing dignity, but no such strategy ever worked with this creature, and since he, Thor, would only end up feeling humiliated and ridiculous whatever posture he adopted, he might as well go with one he felt comfortable with.

"Toe Rag!" he roared, yanked his hammer spinning into the air and hurled it with immense, stunning force at the small creature who was squatting complacently in the shadows on top of a small heap of rubble, leaning forward a little.

Toe Rag caught the hammer and placed it neatly on top of the pile of Thor's clothes that lay next to him. He grinned, and allowed a stray shaft of sunlight to glitter on one of his teeth. These things don't happen by accident. Toe Rag had spent some time while Thor was unconscious working out how long it would take him to recover, then industriously moving the pile of rubble to exactly this spot, checking the height and then calculating the exact angle at which to lean. As a provocateur he regarded himself as a professional.

"Did you do this to me?" roared Thor. "Did you—"

Thor searched for any way of saying "glue me to the floor" that didn't sound like "glue me to floor," but eventually the pause got too long and he had to give up.

"—glue me to the floor?" he demanded at last. He wished he hadn't asked such a stupid question.

"Don't even answer that!" he added angrily and wished he hadn't said that either. He stamped his foot and shook the foundations of the building a little just to make the point. He wasn't certain what the point was, but he felt that it had to be made. Some dust settled gently around him.

Toe Rag watched him with his dancing, glittering eyes.

"I merely carry out the instructions given to me by your father," he said in a grotesque parody of obsequiousness.

"It seems to me," said Thor, "that the instructions my father has been giving since you entered his service have been very odd. I think you have some kind of evil grip on him. I don't know what kind of evil grip it is, but it's definitely a grip, and it's definitely—" synonyms failed him—"evil," he concluded.

Toe Rag reacted like an iguana to whom someone had just complained about the wine.

"Me?" he protested. "How can I possibly have a grip on your father? Odin is the greatest of the Gods of Asgard, and I am his devoted servant in all things. Odin says, 'Do this,' and I do it. Odin says, 'Go there,' and I go there. Odin says, 'Go and get my big stupid son out of the hospital before he causes any more trouble, and then, I don't know, glue him to the floor or something,' and I do exactly as he asks. I am merely the most humble of functionaries. However small or menial the task, Odin's bidding is what I am there to perform."

Thor was not sufficiently subtle a student of human nature or, for that matter, divine or goblin nature, to be able to argue that this was in fact a very powerful grip to hold over anybody, particularly a fallible and pampered old god. He just knew that it was all wrong.

"Well then," he shouted, "take this message back to my father, Odin. Tell him that I, Thor, the God of Thunder, demand to meet him. And not in his damned hospital either! I'm not going to hang about reading magazines and looking at fruit while he has his bed changed! Tell him that Thor, the God of Thunder, will meet Odin, the Father of the Gods of Asgard, tonight, at the Challenging Hour, in the Halls of Asgard!"

"Again?" said Toe Rag, with a sly glance sideways at the Coca-Cola vending machine.

"Er, yes," said Thor. "Yes!" he repeated in a rage. "Again!"

Toe Rag gave a tiny sigh, such as one who felt resigned to carrying out the bidding of a temperamental simpleton might give, and said, "Well, I'll tell him. I don't suppose he will be best pleased."

"It is no matter of yours whether he is pleased or not!" shouted Thor, disturbing the foundations of the building once more. "This is between my father and myself! You may think yourself very clever, Toe Rag, and you may think that I am not—"

Toe Rag arched an eyebrow. He had prepared for this moment. He stayed silent and merely let the stray beam of sunlight glint on his dancing eyes. It was a silence of the most profound eloquence.

"I may not know what you're up to, Toe Rag, I may not know a lot of things, but I do know one thing. I know that I am Thor, the God of Thunder, and that I will not be made a fool of by a goblin!"

"Well," said Toe Rag with a light grin, "when you know two things I expect you'll be twice as clever. Remember to put your clothes on before you go out." He gestured casually at the pile beside him and departed.

10

◆

The trouble with the sort of shop that sells things like magnifying glasses and penknives is that they tend also to sell all kinds of other fascinating things, like the quite extraordinary device with which Dirk eventually emerged after having been hopelessly unable to decide between the knife with the built-in Philips screwdriver, toothpick and ballpoint pen and the one with the 13-tooth gristle saw and the tig-welded rivets.

The magnifying glasses had held him in thrall for a short while, particularly the 25-diopter, high-index, vacuum-deposited, gold-coated glass model with the integral handle and mount and the notchless seal glazing, but then Dirk had happened to catch sight of a small electronic I Ching calculator and he was lost.

He had never before even guessed at the existence of such a thing. And to be able to move from total ignorance of something to total desire for it, and then actually to own the thing all within the space of about forty seconds was, for Dirk, something of an epiphany.

The electronic I Ching calculator was badly made. It had probably been manufactured in whichever of the Southeast Asian countries was busy tooling up to do to South Korea what South Korea was busy doing to Japan. Glue technology had obviously not progressed in that country to the point where things could be successfully held together with it. Already the back had half fallen off and needed to be stuck back on with Sellotape.

It was much like an ordinary pocket calculator, except that the LCD screen was a little larger than usual in order to accommodate the abridged judgements of King Wen on each of the sixty-four hexagrams, and also the commentaries of his son, the Duke of Chou, on each of the lines of each hexagram. These were unusual texts to see marching across the display of a pocket calculator, particularly as they had been translated from the Chinese via the Japanese and seemed to have enjoyed many adventures on the way.

The device also functioned as an ordinary calculator, but only to a limited degree. It could handle any calculation which returned an answer of anything up to 4.

$1 + 1$ it could manage (2) and $1 + 2$ (3) and $2 + 2$ (4) or tan 74 (3.4874145), but anything above 4 it represented merely as "A Suffusion of Yellow." Dirk was not certain if this was a programming error or an insight beyond his ability to fathom, but he was crazy about it anyway, enough to hand over twenty pounds of ready cash for the thing.

"Thank you, sir," said the proprietor. "It's a nice piece, that. I think you'll be happy with it."

"I ab," said Dirk.

"Glad to hear it, sir," replied the proprietor. "Do you know you've broken your nose?"

Dirk looked up from fawning on his new possession.

"Yedth," he said testily, "obf courth I dknow."

The man nodded, satisfied.

"Just that a lot of my customers wouldn't always know about a thing like that," he explained.

Dirk thanked him tersely and hurried out with his purchase. A few minutes later he took up residence at the small corner table of an Islington café, ordered a small but incredibly strong cup of coffee, and attempted to take stock of his day. A moment's reflection told him that he was almost certainly going to need a small but incredibly strong beer as well, and he attempted to add this to his order.

"A wha?" said the waiter. His hair was very black and filled with brilliantine. He was tall, incredibly fit, and too cool to listen to customers or say consonants.

Dirk repeated his order, but what with having the café's music system, a broken nose, and the waiter's insuperable cool to contend with, he eventually found it simpler to write out the order on a napkin with a stub of pencil. The waiter peered at it in an offended manner, and left.

Dirk exchanged a friendly nod with the girl sitting half-reading a book at the next table, who had watched this exchange with sympathy. Then he set about laying out his morning's acquisitions on the table in front of him—

the newspaper, the electronic I Ching calculator and the envelope which he had retrieved from behind the gold disc on Geoffrey Anstey's bathroom wall. He then spent a minute or two dabbing at his nose with a handkerchief and prodding it tenderly to see how much it hurt, which turned out to be quite a lot. He sighed and stuffed the handkerchief back in his pocket.

A few seconds later the waiter returned bearing a herb omelet and a single breadstick. Dirk explained that this wasn't what he had ordered. The waiter shrugged and said that it wasn't his fault.

Dirk had no idea what to say to this, and said so. He was still having a great deal of difficulty speaking. The waiter asked Dirk if he knew that he had broken his nose and Dirk said that yedth, dthagg you berry budge, he did. The waiter said that his friend Neil had once broken his nose and Dirk said that he hobed it hurd like hell, which seemed to draw the conversation to a close. The waiter took the omelet and left, vowing never to return.

When the girl sitting at the next table looked away for a moment, Dirk leaned over and took her coffee. He knew that he was perfectly safe doing this because she would simply not be able to believe that this had happened. He sat sipping at the lukewarm cup and casting his mind back over the day.

He knew that before consulting the I Ching, even an electronic one, he should try and compose his thoughts and allow them to settle calmly.

This was a tough one.

However much he tried to clear his mind and think in a calm and collected way, he was unable to stop Geoffrey Anstey's head revolving incessantly in his mind. It revolved disapprovingly, as if pointing an accusing finger at Dirk. The fact that it did not have an accusing finger with which to point only served to drive the point it was trying to make home all the harder.

Dirk screwed up his eyes and attempted to concentrate instead on the problem of the mysteriously vanished Miss Pearce, but was unable to get much of a grip on it. When she had used to work for him she would often disappear mysteriously for two or three days at a time, but the papers didn't make any kind of fuss about it then. Admittedly, there weren't things exploding around her at the time—at least, not that he was aware of. She had never mentioned anything exploding particularly.

Furthermore, whenever he thought of her face, which he had last seen on the television set in Geoffrey Anstey's house, his thoughts tended instantly to sink toward the head which was busy revolving thirty-three and a third times a minute three floors beneath it. This was not conducive to the calm and contemplative mood he was seeking. Nor was the very loud music on the café's music system.

He sighed and stared at the electronic I Ching calculator.

If he wanted to get his thoughts into some kind of order, then maybe chronological order would be as good a one as any. He decided to cast his mind back to the beginning of the day, before any of these appalling things had happened, or at least before they'd happened to him.

First there had been the fridge.

It seemed to him that by comparison with everything else, the problem of what to do about his fridge had now shrunk to fairly manageable proportions. It still provoked a discernible twinge of fear and guilt, but here, he thought, was a problem which he could face up to with relative calm.

The little book of instructions suggested that he should

simply concentrate "soulfully" on the question which was "besieging" him, write it down, ponder on it, enjoy the silence, and then once he had achieved inner harmony and tranquility he should push the red button.

There wasn't a red button, but there was a blue button marked "Red," and this Dirk took to be the one.

He concentrated for a while on the question, then looked through his pockets for a piece of paper, but was unable to find one. In the end he wrote his question, "Should I buy a new fridge?" on a corner of his napkin. Then he took the view that if he was going to wait until he had achieved inner harmony and tranquility he could be there all night, so he went ahead and pushed the blue button marked "Red" anyway. A symbol flashed up in a corner of the screen, a hexagram which looked like this:

3 : CHUN

The I Ching calculator then scrolled this text across its tiny LCD display:

The Judgment of King Wen:
Chun Signifies Difficulties At Outset, As Of Blade Of Grass Pushing Up Against Stone. The Time Is Full Of Irregularities And Obscurities: Superior Man Will Adjust His Measures As In Sorting The Threads Of The Warp And Woof. Firm Correctness Will Bring At Last Success. Early Advances Should Only Be Made With

Caution. There Will Be Advantage In Appointing Feu-
dal Princes.
Line 6 Changes:
The Commentary of the Duke of Chou:
The Horses and the Chariot Obliged to Retreat.
Streams of Bloody Tears Will Flow.

Dirk considered this for a few moments, and then decided that on balance it appeared to be a vote in favor of
getting the new fridge, which, by a staggering coincidence, was the course of action he himself favored.

There was a pay phone in one of the dark corners where
waiters slouched moodily at one another. Dirk threaded
his way through them, wondering whom it was they reminded him of, and eventually deciding that it was the
small crowd of naked men standing around behind the
Holy Family in Michelangelo's picture of the same name,
for no more apparent reason than that Michelangelo
rather liked them.

He telephoned an acquaintance of his called Nobby
Paxton, or so he claimed, who worked the darker side of
the domestic-appliance supply business. Dirk came
straight to the point.

"Dobby, I deed a fridge."

"Dirk, I been saving one against the day you'd ask me."

Dirk found this highly unlikely.

"Only I wand a good fridge, you thee, Dobby."

"This is the best, Dirk. Japanese. Microprocessor-con-
trolled."

"What would a microprothethor be doing id a fridge,
Dobby?"

"Keeping itself cool, Dirk. I'll get the lads to bring it
round right away. I need to get it off the premises pretty
sharpish for reasons which I won't trouble you with."

"I apprethiade thid, Dobby," said Dirk. "Problem id, I'm not at home at preddent."

"Gaining access to houses in the absence of their owners is only one of the panoply of skills with which my lads are blessed. Let me know if you find anything missing afterwards, by the way."

"I'd be happy to, Dobby. Id fact if your ladth are in a mood for carting thtuff off, I'd be glad if they would thtart with my old fridge. It badly needth throwing away."

"I shall see that it's done, Dirk. There's usually a skip or two on your street these days. Now, do you expect to be paying for this or shall I just get you kneecapped straight off, save everybody time and aggravation all round?"

It was never 100 percent clear to Dirk exactly when Nobby was joking, and he was not keen to put it to the test. He assured him that he would pay him as soon as next they met.

"See you very soon then, Dirk," said Nobby. "By the way, do you know you sound exactly as if someone's broken your nose?"

There was a pause.

"You there, Dirk?" said Nobby.

"Yed," said Dirk. "I wad judd liddening to a reggord."

"Hot Potato!" roared the hi-fi in the café.

"Don't pick it up, pick it up, pick it up,

"Quick, pass it on, pass it on, pass it on."

"I said, do you know you sound exactly as if someone's broken your nose?" repeated Nobby.

Dirk said that he did know this, thanked Nobby for pointing it out, said goodbye, stood thoughtfully for a moment, made another quick couple of phone calls, and then threaded his way back through the huddle of posing waiters to find the girl whose coffee he had appropriated sitting at his table.

"Hello," she said meaningfully.

Dirk was as gracious as he knew how to be.

He bowed to her very politely, doffed his hat, since all this gave him a second or so to recover himself, and requested her permission to sit down.

"Go ahead," she said, "it's your table." She gestured magnanimously.

She was small, her hair was neat and dark, she was in her mid-twenties, and was looking quizzically at the half-empty cup of coffee in the middle of the table.

Dirk sat down opposite her and leant forward conspiratorially. "I expeg," he said in a low voice, "you are enquirigg after your coffee."

"You betcha," said the girl.

"Id very bad for you, you dow."

"Is it?"

"Id id. Caffeide. Cholethderog in the milgg."

"I see—so it was just my health you were thinking of."

"I was thiggigg of meddy thiggs," said Dirk airily.

"You saw me sitting at the next table and you thought, 'There's a nice-looking girl with her health in ruins. Let me save her from herself.'"

"In a nudthell."

"Do you know you've broken your nose?"

"Yeth, of courth I do," said Dirk crossly. "Everybody keepth—"

"How long ago did you break it?" the girl asked.

"Id wad broked for me," said Dirk, "aboud tweddy midddidd ago."

"I thought so," said the girl. "Close your eyes for a moment."

Dirk looked at her suspiciously.

"Why?"

"It's all right," she said with a smile, "I'm not going to hurt you. Now close them."

With a puzzled frown, Dirk closed his eyes just for a moment. In that moment the girl reached over and gripped him firmly by the nose, giving it a sharp twist. Dirk nearly exploded with pain and howled so loudly that he almost attracted the attention of a waiter.

"You widge!" he yelled, staggering wildly back from the table clutching his face. "You double-dabbed widge!"

"Oh, be quiet and sit down," she said. "All right, I lied about it not going to hurt you, but at least it should be straight now, which will save you a lot worse later on. You should get straight round to a hospital to have some splints and padding put on. I'm a nurse, I know what I'm doing. Or at least I think I do. Let's have a look at you."

Panting and spluttering, Dirk sat down once more, his hands cupped round his nose. After a few long seconds he began to prod it tenderly again and then let the girl examine it.

She said, "My name's Sally Mills, by the way. I usually try to introduce myself properly before physical intimacy takes place, but sometimes—" she sighed—"there just isn't time."

Dirk ran his fingers up either side of his nose again.

"I thigg id id trader," Dirk said at last.

"Straighter," Sally said. "Say 'straighter' properly. It'll help you feel better."

"Straighter," said Dirk. "Yed. I thee wad you mead."

"What?"

"I see what you mead."

"Good," she said with a sigh of relief, "I'm glad that

worked. My horoscope this morning said that virtually everything I decided today would be wrong."

"Yes, well, you don't want to believe all that rubbish," said Dirk sharply.

"I don't," said Sally.

"Particularly not The Great Zaganza."

"Oh, you read it too, did you?"

"No. That is, well, not for the same reason."

"My reason was that a patient asked me to read his horoscope to him this morning just before he died. What was yours?"

"Er, a very complicated one."

"I see," said Sally skeptically. "What's this?"

"It's a calculator," said Dirk. "Well, look, I mustn't keep you. I am indebted to you, my dear lady, for the tenderness of your ministrations and the loan of your coffee, but lo! the day wears on, and I am sure you have a heavy schedule of grievous bodily harm to attend to."

"Not at all. I came off night duty at nine o'clock this morning, and all I have to do all day is keep awake so that I can sleep normally tonight. I have nothing better to do than to sit around talking to strangers in cafés. You, on the other hand, should get yourself to a casualty department as soon as possible. As soon as you've paid my bill, in fact."

She leaned over to the table she had originally been sitting at and picked up the running-total lying by her plate. She looked at it, shaking her head disapprovingly.

"Five cups of coffee, I'm afraid. It was a long night on the wards. All sorts of comings and goings in the middle of it. One patient in a coma who had to be moved to a private hospital in the early hours. God knows why it had to be done at that time of night. Just creates unnecessary trouble. I wouldn't pay for the second croissant if I were you. I ordered it but it never came."

She pushed the bill across to Dirk, who picked it up with a reluctant sigh.

"Inordinate," he said, "larcenously inordinate. And, in the circumstances, adding a fifteen percent service charge is tantamount to jeering at you. I bet they won't even bring me a knife."

He turned and tried, without any real hope of success, to summon any of the gaggle of waiters lounging among the sugar bowls at the back.

Sally Mills took her bill and Dirk's and attempted to add them up on Dirk's calculator.

"The total seems to come to 'A Suffusion of Yellow,' " she said.

"Thank you, I'll take that," said Dirk, turning back crossly and relieving her of the electronic I Ching set, which he put into his pocket. He resumed his hapless waving at the tableau of waiters.

"What do you want a knife for, anyway?" asked Sally.

"To open this," said Dirk, waggling the large, heavily Sellotaped envelope at her.

"I'll get you one," she said. A young man sitting on his own at another nearby table was looking away at that moment, so Sally quickly leaned across and nabbed his knife.

"I am indebted to you," said Dirk and put out his hand to take the knife from her.

She held it away from him.

"What's in the envelope?" she said.

"You are an extremely inquisitive and presumptuous young lady," exclaimed Dirk.

"And you," said Sally Mills, "are very strange."

"Only," said Dirk, "as strange as I need to be."

"Humph," said Sally. "What's in the envelope?" She still wouldn't give him the knife.

"The envelope is not yours," proclaimed Dirk, "and its contents are not your concern."

"It looks very interesting though. What's in it?"

"Well, I won't know till I've opened it!"

She looked at him suspiciously, then snatched the envelope from him.

"I insist that you—" expostulated Dirk, incompletely.

"What's your name?" demanded Sally.

"My name is Gently. Mr. Dirk Gently."

"And not Geoffrey Anstey, or any of these other names that have been crossed out?" She frowned, briefly, looking at them.

"No," said Dirk. "Certainly not."

"So you mean the envelope is not yours either?"

"I—that is—"

"Aha! So you are also being extremely . . . what was it?"

"Inquisitive and presumptuous. I do not deny it. But I am a private detective. I am paid to be inquisitive and presumptuous. Not as often or copiously as I would wish, but I am nevertheless inquisitive and presumptuous on a professional basis."

"How sad. I think it's much more fun being inquisitive and presumptuous as a hobby. So you are a professional while I am merely an amateur of Olympic standard. You don't look like a private detective."

"No private detective looks like a private detective. That's one of the first rules of private detection."

"But if no private detective looks like a private detective, how does a private detective know what it is he's supposed not to look like? Seems to me there's a problem there."

"Yes, but it's not one that keeps me awake at nights," said Dirk in exasperation. "Anyway, I am not as other private detectives. My methods are holistic and, in a very proper sense of the word, chaotic. I operate by investigating the fundamental interconnectedness of all things."

Sally Mills merely blinked at him.

"Every particle in the universe," continued Dirk, warming to his subject and beginning to stare a bit, "affects every other particle, however faintly or obliquely. Everything interconnects with everything. The beating of a butterfly's wings in China can affect the course of an Atlantic hurricane. If I could interrogate this table leg in a way that made sense to me, or to the table leg, then it could provide me with the answer to any question about the universe. I could ask anybody I liked, chosen entirely by chance, any random question I cared to think of, and their answer, or lack of it, would in some way bear upon the problem to which I am seeking a solution. It is only a question of knowing how to interpret it. Even you, whom I have met entirely by chance, probably know things that are vital to my investigation, if only I knew what to ask you, which I don't, and if only I could be bothered to, which I can't."

He paused, and said, "Please will you let me have the envelope and the knife?"

"You make it sound as if someone's life depends on it."

Dirk dropped his eyes for a moment.

"I rather think somebody's life did depend on it," he said. He said it in such a way that a cloud seemed to pass briefly over them.

Sally Mills relented and passed the envelope and the knife over to Dirk. A spark seemed to go out of her.

The knife was too blunt and the Sellotape too thickly applied. Dirk struggled with it for a few seconds but was unable to slice through it. He sat back in his seat feeling tired and irritable.

He said, "I'll go and ask them if they've got anything sharper," and stood up, clutching the envelope.

"You should go and get your nose fixed," said Sally Mills quietly.

"Thank you," said Dirk and bowed very slightly to her.

He picked up the bills and set out to visit the exhibition of waiters mounted at the rear of the café. He encountered a certain coolness when he was disinclined to augment the mandatory 15 percent service charge with any voluntary additional token of his personal appreciation, and was told that no, that was the only type of knife they had and that's all there was to it.

Dirk thanked them and walked back through the café.

Sitting in his seat talking to Sally Mills was the young man whose knife she had purloined. He nodded to her, but she was deeply engrossed in conversation with her new friend and did not notice.

". . . in a coma," she was saying, "who had to be moved to a private hospital in the early hours. God knows why it had to be done at that time of night. Just creates unnecessary trouble. Excuse me rabbiting on, but the patient had his own personal Coca-Cola machine and sledgehammer with him, and that sort of thing is all very well in a private hospital, but on a short-staffed NHS ward it just makes me tired, and I talk too much when I'm tired. If I suddenly fall insensible to the floor, would you let me know?"

Dirk walked on, and then noticed that Sally Mills had left the book she had been reading on her original table, and something about it caught his attention.

It was a large book called *Run Like the Devil*. In fact it was extremely large and a little dog-eared, looking more like a puff-pastry cliff than a book. The bottom half of the cover featured the normal woman-in-cocktail-dress-framed-in-the-sights-of-a-gun, while the top half was entirely taken up with the author's name, Howard Bell, embossed in silver.

Dirk couldn't immediately work out what it was about the book that had caught his eye, but he knew that some detail of the cover had struck a chord with him somewhere. He gave a circumspect glance at the girl whose coffee he had purloined, and whose five coffees and two croissants, one undelivered and uneaten, he had subsequently paid for. She wasn't looking, so he purloined her book as well and slipped it into the pocket of his leather coat.

He stepped out onto the street, where a passing eagle swooped out of the sky at him, nearly forcing him into the path of a cyclist, who cursed and swore at him from a moral high ground that cyclists alone seem able to inhabit.

11

◆

Into the well-kempt grounds that lay just on the outskirts of a well-kempt village on the fringes of the well-
kempt Cotswolds turned a less than well-kempt car.

It was a battered yellow Citroën 2CV, which had had
one careful owner but also three suicidally reckless ones.
It made its way up the driveway with a reluctant air as if
all it asked for from life was to be tipped into a restful
ditch in one of the adjoining meadows and there allowed
to settle in graceful abandonment, instead of which, here
it was being asked to drag itself all the way up this long

graveled drive, and would, no doubt, soon be called upon to drag itself all the way back down again, to what possible purpose it was beyond its wit to imagine.

It drew to a halt in front of the elegant stone entrance to the main building, and then began to trundle slowly backward again until its occupant yanked on the handbrake, which evoked from the car a sort of strangled "eek."

A door flopped open, wobbling perilously on its one remaining hinge, and there emerged from the car a pair of the sort of legs which sound-track editors are unable to see without needing to slap a smoky saxophone solo all over, for reasons which no one besides sound-track editors has ever been able to understand. In this particular case, however, the saxophone would have been silenced by the proximity of the kazoo which the same sound-track editor would almost certainly have slapped all over the progress of the vehicle.

The owner of the legs followed them in the usual manner, closed the car door tenderly, and then made her way into the building.

The car remained parked in front of it.

After a few minutes a porter came out and examined it, adopted a disapproving manner and then, for lack of anything more positive to do, went back in.

A short time later, Kate was shown into the office of Mr. Ralph Standish, the chief consultant psychologist and one of the directors of the Woodshead Hospital, who was just completing a telephone conversation.

"Yes, it is true," he was saying, "that sometimes unusually intelligent and sensitive children can appear to be stupid. But, Mrs. Benson, stupid children can sometimes appear to be stupid as well. I think that's something you might have to consider. I know it's very painful, yes. Good day, Mrs. Benson."

He put the phone away into a desk drawer and spent a couple of seconds collecting his thoughts before looking up.

"This is very short notice, Miss, er, Schechter," he said to her at last.

In fact, what he had said was, "This is very short notice, Miss, er—" and then he had paused and peered into another of his desk drawers before saying "Schechter."

It seemed to Kate that it was very odd to keep your visitors' names in a drawer, but then he clearly disliked having things cluttering up his fine but severely designed black ash desk, because there was nothing on it at all. It was completely blank, as was every other surface in his office. There was nothing on the small neat steel-and-glass coffee table which sat squarely between two Barcelona chairs. There was nothing on top of the two expensive-looking filing cabinets which stood at the back of the room.

There were no bookshelves—if there were any books they were presumably hidden away behind the white doors of the large blank built-in cupboards—and although there was one plain black picture frame hanging on the wall, this was presumably a temporary aberration because there was no picture in it.

Kate looked around her with a bemused air.

"Do you have no ornaments in here at all, Mr. Standish?" she asked.

He was, for a moment, somewhat taken aback by her transatlantic directness, but then he answered her.

"Indeed I have ornaments," he said, and pulled open another drawer. He pulled out from this a small china model of a kitten playing with a ball of wool and put it firmly on the desk in front of him.

"As a psychologist I am aware of the important role that ornamentation plays in nourishing the human spirit," he pronounced.

He put the china kitten back in the drawer and slid it closed with a smooth click.

"Now."

He clasped his hands together on the desk in front of him, and looked at her enquiringly.

"It's very good of you to see me at short notice, Mr. Standish—"

"Yes, yes, we've established that."

"—but I'm sure you know what newspaper deadlines are like."

"I know at least as much as I would ever care to know about newspapers, Miss, er—"

He opened his drawer again.

"Miss Schechter, but—"

"Well that's partly what made me approach you," lied Kate charmingly. "I know that you have suffered from some, well, unfortunate publicity here, and thought you might welcome the opportunity to talk about some of the more enlightening aspects of the work at the Woodshead Hospital." She smiled very sweetly.

"It's only because you come to me with the highest recommendation from my very good friend and colleague Mr., er—"

"Franklin, Alan Franklin," prompted Kate, to save the psychologist from having to open his drawer again. Alan Franklin was a therapist whom Kate had seen for a few sessions after the loss of her husband, Luke. He had warned her that Standish, though brilliant, was also peculiar, even by the high standards set by his profession.

"—Franklin," resumed Standish, "that I agreed to see you. Let me warn you instantly that if I see any resumption of this 'Something nasty in the Woodshead' mendacity appearing in the papers as a result of this interview I will, I will—"

" 'do such things—

" 'What they are yet I know not—but they shall be

" 'The terror of the Earth,' " said Kate, brightly.

Standish narrowed his eyes.

"*Lear*, Act Two, Scene Four," he said. "And I think you'll find it's 'terrors' and not 'terror.' "

"Do you know, I think you're right?" replied Kate.

Thank you, Alan, she thought. She smiled at Standish, who relaxed into pleased superiority. It was odd, Kate reflected, that people who needed to bully you were the easiest to push around.

"So you would like to know precisely what, Miss Schechter?"

"Assume," said Kate, "that I know nothing."

Standish smiled, as if to signify that no assumption could possibly give him greater pleasure.

"Very well," he said. "The Woodshead is a research hospital. We specialize in the care and study of patients with unusual or previously unknown conditions, largely in the psychological or psychiatric fields. Funds are raised in various ways. One of our chief methods is quite simply to take in private patients at exorbitantly high fees, which they are happy to pay, or at least happy to complain about. There is in fact nothing to complain about because patients who come to us privately are made fully aware of why our fees are so high. For the money they are paying, they are, of course, perfectly entitled to complain—the right to complain is one of the privileges they are paying for. In some cases we come to a special arrangement under which, in return for being made the sole beneficiaries of a patient's estate, we will guarantee to look after that patient for the rest of his or her life."

"So in effect you are in the business of giving scholarships to people with particularly gifted diseases?"

"Exactly. A very good way of expressing it. We are in the business of giving scholarships to people with particularly gifted diseases. I must make a note of that. Miss Mayhew!"

He had opened a drawer, which clearly contained his office intercom. In response to his summons, one of the cupboards opened and turned out to be a door into a side office—a feature which must have appealed to some architect who had conceived an ideological dislike of doors. From this office there emerged obediently a thin and rather blank-faced woman in her mid-forties.

"Miss Mayhew," said Mr. Standish, "we are in the business of giving scholarships to people with particularly gifted diseases."

"Very good, Mr. Standish," said Miss Mayhew, and retreated backward into her office, pulling the door closed after her. Kate wondered if it was perhaps a cupboard after all.

"And we do have some patients with some really quite outstanding diseases at the moment," enthused the psychologist. "Perhaps you would care to come and see one or two of our current stars?"

"Indeed I would. That would be most interesting, Mr. Standish, you're very kind," said Kate.

"You have to be kind in this job," Standish replied, and flicked a smile on and off at her.

Kate was trying to keep some of the impatience she was feeling out of her manner. She did not take to Mr. Standish, and was beginning to feel that there was a kind of Martian quality to him. Furthermore, the only thing she was actually interested in was discovering whether or not the hospital had accepted a new admission in the early hours of the morning, and if so, where he was and whether she could see him.

She had originally tried the direct approach but had been rebuffed by a mere telephone receptionist on the grounds that she didn't have a name to ask for. Simply asking if they had any tall, well-built, blond men in residence had seemed to create entirely the wrong impression. At least, she insisted to herself that it was entirely the wrong impression. A quick phone call to Alan Franklin had set her up for this altogether more subtle approach.

"Good!" A look of doubt passed momentarily over Mr. Standish's face, and he summoned Miss Mayhew from out of her cupboard again.

"Miss Mayhew, that last thing I just said to you—"

"Yes, Mr. Standish?"

"I assume you realized that I wished you to make a note of it for me?"

"No, Mr. Standish, but I will be happy to do so."

"Thank you," said Mr. Standish with a slightly tense look. "And tidy up in here please. The place looks a—"

He wanted to say that the place looked a mess, but was frustrated by its air of clinical sterility.

"Just tidy up generally," he concluded.

"Yes, Mr. Standish."

The psychologist nodded tersely, brushed a nonexistent speck of dust off the top of his desk, flicked another brief smile on and off at Kate and then escorted her out of his office into the corridor which was immaculately laid with the sort of beige carpet that gave everyone who walked on it electric shocks.

"Here, you see," said Standish, indicating part of the
wall they were walking past with an idle wave of his hand,
but not making it in any way clear what it was he wished
her to see or what she was supposed to understand from
it.

"And this," he said, apparently pointing at a door
hinge.

"Ah," he added, as the door swung open toward them.
Kate was alarmed to find herself giving a little expectant
start every time a door opened anywhere in this place.
This was not the sort of behavior she expected of a
worldly-wise New York journalist, even if she didn't actually live in New York and only wrote travel articles for
magazines. It still was not right for her to be looking for
large blond men every time a door opened.

There was no large blond man. There was instead a
small, sandy-haired girl of about ten years old, being
pushed along in a wheelchair. She seemed very pale, sick
and withdrawn, and was murmuring something sound-
lessly to herself. Whatever it was she was murmuring
seemed to cause her worry and agitation, and she would
flop this way then that in her chair as if trying to escape
from the words coming out of her mouth. Kate was instantly moved by the sight of her, and on an impulse
asked the nurse who was pushing her along to stop.

She squatted down to look kindly into the girl's face,
which seemed to please the nurse a little, but Mr. Standish less so.

Kate did not try to demand the girl's attention, merely
gave her an open and friendly smile to see if she wanted
to respond, but the girl seemed unwilling or unable to.
Her mouth worked away endlessly, appearing almost to
lead an existence that was independent of the rest of her
face.

Now that Kate looked at her more closely it seemed that she looked not so much sick and withdrawn as weary, harassed and unutterably fed up. She needed a little rest, she needed peace, but her mouth kept motoring on.

For a fleeting instant her eyes caught Kate's, and the message Kate received was along the lines of "I'm sorry but you'll just have to excuse me while all this is going on." The girl took a deep breath, half-closed her eyes in resignation and continued her relentless silent murmuring.

Kate leaned forward a little in an attempt to catch any actual words, but she couldn't make anything out. She shot an inquiring look up at Standish.

He said, simply, "Stock market prices."

A look of amazement crept over Kate's face.

Standish added with a wry shrug, "Yesterday's, I'm afraid."

Kate flinched at having her reaction so wildly misinterpreted, and hurriedly looked back at the girl in order to cover her confusion.

"You mean," she said, rather redundantly, "she's just sitting here reciting yesterday's stock market prices?" The girl rolled her eyes past Kate's.

"Yes," said Standish. "It took a lip reader to work out what was going on. We all got rather excited, of course, but then closer examination revealed that they were only yesterday's, which was a bit of a disappointment. Not that significant a case really. Aberrant behavior. Interesting to know why she does it, but—"

"Hold on a moment," said Kate, trying to sound very interested rather than absolutely horrified. "Are you saying that she is reciting—what?—the closing prices over and over, or—"

"No. That's an interesting feature of course. She pretty

much keeps pace with movements in the market over the course of a whole day. Just twenty-four hours out of step."

"But that's extraordinary, isn't it?"

"Oh, yes. Quite a feat."

"A *feat?*"

"Well, as a scientist, I have to take the view that since the information is freely available, she is acquiring it through normal channels. There's no necessity in this case to invent any supernatural or paranormal dimension. Occam's razor. Shouldn't needlessly multiply entities."

"But has anyone seen her studying the newspapers, or copying stuff down over the phone?"

She looked up at the nurse, who shook her head dumbly.

"No, never actually caught her at it," said Standish. "As I said, it's quite a feat. I'm sure a stage magician or memory man could tell you how it was done."

"Have you asked one?"

"No. Don't hold with such people."

"But do you really think that she could possibly be doing this deliberately?" insisted Kate.

"Believe me, if you understood as much about people as I do, Miss, er—you would believe anything," said Standish in his most professionally reassuring tone of voice.

Kate stared into the tired, wretched face of the young girl and said nothing.

"You have to understand," said Standish, "that we have to be rational about this. If it was tomorrow's stock market prices, it would be a different story. That would be a phenomenon of an entirely different character which would merit and demand the most rigorous study. And

I'm sure we'd have no difficulty in funding the research. There would be absolutely no problem about that."

"I see," said Kate, and meant it.

She stood up, a little stiffly, and brushed down her skirt.

"So," she said, and felt ashamed of herself, "who is your newest patient? Who has arrived most recently, then?" She shuddered at the crassness of the non sequitur, but reminded herself that she was there as a journalist, so it would not seem odd.

Standish waved the nurse and the wheelchair with its sad charge on their way. Kate glanced back at the girl once, and then followed Standish through the swing doors and into the next section of corridor, which was identical to the previous one.

"Here, you see," said Standish again, this time apparently in relation to a window frame.

"And this," he said, pointing at a light.

He had obviously either not heard her question or was deliberately ignoring it. Perhaps, thought Kate, he was simply treating it with the contempt it deserved.

It suddenly dawned on her what all this "Here you see" and "And this"-ing was about. He was asking her to admire the quality of the decor. The windows were sashes, with finely made and beautifully painted beads; the light fittings were of a heavy dull metal, probably nickel-plated —and so on.

"Very fine," she said accommodatingly, and then noticed that this had sounded an odd thing to say in her American accent.

"Nice place you've got here," she added, thinking that that would please him.

It did. He allowed himself a subdued beam of pleasure.

"We like to think of it as a quality caring environment," he said.

"You must get a lot of people wanting to come here," Kate continued, plugging away at her theme. "How often do you admit new patients? When was the last—?"

With her left hand she carefully restrained her right hand which wanted to strangle her at this moment.

A door they were passing was slightly ajar, and she tried, unobtrusively, to look in.

"Very well, we'll take a look in here," said Standish immediately, pushing the door fully open, on what transpired to be quite a small room.

"Ah, yes," Standish said, recognizing the occupant. He ushered Kate in.

The occupant of the room was another non-large, non-blond person. Kate was beginning to find the whole visit to be something of an emotionally wearing experience, and she had a feeling that things were not about to ease up in that respect.

The man sitting in the bedside chair while his bed was being made up by a hospital orderly was one of the most deeply and disturbingly tousled people that Kate had ever seen. In fact, it was only his hair that was tousled, but it was tousled to such an extreme degree that it seemed to draw all of his long face up into its distressed chaos.

He seemed quite content to sit where he was, but there was something tremendously vacant about his contentedness—he seemed literally to be content about nothing. There was a completely empty space hanging in the air about eighteen inches in front of his face, and his contentedness, if it sprang from anything, sprang from staring at that.

There was also a sense that he was waiting for something. Whether it was something that was about to happen at any moment or something that was going to happen later in the week, or even something that was going to happen some little while after hell iced over and British Telecom got the phones fixed, was by no means apparent because it seemed to be all the same to him. If it happened he was ready for it and if it didn't—he was content.

Kate found such contentedness almost unbearably distressing.

"What's the matter with him?" she said quietly, and then instantly realized that she was talking as if he wasn't there, when he could probably speak perfectly well for himself. Indeed, at that moment, he suddenly did speak.

"Oh, er, hi," he said. "OK, yeah, thank you."

"Er, hello," she said, in response, though it didn't seem quite to fit. Or rather, what he had said didn't seem quite to fit. Standish made a gesture to her to discourage her from speaking.

"Er, yeah, a bagel would be fine," said the contented man. He said it in a flat kind of tone, as if merely repeating something he had been given to say.

"Yeah, and maybe some juice," he added. "OK, thanks." He then relaxed into his state of empty watchfulness.

"A very unusual condition," said Standish, "that is to say, we can only believe that it is entirely unique. I've certainly never heard of anything remotely like it. It has also proved virtually impossible to verify beyond question that it is what it appears to be, so I'm glad to say that we have been spared the embarrassment of attempting to give the condition a name."

"Would you like me to help Mr. Elwes back to bed?" asked the orderly of Standish. Standish nodded. He didn't bother to waste words on minions.

The orderly bent down to talk to the patient.

"Mr. Elwes?" he said quietly.

Mr. Elwes seemed to swim up out of a reverie.

"Mmmm?" he said, and suddenly looked around. He seemed confused.

"Oh! Oh? What?" he said faintly.

"Would you like me to help you back to bed?"

"Oh. Oh, thank you, yes. Yes, that would be kind."

Though clearly dazed and bewildered, Mr. Elwes was quite able to get himself back into bed, and all the orderly needed to supply was reassurance and encouragement. Once Mr. Elwes was well settled, the orderly nodded politely to Standish and Kate and made his exit.

Mr. Elwes quickly lapsed back into his trancelike state, lying propped up against an escarpment of pillows. His head dropped forward slightly and he stared at one of his knees poking up bonily from under the covers.

"Get me New York," he said.

Kate shot a puzzled glance at Standish, hoping for some kind of explanation, but got none.

"Oh, OK," said Mr. Elwes, "it's five forty-one something. Hold on." He spoke another four digits of a number in his dead, flat voice.

"What is happening here?" asked Kate at last.

"It took us rather a long time to work it out. It was only quite by the remotest chance that someone discovered it. That television was on in the room . . ."

He pointed to the small portable set off to one side of the bed.

". . . tuned to one of those chat program things, which happened to be going out live. Most extraordinary thing. Mr. Elwes was sitting here muttering about how much he hated the BBC—don't know if it was the BBC, perhaps it was one of those other channels they have now—and was expressing an opinion about the host of the program, to the effect that he considered him to be a rectum of some kind, and saying furthermore that he wished the whole thing was over and that, yes, all right, he was coming, and then suddenly what he was saying and what was on the television began in some extraordinary way almost to synchronize."

"I don't understand what you mean," said Kate.

"I'd be surprised if you did," said Standish. "Everything that Elwes said was then said just a moment later on the television by a gentleman by the name of Mr. Dustin Hoffman. It seems that Mr. Elwes here knows everything that this Mr. Hoffman is going to say just a second or so before he says it. It is not, I have to say, something that Mr. Hoffman would be very pleased about if he knew. Attempts have been made to alert the gentleman to the problem, but he has proved to be somewhat difficult to reach."

"Just what the shit is going on here?" asked Mr. Elwes placidly.

"Mr. Hoffman is, we believe, currently making a film on location somewhere on the west coast of America."

Standish looked at his watch.

"I think he has probably just woken up in his hotel and is making his early morning phone calls," he added.

Kate was gazing with astonishment between Standish and the extraordinary Mr. Elwes.

"How long has the poor man been like this?"

"Oh, about five years I think. Started absolutely out of the blue. He was sitting having dinner with his family one day as usual when suddenly he started complaining about his caravan. And then shortly afterward about how he was being shot. He then spent the entire night talking in his sleep, repeating the same apparently meaningless phrases over and over again and also saying that he didn't think much of the way they were written. It was a very trying time for his family, as you can imagine, living with such a perfectionist actor and not even realizing it. It now seems very surprising how long it took them to identify what was occurring. Particularly when he once woke them all up in the early hours of the morning to thank them and the producer and the director for his Oscar."

Kate, who didn't realize that the day was still only softening her up for what was to come, made the mistake of thinking that it had just reached a climax of shock.

"The poor man," she said in a hushed voice. "What a pathetic state to be in. He's just living as someone else's shadow."

"I don't think he's in any pain."

Mr. Elwes appeared to be quietly locked in a bitter argument which seemed to touch on the definitions of the words "points," "gross," "profits" and "limo."

"But the implications of this are *extraordinary*, aren't they?" said Kate. "He's actually saying these things moments *before* Dustin Hoffman?"

"Well, it's all conjecture of course. We've only got a few clear instances of absolute correlation, and we just haven't got the opportunity to do more thorough research. One has to recognize that those few instances of direct correlation were not rigorously documented and could more simply be explained as coincidence. The rest could be merely the product of an elaborate fantasy."

"But if you put this case next to that of the girl we just saw . . ."

"Ah, well, we can't do that, you see. We have to judge each case on its own merits."

"But they're both in the same world . . . "

"Yes, but there are separate issues. Obviously, if Mr.

Elwes here could demonstrate significant precognition of, for instance, the head of the Soviet Union or, better still, the President of the United States, then clearly there would be important defense issues involved, and one might be prepared to stretch a point on the question of what is and what is not coincidence and fantasy, but for a mere screen actor—that is, a screen actor with no apparent designs on political office—I think that, no, we have to stick to the principles of rigorous science.

"So," he added, turning to leave, and drawing Kate with him, "I think that in the cases of both Mr. Elwes and, er, what-was-her-name, the charming girl in the wheelchair, it may be that we are not able to be of much more help to them, and we may need the space and facilities for more deserving cases."

Kate could think of nothing to say to this and followed, seething dumbly.

"Ah, now here we have an altogether much more interesting and promising case," said Standish, forging on ahead through the next set of double doors.

Kate was trying to keep her reactions under control, but nevertheless even someone as glassy and Martian as Mr. Standish could not help but detect that his audience was not absolutely with him. A little extra brusqueness and impatience crept into his demeanor to join forces with the large quantities of brusqueness and impatience which were already there.

They paced down the corridor for a few seconds in silence. Kate was looking for other ways of casually introducing the subject of recent admissions, but was forced to concede to herself that you cannot attempt to introduce the same subject three times in a row without beginning to lose that vital quality of casualness. She glanced as surreptitiously as she could at each door they passed, but most were firmly closed, and the ones that were not revealed nothing of interest.

She glanced out of a window as they walked past it and noticed a van turning into a rear courtyard. It caught her attention in the brief instant that it was within her view because it very clearly wasn't a baker's van or a laundry van. Baker's vans and laundry vans advertise their business and have words like "Bakery" and "Laundry" painted on them, whereas this van was completely blank. It had absolutely nothing to say to anyone, and it said it loudly and distinctly.

It was a large, heavy, serious-looking van that was almost on the verge of being an actual lorry, and it was painted in a uniform dark metallic gray. It reminded Kate of the huge gunmetal-gray freight lorries that thunder through Bulgaria and Yugoslavia on their way from Albania with nothing but the word "Albania" stenciled on their sides. She remembered wondering what it was that the Albanians exported in such an anonymous way, but when on one occasion she had looked it up, she found that their only export was electricity—which, if she remembered her high school physics correctly, was unlikely to be moved around in lorries.

The large, serious-looking van turned and started to reverse toward a rear entrance to the hospital. Whatever it was that the van usually carried, Kate thought, it was about either to pick it up or deliver it. She moved on.

A few moments later Standish arrived at a door, knocked at it gently and looked inquiringly into the room within. He then beckoned to Kate to follow him in.

This was a room of an altogether different sort. Immediately within the door was an anteroom with a very large window through which the main room could be seen. The two rooms were clearly soundproofed from each other, because the anteroom was decked out with monitoring equipment and computers, not one of which but didn't hum loudly to itself, and the main room contained a woman lying in bed, asleep.

"Mrs. Elspeth May," said Standish, and clearly felt that he was introducing the top of the bill. Her room was obviously a very good one—spacious and furnished comfortably and expensively. Fresh flowers stood on every surface, and the bedside table on which Mrs. May's knitting lay was of mahogany.

She herself was a comfortably shaped silver-haired lady of late middle age, and she was lying asleep half propped up in bed on a pile of pillows, wearing a pink woolly cardigan. After a moment it became clear to Kate that though she was asleep she was by no means inactive. Her head lay back peacefully with her eyes closed, but her right hand was clutching a pen which was scribbling away furiously on a large pad of paper that lay beside her. The hand, like the wheelchair girl's mouth, seemed to lead an independent and feverishly busy existence. Some small pinkish electrodes were taped to Mrs. May's forehead just below her hairline, and Kate assumed that these were providing some of the readings dancing across the computer screens in the anteroom in which she and Standish stood. Two white-coated men and a woman sat monitoring the equipment, and a nurse stood watching through the window. Standish exchanged a couple of brief words with them on the current state of the patient, which was universally agreed to be excellent.

Kate could not escape the impression that she ought to know who Mrs. May was, but she didn't, and was forced to ask.

"She is a medium," said Standish a little crossly, "as I assumed you would know. A medium of prodigious powers. She is currently in a trance and engaged in automatic writing. She is taking dictation. Virtually every piece of dictation she receives is of inestimable value. You have not heard of her?"

Kate admitted that she had not.

"Well, you are no doubt familiar with the lady who claimed that Mozart, Beethoven and Schubert were dictating music to her?"

"Yes, I did hear about that. There was a lot of stuff in color supplements about her a few years ago."

"Her claims were, well, interesting, if that's the sort of thing you're interested in. The music was certainly more consistent with what might be produced by each of those gentlemen quickly and before breakfast than it was with what you would expect from a musically unskilled middle-aged housewife."

Kate could not let this pomposity pass.

"That's a rather sexist viewpoint," she said, "George Eliot was a middle-aged housewife."

"Yes, yes," said Standish testily, "but she wasn't taking musical dictation from the deceased Wolfgang Amadeus. That's the point I'm making. Please try and follow the logic of this argument and do not introduce irrelevancies. If I felt for a moment that the example of George Eliot could shed any light on our present problem, you could rely on me to introduce it myself—Where was I?"

"I don't know."

"Mabel. Doris? Was that her name? Let us call her Mabel. The point is that the easiest way of dealing with the Doris problem was simply to ignore it. Nothing very important hinged on it at all. A few concerts. Second-rate material. But here, here we have something of an altogether different nature."

He said this last in hushed tones and turned to study a TV monitor which stood among the bank of computer screens. It showed a close-up of Mrs. May's hand scuttling across her pad of paper. Her hand largely obscured what she had written, but it appeared to be mathematics of some kind.

"Mrs. May is, or so she claims, taking dictation from some of the greatest physicists. From Einstein and from Heisenberg and Planck. And it is very hard to dispute her claims, because the information being produced here, by automatic writing, by this . . . untutored lady, is in fact physics of a very profound order.

"From the late Einstein we are getting more and more refinements to our picture of how time and space work at a macroscopic level, and from the late Heisenberg and Planck we are increasing our understanding of the fundamental structures of matter at a quantum level. And there is absolutely no doubt that this information is edging us closer and closer toward the elusive goal of a Grand Unified Field Theory of Everything.

"Now this produces a very interesting, not to say somewhat embarrassing, situation for scientists because the means by which the information is reaching us seems to be completely contrary to the meaning of the information."

"It's like Uncle Henry," said Kate suddenly.

Standish looked at her blankly.

"Uncle Henry thinks he's a chicken," Kate explained.

Standish looked at her blankly again.

"You must have heard it," said Kate. " 'We're terribly worried about Uncle Henry. He thinks he's a chicken.' 'Well, why don't you send him to the doctor?' 'Well, we would, only we need the eggs.' "

Standish stared at her as if a small but perfectly formed elderberry tree had suddenly sprung unbidden from the bridge of her nose.

"Say that again," he said in a small, shocked voice.

"What, all of it?"

"All of it."

Kate stuck her fist on her hip and said it again, doing the voices with a bit more dash and Southern accents this' time.

"That's brilliant," Standish breathed when she had done.

"You must have heard it before," she said, a little surprised by this response. "It's an old joke."

"No," he said, "I have not. We need the eggs. We need the *eggs*. We *need* the eggs. 'We can't send him to the doctor because *we need the eggs.*' An astounding insight into the central paradoxes of the human condition and of our indefatigable facility for constructing adaptive rationales to account for it. Good God."

Kate shrugged.

"And you say this is a *joke?*" demanded Standish incredulously.

"Yes. It's very old, really."

"And are they all like that? I never realized."

"Well—"

"I'm astounded," said Standish, "utterly astounded. I thought that jokes were things that fat people said on television and I never listened to them. I feel that people have been keeping something from me. Nurse!"

The nurse who had been keeping watch on Mrs. May through the window jumped at being barked at unexpectedly like this.

"Er, yes, Mr. Standish?" she said. He clearly made her nervous.

"Why have you never told me any jokes?"

The nurse stared at him and quivered at the impossibility of even knowing how to think about answering such a question.

"Er, well . . ."

"Make a note of it, will you? In future I will require you and all the other staff in this hospital to tell me all the jokes you have at your disposal, is that understood?"

"Er, yes, Mr. Standish—"

Standish looked at her with doubt and suspicion.

"You do know some jokes, do you, nurse?" he challenged her.

"Er, yes, Mr. Standish, I think, yes, I do."

"Tell me one."

"What, er, now, Mr. Standish?"

"This instant."

"Er, well, um—there's one which is that a patient wakes up after having, well, that is, he's been to, er, to surgery, and he wakes up and, it's not very good, but anyway, he's been to surgery and he says to the doctor when he wakes up, 'Doctor, doctor, what's wrong with me, I can't feel my legs.' And the doctor says, 'Yes, I'm afraid we've had to amputate both your arms.' And that's it really. Er, that's why he couldn't feel his legs, you see."

Mr. Standish looked at her levelly for a moment or two.

"You're on report, nurse," he said.

"Yes, Mr. Standish."

He turned to Kate. "Isn't there one about a chicken crossing a road or some such thing?"

"Er, yes," said Kate doubtfully. She felt she was caught in a bit of a situation here.

"And how does that go?"

"Well," said Kate, "it goes, 'Why did the chicken cross the road?' "

"Yes? And?"

"And the answer is 'To get to the other side.' "

"I see." Standish considered things for a moment. "And what does this chicken do when it arrives at the other side of the road?"

"History does not relate," replied Kate promptly. "I think that falls outside the scope of the joke, which really only concerns itself with the journey of the chicken across the road and the chicken's reasons for making it. It's a little like a Japanese haiku in that respect."

Kate suddenly found she was enjoying herself. She managed a surreptitious wink at the nurse, who had no idea what to make of anything at all.

"I see," said Standish once again, and frowned. "And do these, er, jokes require the preparatory use of any form of artificial stimulant?"

"Depends on the joke, depends on who it's being told to."

"Hmm, well, I must say, you've certainly opened up a rich furrow for me, Miss, er. It seems to me that the whole field of humor could benefit from close and immediate scrutiny. Clearly we need to sort out the jokes which have any kind of genuine psychological value from those which merely encourage drug abuse and should be stopped. Good."

He turned to address the white-coated researcher who was studying the TV monitor on which Mrs. May's scribblings were being tracked.

"Anything fresh of value from Mr. Einstein?" he asked.

The researcher did not move his eyes from the screen. He replied, "It says, 'How would you like your eggs? Poached or boiled?' "

Again Standish paused.

"Interesting," he said, "very interesting. Continue to

make a careful note of everything she writes. Come."
This last he said to Kate and made his way out of the
room.

"Very strange people, physicists," he said as soon as
they were outside again. "In my experience the ones who
aren't actually dead are in some way very ill. Well, the
afternoon presses on, and I'm sure that you are keen to
get away and write your article, Miss, er. I certainly have
things urgently awaiting my attention and patients awaiting my care. So, if you have no more questions—"

"There is just one thing, Mr. Standish." Kate decided,
to hell with it. "We need to emphasize that it's up to the
minute. Perhaps if you could spare a couple more minutes
we could go and see whoever is your most recent admission."

"I think that would be a little tricky. Our last admission
was about a month ago, and she died of pneumonia two
weeks after admission."

"Oh, ah. Well, perhaps that isn't so thrilling. So. No
new admissions in the last couple of days. No admissions
of anyone particularly large or blond or Nordic, with a fur
coat or a sledgehammer perhaps. I mean, just for instance." An inspiration struck her. "A *re*-admission perhaps?"

Standish regarded her with deepening suspicion.

"Miss, er—"

"Schechter."

"Miss Schechter, I begin to get the impression that
your interests in the hospital are not—"

He was interrupted at that moment by the swing doors
just behind them in the corridor being pushed open. He
looked up to see who it was, and as he did so his manner
changed.

He motioned Kate sharply to stand aside while a large

trolley bed was wheeled through the doors by an orderly. A sister and another nurse followed in attendance and gave the impression that they were the entourage in a procession rather than merely nurses about their normal business.

The occupant of the trolley was a delicately frail old man with skin like finely veined parchment.

The rear section of the trolley was inclined upward at a very slight angle so that the old man could survey the world as it passed him, and he surveyed it with a kind of quiet, benevolent horror. His mouth hung gently open and his head lolled very slightly, so that every slightest bump in the progress of the trolley caused it to roll a little to one side or the other. Yet in spite of his fragile listlessness, the air he emanated was that of very quietly, very gently, owning everything.

It was the one eye which conveyed this. Each thing it rested on, whether it was the view through a window or the nurse who was holding back the door so that the trolley could move through it without impediment, or whether it was on Mr. Standish, who suddenly was all obsequious charm and obeisance, all seemed instantly gathered up into the domain ruled by that eye.

Kate wondered for a moment how it was that eyes conveyed such an immense amount of information about their owners. They were, after all, merely spheres of white gristle. They hardly changed as they got older, apart from getting a bit redder and a bit runnier. The iris opened and closed a bit, but that was all. Where did all this flood of information come from? Particularly in the case of a man with only one of them and only a sealed-up flap of skin in place of the other.

She was interrupted in this line of thought by the fact that at that instant the eye in question moved on from

Standish and settled on her. The grip it exerted was so startling that she almost yelped.

With the frailest of faint motions the old man signaled to the orderly who was pushing the trolley to pause. The trolley drew to a halt and when the noise of its rolling wheels was stilled there was, for a moment, no other noise to be heard other than the distant hum of an elevator.

Then the elevator stopped.

Kate returned his look with a little smiling frown as if to say, "Sorry, do I know you?" and then wondered to herself if in fact she did. There was some fleeting familiarity about his face, but she couldn't quite catch it. She was impressed to notice that though this was only a trolley bed he was in, the bed linen that his hands lay on was real linen, freshly laundered and ironed.

Mr. Standish coughed slightly and said, "Miss, er, this is one of our most valued and, er, cherished patients, Mr.—"

"Are you quite comfortable, Mr. Odwin?" interrupted the Sister helpfully. But there was no need. This was one patient whose name Standish most certainly knew.

Odin quieted her with the slightest of gestures.

"Mr. Odwin," said Standish, "this is Miss, er—"

Kate was about to introduce herself once more when she was suddenly taken completely by surprise.

"I know exactly who she is," said Odin in a quiet but distinct voice, and there was in his eye for a moment the sense of an aerosol looking meaningfully at a wasp.

She tried to be very formal and English.

"I'm afraid," she said stiffly, "that you have the advantage of me."

"Yes," said Odin.

He gestured to the orderly, and together they resumed

their leisurely passage down the corridor. Glances were exchanged between Standish and the Sister, and then Kate was startled to notice that there was someone else standing in the corridor there with them.

He had not, presumably, appeared there by magic. He had merely stood still when the trolley moved on, and his height, or rather his lack of it, was such that he had simply hitherto been hidden behind it.

Things had been much better when he had been hidden.

There are some people you like immediately, some whom you think you might learn to like in the fullness of time, and some that you simply want to push away from you with a sharp stick. It was instantly apparent into which category, for Kate, the person of Toe Rag fell. He grinned and stared at her, or rather, appeared to stare at some invisible fly darting round her head.

He ran up, and before she could prevent him, grabbed hold of her right hand in his and shook it wildly up and down.

"I, too, have the advantage of you, Miss Schechter," he said, and gleefully skipped away up the corridor.

12

♦

The large, serious-looking gray van moved smoothly down the driveway, emerged through the stone gates and dipped sedately as it turned off the gravel and onto the asphalt of the public road. The road was a windy country lane lined with the wintry silhouettes of leafless oaks and dead elms. Gray clouds were piled high as pillows in the sky. The van made its stately progress away down the lane and soon was lost among its further twists and turns.

A few minutes later the yellow Citroën made its less stately appearance between the gates. It turned its splayed wheels up onto the camber of the lane and set off at a slow but difficult rate in the same direction.

Kate was rattled.

The last few minutes had been rather unpleasant. Standish was clearly an oddly behaved man at the best of times, but after their encounter with the patient named Odwin, he had turned unequivocally hostile. It was the frightening hostility of one who was himself frightened— of what, Kate did not know.

Who was she? he had demanded to know. How had she wheedled a reference out of Alan Franklin, a respected man in the profession? What was she after? What—and this seemed to be the big one—had she done to arouse the disapprobation of Mr. Odwin?

She held the car grimly to the road as it negotiated the bends with considerable difficulty and the straight sections with only slightly less. The car had landed her in court on one occasion when one of its front wheels had sailed off on a little expedition of its own and nearly caused an accident. The police witness in court had referred to her beloved Citroën as "the alleged car" and the name had subsequently stuck. She was particularly fond of the alleged car for many reasons. If one of its doors, for instance, fell off, she could put it back on herself, which is more than you could say for a BMW.

She wondered if she looked as pale and wan as she felt, but the rearview mirror was rattling around under the seat so she was spared the knowledge.

Standish himself had become quite white and shaky at the very idea of anybody crossing Mr. Odwin and had dismissed out of hand Kate's attempts to deny that she knew anything of him at all. If that were the case, he had demanded of her, why then had Mr. Odwin made it perfectly clear that he knew her? Was she accusing Mr.

Odwin of being a liar? If she was, then she should have a care for herself.

Kate did not know. The encounter with Mr. Odwin was completely inexplicable to her. But she could not deny to herself that the man packed some kind of punch. When he looked at you you stayed looked at. But beneath the disturbing quality of his steady gaze had lain some even more disturbing undercurrents. They were more disturbing because they were undercurrents of weakness and fear.

And as for the other creature . . .

Clearly he was the cause of the stories that had arisen recently in the more extremely abhorrent sectors of the tabloid press about there being "Something Nasty in the Woodshead." The stories had, of course, been offensive and callously insensitive and had largely been ignored by everybody in the country except for those very few millions who were keen on offensive and callously insensitive things.

The stories had claimed that people in the area had been "terrorized" by some repulsively deformed "goblin-like" creature who regularly broke out of the Woodshead and committed an impressively wide range of unspeakable acts.

Like most people, Kate had assumed, insofar as she had thought about it at all, that what had actually happened was that some poor bewildered mental patient had wandered out of the grounds and given a couple of passing old ladies a bit of a turn, and that the slavering hacks of Wapping had done the rest. Now she was a little more shaky and a little less sure.

He—it—had known her name.

What could she make of that?

What she made of it was a wrong turning. In her preoccupation she missed the turning that would take her onto the main road back to London, and she then had to work out what to do about it. She could simply do a three-point turn and go back, but it was a long time since she had last put the car into reverse gear, and she was frankly a bit nervous about how it would take to it.

She tried taking the next two right turns to see if that would set her straight, but she had no great hopes of this actually working, and was right not to have. She drove on for two or three miles, knowing that she was on the wrong road, but at least, judging from the position of the lighter gray smear in the gray clouds, going in the right direction.

After a while she settled down to this new route. A couple of signposts she passed made it clear to her that she was merely taking the B route back to London now, which she was perfectly happy to do. If she had thought about it in advance, she would probably have chosen to do so anyway in preference to the busy trunk road.

The trip had been a total failure, and she would have done far better simply to have stayed soaking in the bath all afternoon. The whole experience had been thoroughly disturbing, verging on the frightening, and she had drawn a complete blank as far as her actual objective was concerned. It was bad enough having an objective that she could hardly bring herself to admit to, without having it completely fall apart on her as well. A sense of stale futility gradually closed in on her along with the general grayness of the sky.

She wondered if she was going very slightly mad. Her life seemed to have drifted completely out of her control in the last few days, and it was distressing to realize just how fragile her grip was when it could so easily be shattered by a relatively minor thunderbolt or meteorite or whatever it was.

The word "thunderbolt" seemed to have arrived in the middle of that thought without warning and she didn't know what to make of it, so she just let it lie there at the bottom of her mind, like the towel lying on her bathroom floor that she hadn't been bothered to pick up.

She longed for some sun to break through. The miles ground along under her wheels, the clouds ground her down, and she found herself increasingly thinking of penguins. At last she felt she could stand it no more and decided that a few minutes' walk was what she needed to shake her out of her mood.

She stopped the car at the side of the road, and the elderly Jaguar which had been following her for the last seventeen miles ran straight into the back of hers, which worked just as well.

13

◆

With a delicious shock of rage Kate leaped, invigorated, out of her car and ran to harangue the driver of the other car, who was, in turn, leaping out of his in order to harangue her.

"Why don't you look where you're going?" she yelled at him. He was a rather overweight man who had been driving wearing a long leather coat and a rather ugly red hat, despite the discomfort this obviously involved. Kate warmed to him for it.

"Why don't I look where *I'm* going?" he replied heatedly. "Don't you look in your rearview mirror?"

"No," said Kate, putting her fists on her hips.

"Oh," said her adversary. "Why not?"

"Because it's under the seat."

"I see," he replied grimly. "Thank you for being so frank with me. Do you have a lawyer?"

"Yes, I do, as a matter of fact," said Kate. She said it with vim and hauteur.

"Is he any good?" said the man in the hat. "I'm going to need one. Mine's popped into prison for a while."

"Well, you certainly can't have mine."

"Why not?"

"Don't be absurd. It would be a clear conflict of interest."

Her adversary folded his arms and leaned back against the bonnet of his car. He took his time to survey the surroundings. The lane was growing dim as the early winter evening began to settle on the land. He then leaned into his car to turn on his hazard-warning indicators. The rear amber lights winked prettily on the scrubby grass of the roadside. The front lights were buried in the rear of Kate's Citroën and were in no fit state to wink.

He resumed his leaning posture and looked Kate up and down appraisingly.

"You are a driver," he said, "and I use the word in the loosest possible sense, i.e., meaning merely somebody who occupies the driving seat of what I will for the moment call—but I use the term strictly without prejudice —a car while it is proceeding along the road, of stupendous, I would even say verging on the superhuman, lack of skill. Do you catch my drift?"

"No."

"I mean you do not drive well. Do you know you've been all over the road for the last seventeen miles?"

"Seventeen miles!" exclaimed Kate. "Have you been following me?"

"Only up to a point," said Dirk. "I've tried to stay on this side of the road."

"I see. Well, thank you, in turn, for being so frank with me. This, I need hardly tell you, is an outrage. You'd better get yourself a damn good lawyer, because mine's going to stick red-hot skewers in him."

"Perhaps I should get myself a kebab instead."

"You look as if you've had quite enough kebabs. May I ask you why you were following me?"

"You looked as if you knew where you were going. To begin with, at least. For the first hundred yards or so."

"What the hell's it got to do with you where I was going?"

"Navigational technique of mine."

Kate narrowed her eyes.

She was about to demand a full and instant explanation of this preposterous remark when a passing white Ford Sierra slowed down beside them.

The driver wound down the window and leaned out. "Had a crash then?" he shouted at them.

"Yes."

"Ha!" he said and drove on.

A second or two later a Peugeot stopped by them.

"Who was that just now?" the driver asked them, in reference to the previous driver who had just stopped.

"I don't know," said Dirk.

"Oh," said the driver. "You look as if you've had a crash of some sort."

"Yes," said Dirk.

—— 155 ——

"Thought so," said the driver and drove on.

"You don't get the same quality of passersby these days, do you?" said Dirk to Kate.

"You get hit by some real dogs, too," said Kate. "I still want to know why you were following me. You realize that it's hard for me not to see you in the role of an extremely sinister sort of a person."

"That's easily explained," said Dirk. "Usually I am. On this occasion, however, I simply got lost. I was forced to take evasive action by a large gray oncoming van which took a proprietorial view of the road. I only avoided it by nipping down a side lane in which I was then unable to reverse. A few turnings later and I was thoroughly lost. There is a school of thought which says that you should consult a map on these occasions, but to such people I merely say, 'Ha! What if you have no map to consult? What if you have a map but it's of the Dordogne?' My own strategy is to find a car, or the nearest equivalent, which looks as if it knows where it's going and follow it. I rarely end up where I was intending to go, but often I end up somewhere that I needed to be. So what do you say to that?"

"Piffle."

"A robust response. I salute you."

"I was going to say that I do the same thing myself sometimes, but I've decided not to admit that yet."

"Very wise," said Dirk. "You don't want to give away too much at this point. Play it enigmatic is my advice."

"I don't want your advice. Where were you trying to get before suddenly deciding that driving seventeen miles in the opposite direction would help you get there?"

"A place called the Woodshead."

"Ah, the mental hospital."

"You know it?"

"I've been driving away from it for the last seventeen miles and I wish it was further. Which ward will you be in? I need to know where to send the repair bill."

"They don't have wards," said Dirk. "And I think they would be distressed to hear you call it a mental hospital."

"Anything that distresses 'em is fine by me."

Dirk looked about him.

"A fine evening," he said.

"No it isn't."

"I see," said Dirk. "You have, if I may say so, the air of one to whom her day has not been a source of joy or spiritual enrichment."

"Too damn right it hasn't," said Kate. "I've had the sort of day that would make Saint Francis of Assisi kick babies. Particularly if you include Tuesday in with today, which is the last time I was actually conscious. And now look. My beautiful car. The only thing I can say in favor of the whole shebang is that at least I'm not in Oslo."

"I can see how that might cheer you."

"I didn't say it cheered me. It just about stops me killing myself. I might as well save myself the bother anyway, with people like you so keen to do it for me."

"You were my able assistant, Miss Schechter."

"*Stop doing that!*"

"Stop doing what?"

"My name! Suddenly every stranger I meet knows my name. Would you guys please just quit knowing my name for one second? How can a girl be enigmatic under these conditions? The only person I met who didn't seem to know my name was the only one I actually introduced myself to. All right," she said, pointing an accusing finger at Dirk, "you're not supernatural, so just tell me how you knew my name. I'm not letting go of your tie till you tell me."

"You haven't got hold of—"

"I have now, buster."

"Unhand me!"

"Why were you following me?" insisted Kate. "How do you know my name?"

"I was following you for exactly the reasons stated. As for your name, my dear lady, you practically told me yourself."

"I did not."

"I assure you, you did."

"I'm still holding your tie."

"If you are meant to be in Oslo but have been unconscious since Tuesday, then presumably you were at the incredible exploding check-in counter at Heathrow Terminal Two. It was widely reported in the press. I expect you missed it through being unconscious. I myself missed it through rampant apathy, but the events of today have rather forced it on my attention."

Kate grudgingly let go of his tie, but continued to eye him with suspicion.

"Oh yeah?" she said. "What events?"

"Disturbing ones," said Dirk, brushing himself down. "Even if what you had told me yourself had not been enough to identify you, then the fact of your having also been today to visit the Woodshead clinched it for me. I gather from your mood of belligerent despondency that the man you were seeking was not there."

"What?"

"Please, have it," said Dirk, rapidly pulling off his tie and handing it to her. "By chance I ran into a nurse from your hospital earlier today. My first encounter with her was one which, for various reasons, I was anxious to terminate abruptly. It was only while I was standing on the pavement a minute or two later, fending off the local wildlife, that one of the words I had heard her say struck me, I may say, somewhat like a thunderbolt. The idea was fantastically, wildly improbable. But like most fantastically, wildly improbable ideas it was at least as worthy of consideration as a more mundane one to which the facts had been strenuously bent to fit.

"I returned to question her further, and she confirmed that a somewhat unusual patient had, in the early hours of the morning, been transferred from the hospital, apparently to the Woodshead.

"She also confided to me that another patient had been almost indecently curious to find out what had become of him. That patient was a Miss Kate Schechter, and I think you will agree, Miss Schechter, that my methods of navigation have their advantages. I may not have gone where I intended to go, but I think I have ended up where I needed to be."

14

♦

After about half an hour a hefty man from the local garage arrived with a pickup truck, a towrope and a son. Having looked at the situation, he sent his son and the pickup truck away to deal with another job, attached the towrope to Kate's now defunct car and pulled it away to the garage himself.

Kate was a little quiet about this for a minute or two, and then said, "He wouldn't have done that if I hadn't been an American."

He had recommended to them a small local pub where

he would come and look for them when he had made his diagnosis on the Citroën. Since Dirk's Jaguar had only lost its front right indicator light, and Dirk insisted that he hardly ever turned right anyway, they drove the short distance there. As Kate, with some reluctance, climbed into Dirk's car, she found the Howard Bell book which Dirk had purloined from Sally Mills in the café, and pounced on it. A few minutes later, walking into the pub, she was still trying to work out if it was one she had read or not.

The pub combined all the traditional English qualities of horse brasses, Formica and surliness. The sound of Michael Jackson in the other bar mingled with the mournful intermittence of the glass-cleaning machine in this one to create an aural ambience which perfectly matched the elderly paintwork in its dinginess.

Dirk bought himself and Kate a drink each, and then joined her at the small corner table she had found away from the fat, T-shirted hostility of the bar.

"I have read it," she announced, having thumbed her way by now through most of *Run Like the Devil*. "At least, I started it and read the first couple of chapters. A couple of months ago, in fact. I don't know why I still read his books. It's perfectly clear that his editor doesn't." She looked up at Dirk. "I wouldn't have thought it was your sort of thing. From what little I know of you."

"It isn't," said Dirk. "I, er, picked it up by mistake."

"That's what everyone says," replied Kate. "He used to be quite good," she added, "if you liked that sort of thing. My brother's in publishing in New York, and he says Howard Bell's gone very strange nowadays. I get the feeling that they're all a little afraid of him and he quite likes that. Certainly no one seems to have the guts to tell him he should cut chapters ten to twenty-seven inclusive. And all the stuff about the goat. The theory is that the reason he sells so many millions of copies is that nobody ever does read them. If everyone who bought them actually read them they'd never bother to buy the next one and his career would be over."

She pushed it away from her.

"Anyway," she said, "you've very cleverly told me why I went to the Woodshead; you haven't told me why you were going there yourself."

Dirk shrugged. "To see what it was like," he said non-committally.

"Oh yes? Well, I'll save you the bother. The place is quite horrible."

"Describe it. In fact start with the airport."

Kate took a hefty swig at her Bloody Mary and brooded silently for a moment while the vodka marched around inside her.

"You want to hear about the airport as well?" she said at last.

"Yes."

Kate drained the rest of her drink.

"I'll need another one, then," she said, and pushed the empty glass across at him.

Dirk braved the bug-eyedness of the barman and returned a minute or two later with a refill for Kate.

"OK," said Kate. "I'll start with the cat."

"What cat?"

"The cat I needed to ask the next-door neighbor to look after for me."

"Which next-door neighbor?"

"The one that died."

"I see," said Dirk. "Tell you what, why don't I just shut up and let you tell me?"

"Yes," said Kate, "that would be good."

Kate recounted the events of the last few days, or at least, those she was conscious of, and then moved on to her impressions of the Woodshead.

Despite the distaste with which she described it, it sounded to Dirk like exactly the sort of place he would love to retire to, tomorrow, if possible. It combined a dedication to the inexplicable, which was his own persistent vice (he could only think of it as such, and sometimes would rail against it with the fury of an addict), with a pampered self-indulgence, a vice to which he would love to be able to aspire if he could ever but afford it.

At last Kate related her disturbing encounter with Mr. Odwin and his repellent minion, and it was as a result of this that Dirk remained sunk in a frowning silence for a minute afterward. A large part of this minute was in fact taken up with an internal struggle about whether or not he was going to cave in and have a cigarette. He had recently foresworn them and the struggle was a regular one and he lost it regularly, often without noticing.

He decided, with triumph, that he would not have one, and then took one out anyway. Fishing out his lighter from the capacious pocket of his coat involved first taking out the envelope he had removed from Geoffrey Anstey's bathroom. He put it on the table next to the book and lit his cigarette.

"The check-in girl at the airport . . . " he said at last.

"She drove me mad," said Kate instantly. "She just went through the motions of doing her job like some kind of blank machine. Wouldn't listen, wouldn't think. I don't know where they find people like that."

"She used to be my secretary, in fact," said Dirk. "They don't seem to know where to find her now, either."

"Oh. I'm sorry," said Kate immediately, and then reflected for a moment.

"I expect you're going to say that she wasn't like that really," she continued. "Well, that's possible. I expect she was just shielding herself from the frustrations of her job. It must drive you insensible working at an airport. I think I would have sympathized if I hadn't been so goddamn frustrated myself. I'm sorry, I didn't know. So that's what you're trying to find out about."

Dirk gave a noncommittal type of nod. "Among other things," he said. Then he added, "I'm a private detective."

"Oh?" said Kate in surprise, and then looked puzzled.

"Does that bother you?"

"It's just that I have a friend who plays the double bass."

"I see," said Dirk.

"Whenever people meet him and he's struggling around with it, they all say the same thing, and it drives him crazy. They all say, 'I bet you wished you played the piccolo.' Nobody ever works out that that's what everybody else says. I was just trying to work out if there was something that everybody would always say to a private detective so that I could avoid saying it."

"No. What happens is that everybody looks very shifty for a moment, and you got that very well."

"I see." Kate looked disappointed. "Well, do you have any clues—that is to say, any idea about what's happened to your secretary?"

"No," said Dirk, "no idea. Just a vague image that I don't know what to make of." He toyed thoughtfully with his cigarette, and then let his gaze wander over the table again and onto the book.

He picked it up and looked it over, wondering what impulse had made him pick it up in the first place.

"I don't really know anything about Howard Bell," he said.

Kate was surprised at the way he suddenly changed the subject, but also a little relieved.

"I only know," said Dirk, "that he sells a lot of books and that they all look pretty much like this. What should I know?"

"Well, there are some very strange stories about him."

"Like what?"

"Like what he gets up to in hotel suites all across America. No one knows the details, of course, they just get the bills and pay them because they don't like to ask. They feel they're on safer ground if they don't know. Particularly about the chickens."

"Chickens?" said Dirk. "What chickens?"

"Well, apparently," said Kate, lowering her voice and leaning forward a little, "he's always having live chickens delivered to his hotel room."

Dirk frowned.

"What on earth for?" he said.

"Nobody knows. Nobody ever knows what happens to them. Nobody ever sees them again. Not," she said, leaning even farther forward, and dropping her voice still lower, "a single feather."

Dirk wondered if he was being hopelessly innocent and naive. "So what do people think he's doing with them?" he asked.

"Nobody," Kate said, "has the faintest idea. They don't even *want* to have the faintest idea. They just don't know."

She shrugged and picked the book up herself.

"The other thing David—that's my brother—says about him is that he has the absolute perfect bestseller's name."

"Really?" said Dirk. "In what way?"

"David says it's the first thing any publisher looks for in a new author. Not, 'Is his stuff any good?' or, 'Is his stuff any good once you get rid of all the adjectives?' but, 'Is his last name nice and short and his first name just a bit longer?' You see? The 'Bell' is done in huge silver letters, and the 'Howard' fits neatly across the top in slightly narrower ones. Instant trademark. It's publishing magic. Once you've got a name like that, then whether you can actually write or not is a minor matter. Which in Howard Bell's case is now a significant bonus. But it's a very ordinary name if you write it down in the normal way, like it is here you see."

"What?" said Dirk.

"Here on this envelope of yours."

"Where? Let me see."

"That's his name there, isn't it? Crossed out."

"Good heavens, you're right," said Dirk, peering at the envelope. "I suppose I didn't recognize it without its trademark shape."

"Is this something to do with him, then?" asked Kate, picking it up and looking it over.

"I don't know what it is, exactly," said Dirk. "It's something to do with a contract, and it may be something to do with a record."

"I can see it might be to do with a record."

"How can you see that?" asked Dirk, sharply.

"Well, this name here is Dennis Hutch, isn't it? See?"

"Oh, yes. Yes, I do," said Dirk, examining it for himself. "Er, should I know that name?"

"Well," said Kate slowly, "it depends if you're alive or not, I suppose. He's the head of the Aries Rising Record Group. Less famous than the Pope, I grant you, but— you know of the Pope, I take it?"

"Yes, yes," said Dirk impatiently. "White-haired chap."

"That's him. He seems to be about the only person of note this envelope hasn't been addressed to at some time. Here's Stan Dubcek, the head of Dubcek, Danton, Heidegger, Draycott. I know they handle the ARRGH! account."

"The—?"

"ARRGH! Aries Rising Record Group Holdings. Getting that account made the agency's fortunes."

She looked at Dirk.

"You have the air," she stated, "of one who knows little of the record business or the advertising business."

"I have that honor," said Dirk, graciously inclining his head.

"So what are you doing with this?"

"When I manage to get it open, I'll know," said Dirk. "Do you have a knife on you?"

Kate shook her head.

"Who's Geoffrey Anstey, then?" she asked. "He's the only name not crossed out. Friend of yours?"

Dirk paled a little and didn't immediately answer. Then he said, "This strange person you mentioned, this 'Something Nasty in the Woodshead' creature. Tell me again what he said to you."

"He said, 'I, too, have the advantage of you, Miss Schechter.' " Kate tried to shrug.

Dirk weighed his thoughts uncertainly for a moment.

"I think it is just possible," he said at last, "that you may be in some kind of danger."

"You mean it's possible that passing lunatics may crash into me in the road? That kind of danger?"

"Maybe even worse."

"Oh yeah?"

"Yes."

"And what makes you think that?"

"It's not entirely clear to me yet," replied Dirk with a frown. "Most of the ideas I have at the moment have to do with things that are completely impossible, so I am wary about sharing them. They are, however, the only thoughts I have."

"I'd get some different ones, then," said Kate. "What was the Sherlock Holmes principle? 'Once you have discounted the impossible, then whatever remains, however improbable, must be the truth.' "

"I reject that entirely," said Dirk sharply. "The impossible often has a kind of integrity to it which the merely improbable lacks. How often have you been presented with an apparently rational explanation of something that works in all respects other than one, which is just that it is hopelessly improbable? Your instinct is to say, 'Yes, but he or she simply wouldn't do that.' "

"Well, it happened to me today, in fact," replied Kate.

"Ah, yes," said Dirk, slapping the table and making the glasses jump, "your girl in the wheelchair—a perfect example. The idea that she is somehow receiving yesterday's stock market prices apparently out of thin air is merely impossible, and therefore *must* be the case, because the idea that she is maintaining an immensely complex and laborious hoax of no benefit to herself is hopelessly improbable. The first idea merely supposes that there is something we don't know about, and God knows there are enough of those. The second, however, runs contrary to something fundamental and human which we do know about. We should therefore be very suspicious of it and all its specious rationality."

"But you won't tell me what you think."

"No."

"Why not?"

"Because it sounds ridiculous. But I think you are in danger. I think you might be in horrible danger."

"Great. So what do you suggest I do about it?" said Kate, taking a sip of her second drink, which otherwise had stayed almost untouched.

"I suggest," said Dirk seriously, "that you come back to London and spend the night in my house."

Kate hooted with laughter and then had to fish out a Kleenex to wipe tomato juice off herself.

"I'm sorry, what is so extraordinary about that?" demanded Dirk, rather taken aback.

"It's just the most wonderfully perfunctory pickup line I've ever heard." She smiled at him. "I'm afraid the answer is a resounding No."

He was, she thought, interesting, entertaining in an eccentric kind of way, but also hideously unattractive to her.

Dirk felt very awkward. "I think there has been some appalling misunderstanding," he said. "Allow me to explain that—"

He was interrupted by the sudden arrival in their midst of the mechanic from the garage with news of Kate's car.

"Fixed it," he said. "In fact there were nothing to fix other than the bumper. Nothing new, that is. The funny noises you mentioned were just the engine. But it'll go all right. You just have to rev her up, let in the clutch, and then wait for a little bit longer than you might normally expect."

Kate thanked him a little stiffly for this advice and then insisted on allowing Dirk to pay the twenty-five pounds he was charging for it.

Outside, in the car park, Dirk repeated his urgent request that Kate should go with him, but she was adamant that all she needed was a good night's sleep and that everything would look bright and clear and easily capable of being coped with in the morning.

Dirk insisted that they should at least exchange phone numbers. Kate agreed to this on condition that Dirk found another route back to London and didn't sit on her tail.

"Be very careful," Dirk called to her as her car grumbled out onto the road.

"I will," shouted Kate, "and if anything impossible happens, I promise you'll be the first to know."

For a brief moment, the yellow undulations of the car gleamed dully in the light leaking from the pub windows and stood out against the heavily hunched grayness of the night sky, which soon swallowed it up.

Dirk tried to follow her, but his car wouldn't start.

15

◆

The clouds sank more heavily over the land, clenching into huge sullen towers, as Dirk, in a sudden excess of alarm, had to call out the man from the garage once again. He was slower to arrive with his truck this time and bad-tempered with drink when at last he did.

He emitted a few intemperate barks of laughter at Dirk's predicament, then fumbled the bonnet of his car open and subjected him to all kinds of muttered talk about manifolds, pumps, alternators and starlings and resolutely would not be drawn on whether or not he was going to be able to get the thing to go again that night.

Dirk was unable to get a meaningful answer, or at least an answer that meant anything to him, as to what was causing the rumpus in the alternator, what ailed the fuel pump, in what way the operation of the starter motor was being disrupted and why the timing was off.

He did at last understand that the mechanic was also claiming that a family of starlings had at some time in the past made their nest in a sensitive part of the engine's workings and had subsequently perished horribly, taking sensitive parts of the engine with them, and at this point Dirk began to cast about himself desperately for what to do.

He noticed that the mechanic's pickup truck was standing nearby with its engine still running, and elected to make off with this instead. Being a slightly less slow and cumbersome runner than the mechanic, he was able to put this plan into operation with a minimum of difficulty.

He swung out into the lane, drove off into the night and parked three miles down the road. He left the van's lights on, let down its tires and hid himself behind a tree. After about ten minutes his Jaguar came hurtling round the corner, passed the van, hauled itself to an abrupt halt and reversed wildly back toward it. The mechanic threw open the door, leaped out and hurried over to reclaim his property, leaving Dirk with the opportunity he needed to leap from behind the tree and reclaim his own.

He spun his wheels pointedly and drove off in a kind of grim triumph, still haunted, nevertheless, by anxieties to which he was unable to give a name or shape.

Kate, in the meantime, had joined the dimly glowing yellow stream that led on eventually through the western suburbs of Acton and Ealing and into the heart of London. She crawled up over the Westway flyover and soon afterward turned north up towards Primrose Hill and home.

She always enjoyed driving up alongside the park, and the dark night shapes of the trees soothed her and made her long for the quietness of her bed.

She found the nearest parking space she could to her front door, which was about thirty yards distant. She climbed out of the car and carefully omitted to lock it. She never left anything of value in it, and she found that it was to her advantage if people didn't have to break anything in order to find that out. The car had been stolen twice, but on each occasion it had been found abandoned twenty yards away.

She didn't go straight home but set off instead in the opposite direction to get some milk and bin liners from the small corner shop in the next street. She agreed with the gentle-faced Pakistani who ran it that she did indeed look tired and should have an early night, but on the way back she made another small diversion to go and lean against the railings of the park, gaze into its darkness for a few minutes, and breathe in some of its cold, heavy night air. At last she started to head back toward her flat. She turned into her own road, and as she passed the first streetlamp it flickered and went out, leaving her in a small pool of darkness.

That sort of thing always gives one a nasty turn.

It is said that there is nothing surprising about the notion, for instance, of a person suddenly thinking about someone he hasn't thought about for years, and then discovering the next day that the person has in fact just died. There are always lots of people suddenly remembering people they haven't thought about for ages, and always lots of people dying. In a population the size of, say,

America, the law of averages means that this particular coincidence must happen at least ten times a day, but it is none the less spooky to anyone who experiences it.

By the same token, there are light bulbs burning out in streetlamps all the time, and a fair few of them must go pop just as someone is passing beneath them. Even so, it still gives the person concerned a nasty turn, especially when the very next streetlamp they pass under does exactly the same thing.

Kate stood rooted to the spot.

If one coincidence can occur, she told herself, then another coincidence can occur. And if one coincidence happens to occur just after another coincidence, then that is just a coincidence. There was absolutely nothing to feel alarmed about in having a couple of streetlamps go pop. She was in a perfectly normal friendly street with houses all around her with their lights on. She looked up at the house next to her, unfortunately just as the lights in its front window chanced to go out. This was presumably because the occupants happened to choose that moment to leave the room, but though it just went to show what a truly extraordinary thing coincidence can be, it did little to improve her state of mind.

The rest of the street was still bathed in a dim yellow glow. It was only the few feet immediately around her that were suddenly dark. The next pool of light was just a few footsteps away in front of her. She took a deep breath, pulled herself together, and walked toward it, reaching its very center at the exact instant that it, too, extinguished itself.

The occupants of the two houses she had passed on the way also happened to choose that moment to leave their front rooms, as did their neighbors on the opposite side of the street.

Perhaps a popular television show had just finished. That's what it was. Everyone was getting up and turning off their TV sets and lights simultaneously, and the resulting power surge was blowing some of the streetlamps. Something like that. The resulting power surge was also making her blood pound a little. She moved on, trying to be calm. As soon as she got home she'd have a look in the paper to see what the program had been that had caused three streetlamps to blow.

Four.

She stopped and stood absolutely still under the dark lamp. More houses were darkening. What she found particularly alarming was that they darkened at the very moment that she looked at them.

Glance—*pop*.

She tried it again.

Glance—*pop*.

Each one she looked at darkened instantly.

Glance—*pop*.

She realized with a sudden start of fear that she must stop herself from looking at the ones that were still lit. The rationalizations she had been trying to construct were now running around inside her head screaming to be let out, and she let them go. She tried to lock her eyes to the ground for fear of extinguishing the whole street, but couldn't help tiny glances to see if it was working.

Glance—*pop*.

She froze her gaze down on to the narrow path forward. Most of the road was dark now.

There were three remaining streetlamps between her and the front door that led to her own flat. Though she kept her eyes averted, she thought she could detect on the periphery of her vision that the lights of the flat downstairs from hers were lit.

Neil lived there. She couldn't remember his last name, but he was a part-time bass player and antiques dealer who used to give her decorating advice she didn't want and also stole her milk—so her relationship with him had always remained at a slightly frosty level. Just at the moment, though, she was praying that he was there to tell her what was wrong with her sofa, and that his light would not go out as her eyes wavered from the pavement in front of her, with its three remaining pools of light spaced evenly along the way she had to tread.

For a moment she tried turning, and looked back the way she had come. All was darkness, shading off into the blackness of the park, which no longer calmed but menaced her, with hideously imagined thick, knotted roots and treacherous, dark, rotting litter.

Again she turned, sweeping her eyes low.

Three pools of light.

The streetlights did not extinguish as she looked at them, only as she passed.

She squeezed her eyes closed and visualized exactly where the lamp of the next streetlight was, above and in front of her. She raised her head and carefully opened her eyes again, staring directly into the orange glow radiating through the thick glass.

It shone steadily.

With her eyes locked fast on it so that it burned squiggles on her retina, she moved cautiously forward, step by step, exerting her will on it to stay burning as she approached. It continued to glow.

She stepped forward again. It continued to glow. Again she stepped. Still it glowed. Now she was almost beneath it, craning her neck to keep it in focus.

She moved forward once more and saw the filament

within the glass flicker and quickly die away, leaving an afterimage prancing madly in her eyes.

She dropped her eyes now and tried looking steadily forward, but wild shapes were leaping everywhere and she felt she was losing control. The next lamp she took a lunging run toward, and again, sudden darkness enveloped her arrival. She stopped there panting, and blinking, trying to calm herself again and get her vision sorted out. Looking toward the last streetlamp, she thought she saw a figure standing beneath it. It was a large form, silhouetted with jumping orange shadows. Huge horns stood upon the figure's head.

She stared with mad intensity into the billowing darkness, and suddenly screamed at it, "Who are you?"

There was a pause, and then a deep answering voice said, "Do you have anything that can get these bits of floorboard off my back?"

16

◆

There was another pause, of a different and slightly disordered quality.

It was a long one. It hung there nervously, wondering which direction it was going to get broken from. The darkened street took on a withdrawn, defensive aspect.

"What?" Kate screamed back at the figure, at last. "I said . . . *what?*"

The great figure stirred. Kate still could not see him properly because her eyes were still dancing with blue shadows, seared there by the orange light.

"I was," said the figure, "glued to the floor. My father—"

"Did *you* . . . are *you* . . . " Kate quivered with incoherent rage, "are you responsible . . . for all *this?*" She turned and swept an angry hand around the street to indicate the nightmare she had just traversed.

"It is important that you know who I am."

"Oh yeah?" said Kate. "Well let's get the name down right now so I can take it straight to the police and get you done for breach of something willful or other. Intimidation. Interfering with—"

"I am Thor. I am the God of Thunder. The God of Rain. The God of the High Towering Clouds. The God of Lightning. The God of the Flowing Currents. The God of the Particles. The God of the Shaping and the Binding Forces. The God of the Wind. The God of the Growing Crops. The God of the Hammer Mjollnir."

"Are you?" simmered Kate. "Well, I've no doubt that if you'd picked a slack moment to mention all that, I might have taken an interest, but right now it just makes me very angry. Turn the damn lights on!"

"I am—"

"I said, Turn the lights on!"

With something of a sheepish glow, the streetlights all came back on, and the windows of the houses all quietly illuminated themselves once more. The lamp above Kate popped again almost immediately. She shot him a warning look.

"It was an old light, and infirm," he said.

She simply continued to glare at him.

"See," he said, "I have your address." He held out the piece of paper she had given him at the airport, as if that somehow explained everything and put the world to rights.

"I—"

"Back!" he shouted, throwing up his arms in front of his face.

"What?"

With a huge rush of wind, a swooping eagle dropped from out of the night sky with its talons outspread to catch at him. Thor beat and thrashed at it until the great bird flailed backward, turned, nearly crashed to the ground, recovered itself, and with great slow beats of its wings heaved itself back up through the air and perched on top of the streetlamp. It grasped the lamp hard with its talons and steadied itself, making the whole lamppost quiver very slightly in its grip.

"Go!" Thor shouted at it.

The eagle sat there and peered down at him. A monstrous creature made more monstrous by the effect of the orange light on which it perched, casting huge, flapping shadows on the nearby houses, it had strange circular markings on its wings. These were markings that Kate wondered if she had seen before, only in a nightmare, but then again she was by no means certain that she was not in a nightmare now.

There was no doubt that she had found the man she was looking for. The same huge form, the same glacial eyes, the same look of arrogant exasperation and slight muddle, only this time his feet were plunged into huge hide boots, great furs, straps and thongs hung from his shoulders, a huge steel horned helmet stood on his head, and his exasperation was directed this time not at an airline check-in girl but at a huge eagle perched on a lamppost in the middle of Primrose Hill.

"Go," he shouted at it again. "The matter is beyond my power! All that I can do I have done! Your family is provided for. You I can do nothing more for! I myself am powerless and sick."

Kate was suddenly shocked to see that there were great gouges on the big man's left forearm where the eagle had got its talons into him and ripped them through his skin. Blood was welling up out of them like bread out of a baking tin.

"Go!" he shouted again. With the edge of one hand he scraped the blood off his other arm and flung the heavy drops at the eagle, which reared back, flapping, but retained its hold. Suddenly the man leaped high into the air and grappled himself to the top of the lamppost, which now began to shake dangerously under their combined weight. With loud cries the eagle pecked viciously at him while he tried with great swings of his free arm to sweep it from its perch.

A door opened. It was the front door of Kate's house, and a man with gray-rimmed spectacles and a neat moustache looked out. It was Neil, Kate's downstairs neighbor, in a mood.

"Look, I really think—" he started. However, it quickly became clear that he simply didn't know what to think, and he retreated back indoors, taking his mood, unsatisfied, with him.

The big man braced himself, and with a huge leap hurled himself through the air and landed with a slight, controlled wobble on top of the next lamppost, which bent slightly under his weight. He crouched, glaring at the eagle, which glared back.

"Go!" he shouted again, brandishing his arm at it.

"Gaarh!" it screeched back at him.

With another swing of his arm he pulled from under his furs a great short-handled sledgehammer and hefted its great weight meaningfully from one hand to another. The head of the hammer was a roughly cast piece of iron about the size and shape of a pint of beer in a big glass mug, and its shaft was a stocky, wrist-thick piece of ancient oak with leather strapping bound about its handle.

"Gaaarrrh!" screeched the eagle again, but regarded the sledgehammer with keen-eyed suspicion. As Thor began slowly to swing the hammer, the eagle shifted its weight tensely from one leg to the other, in time to the rhythm of the swings.

"Go!" said Thor again, more quietly, but with greater menace. He rose to his full height on top of the lamppost and swung the hammer faster and faster in a great circle. Suddenly he hurled it directly toward the eagle. In the same instant a bolt of high-voltage electricity erupted from the lamp on which the eagle was sitting, causing it to leap with loud cries wildly into the air. The hammer sailed harmlessly under the lamp, swung up into the air and out over the darkness of the park, while Thor, released of its weight, wobbled and tottered on top of his lamppost, spun round and regained his balance. Flailing madly at the air with its huge wings, the eagle, too, regained control of itself, flew upward, made one last diving attack on Thor, which the god leaped backward off the lamppost to avoid, and then climbed up and away into the night sky, in which it quickly became a small, dark speck and then at last was gone.

The hammer came bounding back from out of the sky, scraped flying sparks from the paving stones with its head, turned over twice in the air and then dropped its head back to the ground next to Kate and rested its shaft gently against her leg.

An elderly lady who had been waiting patiently with her dog in the shadows beneath the streetlamp, which was now defunct, sensed, correctly, that all of the excitement was now over and proceeded quietly past them. Thor waited politely till they had passed and then approached Kate, who stood with her arms folded watching him. After all the business of the last two or three minutes he seemed suddenly not to have the faintest idea what to say and for the moment merely gazed thoughtfully into the middle distance.

Kate formed the distinct impression that thinking was, for him, a separate activity from everything else, a task that needed its own space. It could not easily be combined with other activities such as walking or talking or buying airline tickets.

"We'd better take a look at your arm," she said, and led the way up the steps to her house. He followed, docile.

As she opened the front door she found Neil in the hall leaning his back against the wall and looking with grim pointedness at a Coca-Cola vending machine standing against the opposite wall and taking up an inordinate amount of space in the hallway.

"I don't know what we're going to do about this, I really don't," he said.

"What's it doing there?" asked Kate.

"Well, that's what I'm asking you, I'm afraid," said Neil. "I don't know how you're going to get it up the stairs. Don't see how it can be done, to be perfectly frank with you. And let's face it, I don't think you're going to like it once you've got it up there. I know it's very modern and American, but think about it, you've got that nice French cherrywood table, that sofa which will be very nice once you've taken off that dreadful Collier Campbell covering like I keep on saying you should, only you won't listen, and I just don't see that it's going to fit in, not in either sense. And I'm not even sure that I should allow it, I mean it's a very heavy object, and you know what

I've said to you about the floors in this house. I'd think again, I really would, you know."

"Yes, Neil, how did it get here?"

"Well, your friend here delivered it just an hour or so ago. I don't know where he's been working out, but I must say I wouldn't mind paying his gym a visit. I said I thought the whole thing was very doubtful, but he would insist and in the end I even had to give him a hand. But I must say that I think we need to have a very serious think about the whole topic. I asked your friend if he liked Wagner but he didn't respond very well. So, I don't know, what do you want to do about it?"

Kate took a deep breath. She suggested to her huge guest that he carry on upstairs and she would see him in just a moment. Thor lumbered past, and was an absurd figure mounting the stairs.

Neil watched Kate's eyes very closely for a clue as to what, exactly, was going on, but Kate was as blank as she knew how to be.

"I'm sorry, Neil," she said matter-of-factly. "The Coke machine will go. It's all a misunderstanding. I'll get this sorted out by tomorrow."

"Yes, that's all very well," said Neil, "but where does all this leave me? I mean, you see my problem."

"No, Neil, I don't."

"Well, I've got this . . . thing out here, you've got that . . . person upstairs, and the whole thing is just a total disruption."

"Is there anything I can do to make anything any better?"

"Well it's not as easy as that, is it? I mean, I think you should just think about it a bit, that's all. I mean, all this. You told me you were going away. I heard the bath running this afternoon. What was I to think? And after you had gone on about the cat, and you know I won't work with cats."

"I know, Neil. That's why I asked Mrs. Grey next door to look after her."

"Yes, and look what happened to her. Died of a heart attack. Mr. Grey's very upset, you know."

"I don't think it had anything to do with me asking her if she would look after my cat."

"Well, all I can say is that he's *very* upset."

"Yes, Neil. His wife's died."

"Well, I'm not saying anything. I'm just saying I think you should think about it. And what on earth are we going to do about all this?" he added, readdressing his attention to the Coca-Cola machine.

"I've said that I will make sure it's gone in the morning, Neil," said Kate. "I'm quite happy to stand here and scream very loudly if you think it will help in any way, but—"

"Listen, love, I'm only making the point. And I hope you're not going to be making a lot of noise up there because I've got to practice my music tonight, and you know that I need quiet to concentrate." He gave Kate a meaningful look over the top of his glasses and disappeared into his flat.

Kate stood and silently counted as much of one to ten as she could currently remember and then headed staunchly up the stairs in the wake of the God of Thunder, feeling that she was not in a mood for either weather or theology. The house began to throb and shake to the sound of the main theme of "The Ride of the Valkyries" being played on a Fender Precision bass.

17

◆

As Dirk edged his way along the Euston Road, caught in the middle of a rush hour traffic jam that had started in the late nineteen seventies and which, at a quarter to ten on this Thursday evening, still showed no signs of abating, he thought he caught sight of something he recognized.

It was his subconscious which told him this—that infuriating part of a person's brain which never responds to interrogation, merely gives little meaningful nudges and then sits humming quietly to itself, saying nothing.

"Well, of course, I've just seen something I recognize," Dirk muttered mentally to his subconscious. "I drive along this benighted thoroughfare twenty times a month. I expect I recognize every single matchstick lying in the gutter. Can't you be a little more specific?" His subconscious would not be hectored though, and was dumb. It had nothing further to add. The city was probably full of gray vans anyway. Very unremarkable.

"Where?" muttered Dirk to himself fiercely, twisting around in his seat this way and that. "Where did I see a gray van?"

Nothing.

He was thoroughly hemmed in by the traffic and could not maneuver in any direction, least of all forward. He erupted from his car and started to jostle his way back through the jammed cars bobbing up and down to try and see where, if anywhere, he might have caught a glimpse of a gray van. If he had seen one, it eluded him now. His subconscious sat and said nothing.

The traffic was still not moving, so he tried to thread his way farther back, but was obstructed by a large motorcycle courier edging his way forward on a huge grimy Kawasaki. Dirk engaged in a brief altercation with the courier, but lost it because the courier was unable to hear Dirk's side of the altercation; eventually Dirk retreated through the tide of traffic which now was beginning slowly to move in all lanes other than the one in which his car sat, driverless, immobile and hooted at.

He felt suddenly elated by the braying of the motor horns, and as he swayed and bobbed his way back through the snarled-up columns of cars, he suddenly found that he reminded himself of the crazies he had seen on the streets of New York, who would career out into the road to explain to the oncoming traffic about the Day of Judgement, imminent alien invasions and incompetence and corruption in the Pentagon. He put his hands above his head and started to shout out, "The Gods are walking the Earth! The Gods are walking the Earth!"

This further inflamed the feelings of those who were beeping their horns at his stationary car, and quickly the whole rose through a crescendo of majestic cacophony, with Dirk's voice ringing out above it.

"The Gods are walking the Earth! The Gods are walking the Earth!" he hollered. "The Gods are walking the Earth! Thank you!" he added, and ducked down into his car, put it into drive and pulled away, allowing the whole jammed mass at last to seethe easily forward.

He wondered why he was so sure. An "act of God." Merely a chance, careless phrase by which people were able to dispose conveniently of awkward phenomena that would admit of no more rational explanation. But it was the chance carelessness of it which particularly appealed to Dirk because words used carelessly, as if they did not matter in any serious way, often allowed otherwise well-guarded truths to seep through.

An inexplicable disappearance. Oslo and a hammer: a tiny, tiny coincidence which struck a tiny, tiny note. However, it was a note which sang in the midst of the daily hubbub of white noise, and other tiny notes were singing at the same pitch. An act of God, Oslo, and a hammer. A man with a hammer, trying to go to Norway, is prevented, loses his temper, and as a result there is an "act of God."

If, thought Dirk, if a being were immortal he would still be alive today. That, quite simply, was what "immortal" meant.

How would an immortal being have a passport?

Quite simply, how? Dirk tried to imagine what might

happen if—to pick a name quite at random—the God Thor, he of the Norwegian ancestry and the great hammer, were to arrive at the passport office and try to explain who he was and how come he had no birth certificate. There would be no shock, no horror, no loud exclamations of astonishment, just blank, bureaucratic impossibility. It wouldn't be a matter of whether anybody believed him or not, it would simply be a question of producing a valid birth certificate. He could stand there wreaking miracles all day if he liked but at close of business, if he didn't have a valid birth certificate, he would simply be asked to leave.

And credit cards.

If, to sustain for a moment the same arbitrary hypothesis, the God Thor were alive and for some reason at large in England, then he would probably be the only person in the country who did not receive the constant barrage of invitations to apply for an American Express card, crude threats by the same post to take their American Express cards away, and gift catalogues full of sumptuously unpleasant things, lavishly tooled in naff brown plastic.

Dirk found the idea quite breathtaking.

That is, if he were the only god at large—which, once you were to accept the first extravagant hypothesis, was hardly likely to be the case.

But imagine for a moment such a person attempting to leave the country, armed with no passport, no credit cards, merely the power to throw thunderbolts and who knew what else. You would probably have to imagine a scene very similar to the one that did in fact occur at Terminal Two, Heathrow.

But why, if you were a Norse god, would you be needing to leave the country by means of a scheduled airline? Surely there were other means? Dirk rather thought that one of the perks of being an immortal divine might be the ability to fly under your own power. From what he remembered of his reading of the Norse legends many years ago, the gods were continually flying all over the place, and there was never any mention of them hanging around in departure lounges eating crummy buns. Admittedly, the world was not, in those days, bristling with air-traffic controllers, radar, missile-warning systems and such like. Still, a quick hop across the North Sea shouldn't be that much of a problem for a god, particularly if the weather was in your favor, which, if you were the God of Thunder, you would pretty much expect it to be, or want to know the reason why. Should it?

Another tiny note sang in the back of Dirk's mind and then was lost in the hubbub.

He wondered for a moment what it was like to be a whale. Physically, he thought, he was probably well placed to get some good insights, though whales were better adapted for their lives of gliding about in the vast pelagic blueness than he was for his of struggling up through the Pentonville Road traffic in a weary old Jaguar—but what he was thinking of, in fact, was the whales' songs. In the past the whales had been able to sing to each other across whole oceans, even from one ocean to another because sound travels such huge distances underwater. But now, again because of the way in which sound travels, there is no part of the ocean that is not constantly jangling with the hubbub of ships' motors, through which it is now virtually impossible for the whales to hear each other's songs or messages.

So fucking what, is pretty much the way that people tend to view this problem, and understandably so, thought Dirk. After all, who wants to hear a bunch of fat fish, oh, all right, mammals, burping at each other?

But for a moment Dirk had a sense of infinite loss and sadness that somewhere among the frenzy of information noise that daily rattled the lives of men he thought he might have heard a few notes that denoted the movements of gods.

As he turned north into Islington and began the long haul up past the pizza restaurants and estate agents, he felt almost frantic at the idea of what their lives must now be like.

18

◆

Thin fingers of lightning spread out across the heavy underside of the great clouds which hung from the sky like a sagging stomach. A small crack of fretful thunder nagged at it and dragged from it a few mean drops of greasy drizzle.

Beneath the sky ranged a vast assortment of wild turrets, gnarled spires and pinnacles, which prodded at it, goaded and inflamed it till it seemed it would burst and drown them in a flood of festering horrors.

High in the flickering darkness, silent figures stood

guard behind long shields, dragons crouched gaping at the foul sky as Odin, father of the Gods of Asgard, approached the great iron portals through which led to his domain and on into the vaulted halls of Valhalla. The air was full of the noiseless howls of great winged dogs, welcoming their master to the seat of his rule. Lightning searched among the towers and turrets.

The great, ancient and immortal God of Asgard was returning to the current site of his domain in a manner that would have surprised even him centuries ago in the years of the prime of his life—for even the immortal gods have their primes, when their powers are rampant and they both nourish and hold sway over the world of men, the world whose needs give them birth—he was returning in a large, unmarked gray Mercedes van.

The van drew to a halt in a secluded area.

The cab door opened and there climbed down from it a dull, slow-faced man in an unmarked gray uniform. He was a man who was charged with the work he did in life because he was not one to ask questions—not so much on account of any natural quality of discretion as because he simply could never think of any questions to ask. Moving with a slow, rolling gait, like a paddle being pulled through porridge, he made his way to the rear of the van and opened the rear doors—an elaborate procedure involving the coordinated manipulation of many sliders and levers.

At length the doors swung open, and if Kate had been present she might for a moment have been jolted by the thought that perhaps the van was carrying Albanian electricity after all. A haze of light greeted Hillow—the man's name was Hillow—but nothing about this struck him as odd. A haze of light was simply what he expected to see whenever he opened this door. The first time ever he had opened it he had simply thought to himself, "Oh. A haze of light. Oh well," and more or less left it at that, on the strength of which he had guaranteed himself regular employment for as long as he cared to live.

The haze of light subsided and coalesced into the shape of an old, old man in a trolley bed attended by a short little figure whom Hillow would probably have thought was the most evil-looking person he had ever seen if he had had a mind to recall the other people he had seen in his life and run through them all one by one, making the comparison. That, however, was harder than Hillow wished to work. His only concern at present was to assist the small figure with the decanting of the old man's bed onto ground level.

This was fluently achieved. The legs and wheels of the bed were a miracle of smoothly operating stainless-steel technology. They unlocked, rolled, swiveled, in elaborately interlocked movements which made the negotiating of steps or bumps all part of the same fluid, gliding motion.

To the right of this area lay a large antechamber paneled in finely carved wood, with great marble torch holders standing proudly from the walls. This in turn led into the great vaulted hall itself. To the left, however, lay the entrance to the majestic inner chambers where Odin would go to prepare himself for the encounters of the night.

He hated all this. Hounded from his bed, he muttered to himself, though in truth he was bringing his bed with him. Made to listen once again to all kinds of self-indulgent claptrap from his boneheaded thunderous son who would not accept, could not accept, simply did not have the intelligence to accept, the new realities of life. If he would not accept them, then he must be extinguished, and tonight Asgard would see the extinction of an immortal god. It was all, thought Odin fractiously, too much for someone at his time of life, which was extremely advanced, but not in any particular direction.

He wanted merely to stay in his hospital, which he loved. The arrangement which had brought him to that place was of the sweetest kind, and though it was not without its cost, it was a cost that simply had to be borne and that was all there was to it. There were new realities, and he had learned to embrace them. Those who did not would simply have to suffer the consequences. Nothing came of nothing, even for a god.

After tonight he could return to his life in the Woodshead indefinitely, and that would be good. He said as much to Hillow.

"Clean white sheets," he said to Hillow, who merely nodded blankly. "Linen sheets. Every day, clean sheets."

Hillow maneuvered the bed around and up a step.

"Being a god, Hillow," continued Odin, "being a god, well, it was unclean, you hear what I'm saying? There was no one who took care of the sheets. I mean really took care of them. Would you think that? In a situation like mine? Father of the Gods? There was no one, absolutely no one, who came in and said, 'Mr. Odwin' "—he chuckled to himself—"they call me Mr. Odwin there, you know. They don't quite know who they're dealing with. I don't think they could handle it, do you, Hillow? But there was no one in all that time who came in and said, 'Mr. Odwin, I have changed your bed and you have clean sheets.' No one. There was constant talk about hewing things and ravaging things and splitting things asunder. Lots of big talk of things being mighty, and of things being riven, and of things being in thrall to other things, but very little attention given, as I now realize, to the laundry. Let me give you an example . . ."

His reminiscences were for a moment interrupted, however, by the arrival of his vehicle at a great doorway which was guarded by a great sweaty splodge of a being who stood swaying, arms akimbo, in their path. Toe Rag, who had been preserving an intense silence as he stalked along just ahead of the bed, hurried forward and had a quick word with the sweating creature, who had to bend, red-faced, to hear him. Then instantly the sweaty creature shrank back with glistening obsequiousness into its yellow lair, and the sacred trolley rolled forward into the great halls, chambers and corridors from which great gusty echoes roared and fetid odors blew.

"Let me give you an example, Hillow," continued Odin. "Take this place, for example. Take Valhalla . . ."

19

◆

Turning north was a maneuver which normally had the effect of restoring a sense of reason and sanity to things, but Dirk could not escape a sense of foreboding.

Furthermore, it came on to rain a little, which should have helped, but it was such mean and wretched rain to come from such a heavy sky that it only increased the sense of claustrophobia and frustration that gripped the night. Dirk turned on the car wipers, which grumbled because they didn't have quite enough rain to wipe away, so he turned them off again. Rain quickly speckled the windscreen.

He turned on the wipers again, but they still refused to feel that the exercise was worthwhile, and scraped and squeaked in protest. The streets turned treacherously slippery.

Dirk shook his head. He was being quite absurd, he told himself, in the worst possible way. He had allowed himself to become fanciful in a manner that he quite despised. He astounded himself at the wild fantasies he had built on the flimsiest amount of, well he would hardly call it evidence, mere conjecture.

An accident at an airport. Probably a simple explanation.

A man with a hammer. So what?

A gray van which Kate Schechter had seen at the hospital. Nothing unusual about that. Dirk had nearly collided with it, but again, that was a perfectly commonplace occurrence.

A Coca-Cola machine: he hadn't taken that into account.

Where did a Coca-Cola machine fit into these wild notions about ancient gods? The only idea he had about that was simply too ridiculous for words and he refused even to acknowledge it to himself.

At that point Dirk found himself driving past the house where, that very morning, he had encountered a client of his who had had his severed head placed on a revolving record turntable by a green-eyed devil-figure waving a scythe and a blood-signed contract, who had then vanished into thin air.

He peered at it as he passed, and when a large dark-blue BMW pulled out from the curb just ahead of him, he ran straight into the back of it, and for the second time that day he had to leap out of his car, already shouting.

"For God's sake can't you look where you're going?" he exclaimed, in the hope of bagging his adversary's best lines from the outset. "Stupid people!" he continued, without pausing for breath. "Careering all over the place. Driving without due care and attention! Reckless assault!" Confuse your enemy, he thought. It was a little like phoning somebody up, and saying "Yes? Hello?" in a testy voice when they answered, which was one of Dirk's favorite methods of whiling away long, hot summer afternoons. He bent down and examined the palpable dent in the rear of the BMW, which was quite obviously, damn it, a brand-new one. Blast and bugger it, thought Dirk.

"Look what you've done to my bumper!" he cried. "I hope you have a good lawyer!"

"I am a good lawyer," said a quiet voice, which was followed by a quiet click. Dirk looked up in momentary apprehension. The quiet click was only the sound of the car door closing.

The man was wearing an Italian suit, which was also quiet. He had quiet glasses, quietly cut hair, and though a bow tie is not, by its very nature, a quiet object, the particular bow tie he wore was, nevertheless, a very quietly spotted example of the genre. He drew a slim wallet from his pocket and also a slim silver pencil. He walked without fuss to the rear of Dirk's Jaguar and made a note of the registration number.

"Do you have a card?" he inquired as he did so, without looking up. "Here's mine," he added, taking one from his wallet. He made a note on the back of it. "My registration number," he said, "and the name of my insurance company. Perhaps you would be good enough to let me have the name of yours. If you don't have it with you, I'll get my girl to call you."

Dirk sighed, and decided there was no point in putting up a fight on this one. He fished out his wallet and leafed through the various business cards that seemed to accumulate in it as if from nowhere. He toyed for a second with the idea of being Wesley Arlott, an ocean-going yacht navigation consultant from, apparently, Arkansas, but then thought better of it. The man had, after all, taken his registration number, and although Dirk had no particular recollection of paying an insurance premium of late, he also had no particular recollection of not paying one either, which was a reasonably promising sign. He handed over a bona fide card with a wince. The man looked at it.

"Mr. Gently," he said. "Private investigator. I'm sorry, private *holistic* investigator. OK."

He put the card away, taking no further interest.

Dirk had never felt so patronized in his life. At that moment there was another quiet click from the other side of the car. Dirk looked across to see a woman with red spectacles standing there giving him a frozen half-smile. She was the woman he had spoken with over Geoffrey Anstey's garden wall this morning, and the man, Dirk therefore supposed, was probably her husband. He wondered for a second whether he should wrestle them to the ground and question them rigorously and violently, but he was suddenly feeling immensely tired and run-down.

He acknowledged the woman in red spectacles with a minute inclination of his head.

"All done, Cynthia," said the man and flicked a smile on and off at her. "It's all taken care of."

She nodded faintly, and the two of them climbed back into their BMW and after a moment or two pulled away without fuss and disappeared away down the road. Dirk looked at the card in his hand. Clive Draycott. He was with a good firm of City solicitors. Dirk stuck the card away in his wallet, climbed despondently back into his car, and drove on back to his house, where he found a large golden eagle sitting patiently on his doorstep.

20

$\diamond$

Kate rounded on her guest as soon as they were both inside her flat with the door closed and Kate could be reasonably certain that Neil wasn't going to sneak back out of his flat and lurk disapprovingly halfway up the stairs. The continuing thumping of his bass was at least her guarantee of privacy.

"All right," she said fiercely, "so what is the deal with the eagle then? What is the deal with all the streetlights? Huh?"

The Norse God of Thunder looked at her awkwardly.

He had to remove his great horned helmet because it was banging against the ceiling and leaving scratch marks in the plaster. He tucked it under his arm.

"What is the deal," continued Kate, "with the Coca-Cola machine? What is the deal with the hammer? What, in short, is the big deal? Huh?"

Thor said nothing. He frowned for a second in arrogant irritation, then frowned in something that looked somewhat like embarrassment, and then simply stood there and bled at her.

For a few seconds she resisted the impending internal collapse of her attitude, and then realized it was just going to go to hell anyway so she might as well go with it.

"OK," she muttered, "let's get all that cleaned up. I'll find some antiseptic."

She went to rummage in the kitchen cupboard and returned with a bottle to find Thor saying "No" at her.

"No what?" she said crossly, putting the bottle down on the table with a bit of a bang.

"That," said Thor, and pushed the bottle back at her. "No."

"What's the matter with it?"

Thor just shrugged and stared moodily at a corner of the room. There was nothing that could be considered remotely interesting in that corner of the room, so he was clearly looking at it out of sheer bloody-mindedness.

"Look, buster," said Kate, "if I can call you buster, what—"

"Thor," said Thor, "God of—"

"Yes," said Kate, "you've told me all the things you're God of. I'm trying to clean up your arm."

"Sedra," said Thor, holding his bleeding arm out, but away from her. He peered at it anxiously.

"What?"

"Crushed leaves of sedra. Oil of the kernel of the apricot. Infusion of bitter orange blossom. Oil of almonds. Sage and comfrey. Not this."

He pushed the bottle of antiseptic off the table and sank into a mood.

"Right!" said Kate, picked up the bottle and hurled it at him. It rebounded off his cheekbone leaving an instant red mark. Thor lunged forward in a rage, but Kate simply stood her ground with a finger pointed at him.

"You stay right there, buster!" she said, and he stopped. "Anything special you need for that?"

Thor looked puzzled for a moment.

"That!" said Kate, pointing at the blossoming bruise on his cheek.

"Vengeance," said Thor.

"I'll have to see what I can do," said Kate. She turned on her heel and stalked out of the room.

After about two minutes of unseen activity Kate returned to the room, trailed by wisps of steam.

"All right," she said, "come with me."

She led him into her bathroom. He followed her with a great show of reluctance, but he followed her. Kate had been trailed by wisps of steam because the bathroom was full of it. The bath itself was overflowing with bubbles and gunk.

There were some bottles and pots, mostly empty, lined up along a small shelf above the bath. Kate picked them up one by one and displayed them at him.

"Apricot kernel oil," she said, and turned it upside down to emphasize its emptiness. "All in there," she added, pointing at the foaming bath.

"Neroli oil," she said, picking up the next one, "distilled from the blossom of bitter oranges. All in there."

She picked up the next one. "Orange cream bath oil. Contains almond oil. All in there."

She picked up the pots.

"Sage and comfrey," she said of one, "and sedra oil. One of them's a hand cream and the other's hair conditioner, but they're all in there, along with a tube of Aloe Lip Preserver, some Cucumber Cleansing Milk, Honeyed Beeswax and Jojoba Oil Cleanser, Rhassoul Mud, Seaweed and Birch Shampoo, Rich Night Cream with Vitamin E, and a very great deal of cod liver oil. I'm afraid I haven't got anything called Vengeance, but here's some Calvin Klein Obsession."

She took the stopper from a bottle of perfume and threw the bottle in the bath.

"I'll be in the next room when you're done."

With that she marched out, and slammed the door on him. She waited in the other room, firmly reading a book.

21

◆

For about a minute Dirk remained sitting motionless in his car a few yards away from his front door. He wondered what his next move should be. A small, cautious one, he rather thought. The last thing he wanted to have to contend with at the moment was a startled eagle.

He watched it intently. It stood there with a pert magnificence about its bearing, its talons gripped tightly round the edge of the stone step. From time to time it preened itself and then peered sharply up the street and down the street, dragging one of its great talons across the stone in a deeply worrying manner. Dirk admired the creature greatly for its size and its plumage and its general sense of extreme airworthiness, but, asking himself if he liked the way that the light from the streetlamp glinted in its great glassy eye or on the huge hook of its beak, he had to admit that he did not.

The beak was a major piece of armory.

It was a beak that would frighten any animal on earth, even one that was already dead and in a tin. Its talons looked as if they could rip up a small Volvo. And it was sitting waiting on Dirk's doorstep, looking up and down the street with a gaze that was at once meaningful and mean.

Dirk wondered if he should simply drive off and leave the country. Did he have his passport? No. It was at home. It was behind the door which was behind the eagle, in a drawer somewhere or, most likely, lost.

He could sell up. The ratio of estate agents to actual houses in the area was rapidly approaching parity. One of their lot could come and deal with the house. He'd had enough of it, with its fridges and its wildlife and its ineradicable position on the mailing lists of the American Express company.

Or he could, he supposed with a slight shiver, just go and see what it was the eagle wanted. There was a thought. Rats, probably, or a small whippet. All Dirk had, to his knowledge, was some Rice Krispies and an old muffin, and he didn't see those appealing to this magisterial creature of the air. He rather fancied that he could make out fresh blood congealing on the bird's talons, but he told himself firmly not to be so ridiculous.

He was just going to have to go and face up to the thing, explain that he was fresh out of rats, and take the consequences.

Quietly, infinitely quietly, he pushed open the door of his car and stole out of it, keeping his head down. He peered at the eagle from over the bonnet of the car. It hadn't moved. That is to say, it hadn't left the district. It was still looking this way and that around itself with, possibly, a heightened sense of alertness. Dirk didn't know in what remote mountain eyrie the creature had learned to listen out for the sound of Jaguar car-door hinges revolving in their sockets, but the sound had clearly not escaped its attention.

Cautiously, Dirk bobbed along behind the line of cars that had prevented him from being able to park directly outside his own house. In a couple of seconds all that separated him from the extraordinary creature was a small blue Renault.

What next?

He could simply stand up and, as it were, declare himself. He would be saying, in effect, "Here I am, do what you will." Whatever then transpired, the Renault could probably bear the brunt.

There was always the possibility, of course, that the eagle would be pleased to see him, that all this swooping it had been directing at him had been just its way of being matey. Assuming, of course, that it was the same eagle. That was not such an enormous assumption. The number of golden eagles at large in North London at any one time was, Dirk guessed, fairly small.

Or maybe it was just resting on his doorstep completely by chance, enjoying a quick breather prior to having another hurtle through the sky in pursuit of whatever it is that eagles hurtle through the sky after.

Whatever the explanation, now, Dirk realized, was the time that he had simply to take his chances. He steeled himself, took a deep breath and arose from behind the Renault like a spirit rising from the deep.

The eagle was looking in another direction at the time, and it was a second or so before it looked back to the front and saw him, at which point it reacted with a loud screech and stepped back an inch or two, a reaction which Dirk felt a little put out by. It then blinked rapidly a few times and adopted a sort of perky expression of which Dirk did not have the faintest idea what to make.

He waited for a second or two until he felt the situation had settled down again after all the foregoing excitement, and then stepped forward tentatively, around the front of the Renault. A number of quiet, interrogative cawing noises seemed to float uncertainly through the air, and then after a moment Dirk realized that he was making them himself, and made himself stop. This was an eagle he was dealing with, not a budgie.

It was at this point that he made his mistake.

With his mind entirely taken up with eagles, the possible intentions of eagles, and the many ways in which eagles might be considered to differ from small kittens, he did not concentrate enough on what he was doing as he stepped up out of the road and on to a pavement that was slick with the recent drizzle. As he brought his rear foot forward it caught on the bumper of the car; he wobbled, slipped, and then did that thing which one should never do to a large eagle of uncertain temper, which was to fling himself headlong at it with his arms outstretched.

The eagle reacted instantly.

Without a second's hesitation it hopped neatly aside and allowed Dirk the space he needed to collapse heavily onto his own doorstep. It then peered down at him with a scorn that would have withered a lesser man, or at least a man who had been looking up at that moment.

Dirk groaned.

He had sustained a blow to the temple from the edge of the step, and it was a blow, he felt, that this evening he could just as easily have done without. He lay there gasping for a second or two, then at last rolled over heavily, clasping one hand to his forehead, the other to his nose, and looked up at the great bird in apprehension, reflecting bitterly on the conditions under which he was expected to work.

When it became clear to him that he appeared for the moment to have nothing to fear from the eagle, who was merely regarding him with a kind of quizzical, blinking doubt, he sat up, and then slowly dragged himself back to his feet and wiped and smacked some of the dirt off his coat. Then he hunted through his pockets for his keys and unlocked the front door, which seemed a little loose. He waited to see what the eagle would do next.

With a slight rustle of its wings it hopped over the lintel and into his hall. It looked around itself and seemed to regard what it saw with a little distaste. Dirk didn't know what it was that eagles expected of people's hallways, but had to admit to himself that it wasn't only the eagle which reacted like that. The disorder was not that great, but there was a grimness to it which tended to cast a pall over visitors, and the eagle was clearly not immune to this effect.

Dirk picked up a large flat envelope lying on his doormat, looked inside it to check that it was what he had been expecting, then noticed that a picture was missing from the wall. It wasn't a particularly wonderful picture, merely a small Japanese print that he had found in Camden Passage and quite liked, but the point was that it was missing. The hook on the wall was empty. There was a chair missing as well, he realized.

The possible significance of this suddenly struck him, and he hurried through to the kitchen. Many of his assorted kitchen implements had clearly gone. The rack of largely unused Sabatier knives, the food processor and his radio cassette player had all vanished, but he did, however, have a new fridge. It had obviously been delivered by Nobby Paxton's felonious thugs, and he would just have to make the usual little list.

Still, he had a new fridge, and that was a considerable load off his mind. Already the whole atmosphere in the kitchen seemed easier. The tension had lifted. There was a new sense of lightness and springiness in the air that had even communicated itself to the pile of old pizza boxes which seemed now to recline at a jaunty rather than an oppressive angle.

Dirk cheerfully threw open the door to the new fridge and was delighted to find it completely and utterly empty. Its inner light shone on perfectly clean blue-and-white walls and on gleaming chrome shelves. He liked it so much that he instantly determined to keep it like that. He would put nothing in it at all. His food would just have to go off in plain view.

Good. He closed it again.

A screech and a flap behind him reminded him that he was entertaining a visiting eagle. He turned to find it glaring at him from on top of the kitchen table.

Now that he was getting a little more accustomed to it, and had not actually been viciously attacked as he had suspected he might be, it seemed a little less fearsome than it had at first. It was still a serious amount of eagle, but perhaps an eagle was a slightly more manageable proposition than he had originally supposed. He relaxed a little and took off his hat, pulled off his coat, and threw them on to a chair.

The eagle seemed at this juncture to sense that Dirk might be getting the wrong idea about it and flexed one of its claws at him. With sudden alarm Dirk saw that it did indeed have something that closely resembled congealed blood on the talons. He backed away from it hurriedly. The eagle then rose up to its full height on its talons and began to spread its great wings out, wider and wider, beating them very slowly and leaning forward so as to keep its balance. Dirk did the only thing he could think to do under the circumstances and bolted from the room, slamming the door behind him and jamming the hall table up against it.

A terrible cacophony of screeching and scratching and buffeting arose instantly from behind it. Dirk sat leaning back against the table, panting and trying to catch his breath, and then after a while began to get a worrying feeling about what the bird was up to now.

It seemed to him that the eagle was actually dive-bombing itself against the door. Every few seconds the pattern would repeat itself—first a great beating of wings, then a rush, then a terrible cracking thud. Dirk didn't think it would get through the door, but was alarmed that it might beat itself to death trying. The creature seemed to be quite frantic about something, but what, Dirk could not even begin to imagine. He tried to calm himself down and think clearly, to work out what he should do next.

He should phone Kate and make certain she was all right.

Whoosh, thud!

He should finally open up the envelope he had been carrying with him all day and examine its contents.

Whoosh, thud!

For that he would need a sharp knife.

Whoosh, thud!

Three rather awkward thoughts then struck him in fairly quick succession.

Whoosh, thud!

First, the only sharp knives in the place, assuming Nobby's removal people had left him with any at all, were in the kitchen.

Whoosh, thud!

That didn't matter so much in itself, because he could probably find something in the house that would do.

Whoosh, thud!

The second thought was that the actual envelope itself was in the pocket of his coat, which he had left lying over the back of a chair in the kitchen.

Whoosh, thud!

The third thought was very similar to the second and had to do with the location of the piece of paper with Kate's telephone number on it.

Whoosh, thud!

Oh God.

Whoosh, thud!

Dirk began to feel very, very tired at the way the day was working out. He was deeply worried by the sense of impending calamity, but was still by no means able to divine what lay at the root of it.

Whoosh, thud!

Well, he knew what he had to do now . . .

Whoosh, thud!

. . . so there was no point in not getting on with it. He quietly pulled the table away from the door.

Whoosh—

He ducked and yanked the door open, passing smoothly under the eagle as it hurtled out into the hallway and hit the opposite wall. He slammed the door closed behind him from inside the kitchen, pulled his coat off the chair and jammed the chair back up under the handle.

Whoosh, thud!

The damage done to the door on this side was both considerable and impressive, and Dirk began seriously to worry about what this behavior said about the bird's state of mind, or what the bird's state of mind might become if it maintained this behavior for very much longer.

Whoosh . . . scratch . . .

The same thought seemed to have occurred to the bird at that moment, and after a brief flurry of screeching and of scratching at the door with its talons it lapsed into a grumpy and defeated silence, which, after having gone on for about a minute, became almost as disturbing as the previous batterings.

Dirk wondered what the eagle was up to.

He approached the door cautiously and very, very quietly moved the chair back a little so that he could see through the keyhole. He squatted down and peered through it. At first it seemed to him that he could see nothing, that it must be blocked by something. Then, a slight flicker and glint close up on the other side suddenly revealed the startling truth, which was that the eagle also had an eye up at the keyhole and was busy looking back at him. Dirk almost toppled backward with the shock of the realization, and backed away from the door with a sense of slight horror and revulsion.

This was extremely intelligent behavior for an eagle, wasn't it? Was it? How could he find out? He couldn't think of any ornithological experts to phone. All his reference books were piled up in other rooms of the house, and he didn't think he'd be able to keep on pulling off the same stunt with impunity, certainly not when he was dealing with an eagle which had managed to figure out what keyholes were for.

He retreated to the kitchen sink and found a kitchen towel. He folded it into a wad, soaked it, and dabbed it first on his bleeding temple, which was swelling up nicely, and then on his nose, which was still very tender and had been a considerable size for most of the day now. Maybe the eagle was an eagle of delicate sensibilities and had reacted badly to the sight of Dirk's face in its current, much-abused state and had simply lost its mind. Dirk sighed and sat down.

Kate's telephone, which was the next thing he turned his attention to, was answered by a machine when he tried to ring it. Her voice told him, very sweetly, that he was welcome to leave a message after the beep, but warned that she hardly ever listened to them and that it was much better to talk to her directly, only he couldn't because she wasn't in, so he'd best try again.

Thank you very much, he thought, and put the phone down.

He realized that the truth of the matter was this: He had spent the day putting off opening the envelope because of what he was worried about finding in it. It wasn't that the idea was frightening, though indeed it was frightening that a man should sell his soul to a green-eyed man with a scythe, which is what circumstances were trying very hard to suggest had happened. It was just that it was extremely depressing that he should sell it to a green-eyed man with a scythe in exchange for a share in the royalties of a hit record.

That was what it looked like on the face of it. Wasn't it?

Dirk picked up the other envelope, the one which had

been waiting for him on his doormat, delivered there by courier from a large London bookshop where Dirk had an account. He pulled out the contents, which were a copy of the sheet music of "Hot Potato," written by Colin Paignton, Phil Mulville and Geoff Anstey.

The lyrics were, well, straightforward. They provided a basic repetitive bit of funk rhythm and a simple sense of menace and cheerful callousness which had caught the mood of last summer. They went:

Hot Potato,
Don't pick it up, pick it up, pick it up.
Quick, pass it on, pass it on, pass it on.
You don't want to get caught, get caught, get caught.
Drop it on someone. Who? Who? Anybody.
You better not have it when the big one comes.
I said you better not have it when the big one comes.
It's a Hot Potato.

And so on. The repeated phrases got tossed back and forward between the two members of the band, the drum machine got heavier and heavier, and there had been a dance video.

Was that all it was going to be? Big deal. A nice house in Lupton Street with polyurethaned floors and a broken marriage?

Things had certainly come down a long way since the great days of Faust and Mephistopheles, when a man could gain all the knowledge of the universe, achieve all the ambitions of his mind and all the pleasures of the flesh for the price of his soul. Now it was a few record royalties, a few pieces of trendy furniture, a trinket to stick on your bathroom wall and, whap, your head comes off.

So what exactly was the deal? What was the "Potato" contract? Who was getting what and why?

Dirk rummaged through a drawer for the breadknife, sat down once more, took the envelope from his coat pocket and ripped through the congealed strata of Sellotape which held the end of it together.

Out fell a thick bundle of papers.

22

◆

At exactly the moment that the telephone rang, the door to Kate's sitting room opened. The Thunder God attempted to stomp in through it, but in fact he wafted. He had clearly soaked himself very thoroughly in the stuff Kate had thrown into the bath, then redressed, and torn up a nightgown of Kate's to bind his forearm with. He casually tossed a handful of softened oak shards away into the corner of the room. Kate decided for the moment to ignore both the deliberate provocations and the telephone. The former she could deal with and the latter she had a machine for dealing with.

"I've been reading about you," she challenged the Thunder God. "Where's your beard?"

He took the book, a one-volume encyclopedia, from her hands and glanced at it before tossing it aside contemptuously.

"Ha," he said, "I shaved it off. When I was in Wales." He scowled at the memory.

"What were you doing in Wales, for heaven's sake?"

"Counting the stones," he said with a shrug, and went to stare out of the window.

There was a huge, moping anxiety in his bearing. It suddenly occurred to Kate with a spasm of something not entirely unlike fear that sometimes when people got like that, it was because they had picked up their mood from the weather. With a Thunder God it presumably worked the other way round. The sky outside certainly had a restless and disgruntled look.

Her reactions suddenly started to become very confused.

"Excuse me if this sounds like a stupid question," said Kate, "but I'm a little at sea here. I'm not used to spending the evening with someone who's got a whole day named after them. What stones were you counting in Wales?"

"All of them," said Thor in a low growl. "All of them between this size—" he held the tip of his forefinger and thumb about a quarter of an inch apart—"and this size." He held his two hands about a yard apart, and then put them down again.

Kate stared at him blankly.

"Well . . . how many were there?" she asked. It seemed only polite to ask.

He rounded on her angrily.

"Count them yourself if you want to know!" he shouted. "What's the point in my spending years and years and years counting them, so that I'm the only person who knows, and who will ever know, if I just go and tell somebody else? Well?"

He turned back to the window.

"Anyway," he said, "I've been worried about it. I think I may have lost count somewhere in Mid-Glamorgan. But I'm not," he shouted, "going to do it again!"

"Well, why on earth would you do such an extraordinary thing in the first place?"

"It was a burden placed on me by my father. A punishment. A penance." He glowered.

"Your father?" said Kate. "Do you mean Odin?"

"The All-Father," said Thor. "Father of the Gods of Asgard."

"And you're saying he's alive?"

Thor turned to look at her as if she was stupid.

"We are immortals," he said, simply.

Downstairs, Neil chose that moment to conclude his thunderous performance on the bass, and the house seemed to sing in its aftermath with an eerie silence.

"Immortals are what you wanted," said Thor in a low, quiet voice. "Immortals are what you got. It is a little hard on us. You wanted us to be forever, so we are forever. Then you forget about us. But still we are forever. Now at last, many are dead, many dying," he then added in a quiet voice, "but it takes a special effort."

"I can't even begin to understand what you're talking about," said Kate, "you say that I, we—"

"You *can* begin to understand," said Thor angrily, "which is why I have come to you. Do you know that most people hardly see me? Hardly notice me at all? It is not that we are hidden. We are here. We move among you. My people. Your gods. You gave birth to us. You made us be what you would not dare to be yourselves. Yet you will not acknowledge us. If I walk along one of your .streets in this . . . world you have made for yourselves without us, then barely an eye will once flicker in my direction."

"Is this when you're wearing the helmet?"

"Especially when I'm wearing the helmet!"

"Well—"

"You make fun of me!" roared Thor.

"You make it very easy for a girl," said Kate. "I don't know what—"

Suddenly the room seemed to quake and then to catch its breath. All of Kate's insides wobbled violently and then held very still. In the sudden horrible silence, a blue china table lamp slowly toppled off the table, hit the floor and crawled off to a dark corner of the room where it sat in a worried little defensive huddle.

Kate stared at it and tried to be calm about it. She felt as if cold, soft jelly was trickling down her skin.

"Did you do that?" she said shakily.

Thor was looking livid and confused. He muttered, "Do not make me angry with you. You were very lucky." He looked away.

"What are you *saying?*"

"I'm saying that I wish you to come with me."

"What? What about *that?*" She pointed at the small, befuddled kitten under the table which had so recently and so confusingly been a blue china table lamp.

"There's nothing I can do for it."

Kate was suddenly so tired and confused and frightened that she found she was nearly in tears. She stood biting her lip and trying to be as angry as she could.

"Oh yeah?" she said. "I thought you were meant to be a god. I hope you haven't got into my home under false pretenses, I . . ." She stumbled to a halt, and then resumed in a different tone of voice.

"Do you mean," she said in a small voice, "that you have been here, in the world, *all this time?*"

"Here, and in Asgard," said Thor.

"Asgard," said Kate. "The home of the gods?"

Thor was silent. It was a grim silence that seemed to be full of something that bothered him deeply.

"Where is Asgard?" demanded Kate.

Again Thor did not speak. He was a man of very few words and enormously long pauses. When at last he did answer, it wasn't at all clear whether he had been thinking all that time or just standing there.

"Asgard is also here," he said. "All worlds are here."

He drew out from under his furs his great hammer and studied its head deeply and with an odd curiosity, as if something about it was very puzzling. Kate wondered why she found such a gesture familiar. She found that it instinctively made her want to duck. She stepped back very slightly and was watchful.

When he looked up again, there was an altogether new focus and energy in his eyes, as if he was gathering himself up to hurl himself at something.

"Tonight I must be in Asgard," he said. "I must confront my father, Odin, in the great hall of Valhalla and bring him to account for what he has done."

"You mean, for making you count Welsh pebbles?"

"No!" said Thor. "For making the Welsh pebbles not worth counting!"

Kate shook her head in exasperation. "I simply don't know what to make of you at all," she said. "I think I'm just too tired. Come back tomorrow. Explain it all in the morning."

"No," said Thor. "You must see Asgard yourself, and then you will understand. You must see it tonight." He gripped her by the arm.

"I don't want to go to Asgard," she insisted. "I don't go to mythical places with strange men. You go. Call me up and tell me how it went in the morning. Give him hell about the pebbles."

She wrested her arm from his grip. It was very, very clear to her that she only did this with his permission.

"Now please go, and let me sleep!" She glared at him.

At that moment the house seemed to erupt as Neil launched into a thumping bass rendition of Siegfried's "Rheinfahrt" from Act 1 of *Götterdämmerung*, just to prove it could be done. The walls shook, the windows rattled. From under the table the sound of the table lamp mewing pathetically could just be heard.

Kate tried to maintain her furious glare, but it simply couldn't be kept up for very long in the circumstances.

"OK," she said at last, "how do we get to this place?"

"There are as many ways as there are tiny pieces."

"I beg your pardon?"

"Tiny things." He held up his thumb and forefinger again to indicate something very small. "Molecules," he added, seeming to be uncomfortable with the word. "But first let us leave here."

"Will I need a coat in Asgard?"

"As you wish."

"Well, I'll take one anyway. Wait a minute."

She decided that the best way to deal with the astonishing rigmarole which currently constituted her life was to be businesslike about it. She found her coat, brushed her hair, left a new message on her telephone answering machine and put a saucer of milk firmly under the table.

"Right," she said, and led the way out of the flat, locking it carefully after them, and making shushing noises as they passed Neil's door. For all the uproar he was currently making he was almost certainly listening out for the slightest sound, and would be out in a moment if he heard them going by, to complain about the Coca-Cola machine, the lateness of the hour, man's inhumanity to man, the weather, the noise, and the color of Kate's coat, which was a shade of blue that Neil for some reason disapproved of most particularly. They stole past successfully and closed the front door behind them with the merest click.

23

◆

The sheets which tumbled out onto Dirk's kitchen table were made of thick heavy paper folded together, and had obviously been much handled.

He sorted them out one by one, separating them from each other, smoothing them out with the flat of his hand and laying them out neatly in rows on the kitchen table, clearing a space, as it became necessary, among the old newspapers, ashtrays and dirty cereal bowls which Elena the cleaner always left exactly where they were, claiming, when challenged on this, that she thought he had put them there specially.

He pored over the papers for several minutes, moving from one to another, comparing them with each other, studying them carefully, page by page, paragraph by paragraph, line by line.

He couldn't understand a word of them.

It should have occurred to him, he realized, that the green-eyed, hairy, scythe-waving giant might differ from him not only in general appearance and personal habits, but also in such matters as the alphabet he favored.

He sat back in his seat, disgruntled and thwarted, and reached for a cigarette, but the packet in his coat was now empty. He picked up a pencil and tapped it in a cigarette-like way, but it wasn't able to produce the same effect.

After a minute or two he became acutely conscious of the fact that he was probably still being watched through the keyhole by the eagle, and he found that this made it impossibly hard to concentrate on the problem before him, particularly without a cigarette. He scowled to himself. He knew there was still a packet upstairs by his bed, but he didn't think he could handle the sheer ornithology involved in going to get it.

He tried to stare at the papers for a little longer. The writing, apart from being written in some kind of small, crabby and indecipherable runic script, was mostly hunched up toward the left-hand side of the paper as if swept there by a tide. The right-hand side was largely clear except for an occasional group of characters which were lined up underneath each other. All of it, except for a slight sense of undefinable familiarity about the layout, was completely meaningless to Dirk.

He turned his attention back to the envelope instead

and tried once more to examine some of the names which
had been so heavily crossed out.

Howard Bell, the incredibly wealthy best-selling nov-
elist who wrote bad books which sold by the warehouse-
load despite—or perhaps because of—the fact that
nobody read them.

Dennis Hutch, record-company magnate. Now that he
had a context for the name, Dirk knew it perfectly well.
The Aries Rising Record Group, which had been founded
on Sixties ideals, or at least on what passed for ideals in
the Sixties, grown in the Seventies and then embraced
the materialism of the Eighties without missing a beat,
was now a massive entertainment conglomerate on both
sides of the Atlantic. Dennis Hutch had stepped up into
the top seat when its founder had died of a lethal overdose
of brick wall, taken while under the influence of a Ferrari
and a bottle of tequila. ARRGH! was also the record label
on which "Hot Potato" had been released.

Stan Dubcek, senior partner in the advertising company with the silly name which now owned most of the
British and American advertising companies which had
not had names which were quite as silly, and had therefore been swallowed whole.

And here, suddenly, was another name that was instantly recognizable, now that Dirk was attuned to the
sort of names he should be looking for. Roderick Mercer,
the world's greatest publisher of the world's sleaziest
newspapers. Dirk hadn't at first spotted the name with
the unfamiliar ". . . erick" in place after the "Rod." Well,
well, well . . .

Now here were people, thought Dirk suddenly, who
had really got something. Certainly they had got rather
more than a nice little house in Lupton Road with some
dried flowers lying around the place. They also had the

great advantage of having heads on their shoulders as well, unless Dirk had missed something new and dramatic on the news. What did that all mean? What was this contract? How come everybody whose hands it had been through had been so astoundingly successful except for one, Geoffrey Anstey? Everybody whose hands it had passed through had benefited from it except for the one who had it last. Who had still got it.

It was a hot potato.

You better not have it when the big one comes.

The notion suddenly formed in Dirk's mind that it might have been Geoffrey Anstey himself who had overheard a conversation about a hot potato, about getting rid of it, passing it on. If he remembered correctly the interview he had read with Pain, he didn't say that he himself had overheard the conversation.

You better not have it when the big one comes.

The notion was a horrible one and ran on like this: Geoffrey Anstey had been pathetically naive. He had overheard this conversation, between—who? Dirk picked up the envelope and ran over the list of names—and had thought that it had a good dance rhythm. Anstey had not for a moment realized that what he was listening to was a conversation that would result in his own hideous death. He had got a hit record out of it, and when the real hot potato was actually handed to him he had picked it up.

Don't pick it up, pick it up, pick it up.

And instead of taking the advice he had recorded in the words of the song . . .

Quick, pass it on, pass it on, pass it on.

. . . he had stuck it behind the gold record award on his bathroom wall.

You better not have it when the big one comes.

Dirk frowned and took a long, slow thoughtful drag on his pencil.

This was ridiculous.

He had to get some cigarettes if he was going to think this through with any intellectual rigor. He pulled on his coat, stuffed his hat on his head and made for the window.

The window hadn't been opened for—well, certainly not during his ownership of the house, and it struggled and screamed at the sudden unaccustomed invasion of its space and independence. Once he had forced it wide enough, Dirk struggled out onto the windowsill, pulling swathes of leather coat out with him. From here it was a bit of a jump to the pavement since there was a lower ground floor to the house with a narrow flight of steps leading down to it in the front. A line of iron railings separated these from the pavement, and Dirk had to get clear over them.

Without hesitating for a moment, he made the jump, and it was in mid-bound that he realized he had not picked up his car keys from the kitchen table where he'd left them.

He considered as he sailed gracelessly through the air whether or not to execute a wild midair twist, make a desperate grab backward for the window and hope that he might just manage to hold onto the sill, but decided on mature reflection that an error at this point might just conceivably kill him, whereas the walk would probably do him good.

He landed heavily on the far side of the railings, but the tails of his coat became entangled with them and he had to pull them off, tearing part of the lining in the process. Once the ringing shock in his knees had subsided and he had recovered what little composure the events of the day had left him with, he realized that it was now well after eleven o'clock and the pubs would be shut, and he might have a longer walk than he had bargained for to find some cigarettes.

He considered what to do.

The current outlook and state of mind of the eagle was a major factor to be taken into account here. The only way to get his car keys now was back through the front door into his eagle-infested hallway.

Moving with great caution he tiptoed back up the steps to his front door, squatted down and, hoping that the damn thing wasn't going to squeak, gently pushed up the flap of the letter box and peered through.

In an instant a talon was hooked into the back of his hand and a great screeching beak slashed at his eye, narrowly missing it but scratching a great gouge across his much-abused nose.

Dirk howled with pain and lurched backward, not getting very far because he still had a talon hooked in his hand. He lashed out desperately and hit at the talon, which hurt him considerably, dug the sharp point even further into his flesh and caused a great, barging flurry on the far side of the door, each tiniest movement of which tugged heavily in his hand.

He grabbed at the great claw with his free hand and tried to tug it back out of himself. It was immensely strong, and was shaking with the fury of the eagle, which was as trapped as he was. At last, quivering with pain, he managed to release himself, and pulled his injured hand back, nursing and cuddling it with the other.

The eagle pulled its claw back sharply, and Dirk heard it flapping away back down his hallway, emitting terrible screeches and cries, its great wings colliding with and scraping the walls.

Dirk toyed with the idea of burning the house down, but once the throbbing in his hand had begun to subside a little he calmed down and tried, if he could, to see things from the eagle's point of view.

He couldn't.

He had not the faintest idea how things appeared to eagles in general, much less to this particular eagle, which seemed to be a seriously deranged example of the species.

After a minute or so more of nursing his hand, curiosity —allied to a strong sense that the eagle had definitely retreated to the far end of the hall and stayed there— overcame him, and he bent down once more to the letter box. This time he used his pencil to push the flap back upward and scanned the hallway from a safe position a good few inches back.

The eagle was clearly in view, perched on the end of the banister rail, regarding him with resentment and opprobrium, which Dirk felt was a little rich coming from a creature which had only a moment or two ago been busily engaged in trying to rip his hand off.

Then, once the eagle was certain that it had got Dirk's attention, it slowly raised itself up on its feet and slowly shook its great wings out, beating them gently for balance. It was this gesture that had previously caused Dirk to bolt prudently from the room. This time, however, he was safely behind a couple of good solid inches of wood, and he stood, or rather, squatted, his ground. The eagle stretched its neck upward as well, jabbing its tongue out at the air and cawing plaintively, which surprised Dirk.

Then he noticed something else rather surprising about the eagle, which was that its wings had strange, un-eagle-like markings on them. They were large concentric circles.

The differences of coloration which delineated the circles were very slight, and it was only the absolute geometric regularity of them which made them stand out as clearly as they did. Dirk had the very clear sense that the eagle was showing him these circles, and that that was what it had wanted to attract his attention to all along. Each time the bird had dived at him, he realized, as he thought back, it had then started on a strange kind of flapping routine which had involved opening its wings right out. However, each time it had happened Dirk had been too busily engaged with the business of turning around and running away to pay this exhibition the appropriate attention.

"Have you got the money for a cup of tea, mate?"

"Er, yes, thank you," said Dirk, "I'm fine." His attention was fully occupied with the eagle, and he didn't immediately look around.

"No, I meant can you spare me a bob or two, just for a cup of tea?"

"What?" This time Dirk looked around, irritably.

"Or just a fag, mate. Got a fag you can spare?"

"No, I was just going to go and get some myself," said Dirk.

The man on the pavement behind him was a tramp of indeterminate age. He was standing there, slightly wobbly, with a look of wild and continuous disappointment bobbing in his eyes.

Not getting an immediate response from Dirk, the man dropped his eyes to the ground about a yard in front of him, and swayed back and forth a little. He was holding his arms out, slightly open, slightly away from his body, and just swaying. Then he frowned suddenly at the ground. Then he frowned at another part of the ground. Then, holding himself steady while he made quite a major

realignment of his head, he frowned away down the
street.

"Have you lost something?" said Dirk.

The man's head swayed back toward him.

"Have I *lost* something?" he said in querulous astonishment. "Have I *lost* something?"

It seemed to be the most astounding question he had
ever heard. He looked away again for a while, and seemed
to be trying to balance the question in the general scale
of things. This involved a fair bit more swaying and a fair
few more frowns. At last he seemed to come up with
something that might do service as some kind of answer.

"The sky?" he said, challenging Dirk to find this a good
enough answer. He looked up toward it carefully, so as
not to lose his balance. He seemed not to like what he saw
in the dim, orange, street-lit pallor of the clouds, and
slowly looked back down again till he was staring at a
point just in front of his feet.

"The ground?" he said, with evident great dissatisfac-
tion, and then was struck with a sudden thought.

"Frogs?" he said, wobbling his gaze up to meet Dirk's
rather bewildered one. "I used to like . . . frogs," he said,
and left his gaze sitting on Dirk as if that was all he had
to say, and the rest was entirely up to Dirk now.

Dirk was completely flummoxed. He longed for the
times when life had been easy, life had been carefree, the
great times he'd had with a mere homicidal eagle, which
seemed now to be such an easygoing and amiable companion. Aerial attack he could cope with, but not this nameless roaring guilt that came howling at him out of
nowhere.

"What do you want?" he said in a strangled voice.

"Just a fag, mate," said the tramp, "or something for a
cup of tea."

Dirk pressed a pound coin into the man's hand and lunged off down the street in a panic, passing, twenty yards farther on, a builder's skip from which the shape of his old fridge loomed at him menacingly.

24

♦

As Kate came down the steps from her house she noticed that the temperature had dropped considerably. The clouds sat heavily on the land and loured at it. Thor set off briskly in the direction of the park, and Kate trotted along in his wake.

As he strode along, an extraordinary figure on the streets of Primrose Hill, Kate could not help but notice that he had been right. They passed three different people on the way, and she saw distinctly how their eyes avoided looking at him, even as they had to make allowance for his great bulk as he passed them. He was not invisible, far from it. He simply didn't fit.

The park was closed for the night, but Thor leaped quickly over the spiked railings and then lifted her over in turn as lightly as if she had been a bunch of flowers.

The grass was damp and mushy, but still worked its magic on city feet. Kate did what she always did when entering the park, which was to bob down and put the flats of her hands down on the ground for a moment. She had never quite worked out why she did this, and often she would adjust a shoe or pick up a piece of litter as a pretext for the movement, but all she really wanted was to feel the grass and the wet earth on her palms.

The park from this viewpoint was simply a dark shoulder that rose up before them, obscuring itself. They mounted the hill and stood on the top of it, looking over the darkness of the rest of the park to where it shaded off into the hazy light of the heart of London which lay to the south. Ugly towers and blocks stuck yobbishly up out of the skyline, dominating the park, the sky and the city.

A cold, damp wind moved across the park, flicking at it from time to time like the tail of a dark and broody horse. There was an unsettled, edgy quality to it. In fact, the night sky seemed to Kate to be like a train of restless, irritable horses, their traces flapping and slapping in the wind. It also seemed to her as if the traces all radiated loosely from a single center, and that the center was very close by her. She reprimanded herself for absurd suggestibility, but nevertheless it still seemed that all the weather was gathered and circling around them, waiting on them.

Thor once more drew out his hammer and held it before him in the thoughtful and abstracted manner she had seen a few minutes before in her flat. He frowned and seemed to be picking tiny invisible pieces of dust off it. It was a little like a chimpanzee grooming its mate, or—that was it!—the comparison was extraordinary, but it explained why she had tensed herself so watchfully when last he had done it. It was like Jimmy Connors minutely adjusting the strings of his racquet before preparing to serve.

Thor looked up sharply once again, drew his arm back, turned fully once, twice, three times, twisting his heels heavily in the mud, and then hurled his hammer with astonishing force up to the heavens.

It vanished almost instantly into the murky haze of the sky. Damp flashes sparked deep within the clouds, tracking its path in a long parabola through the night. At the farthest extent of the parabola it swung down out of the clouds, a distant tiny pinpoint, moving slowly now, gathering and redirecting its momentum for the return flight. Kate watched, breathless, as the speck crept behind the dome of Saint Paul's. It then seemed almost as if it had halted altogether, hanging silently and improbably in the air, before gradually beginning to increase microscopically in size as it accelerated back toward them.

Then, as it returned, it swung aside in its path, no longer describing a simple parabola, but following instead a new path that seemed to lie along the perimeter of a gigantic Möbius strip, which took it around the other side of the Telecom Tower. Then suddenly it was swinging back in a path directly toward them, hurtling out of the night with impossible weight and speed like a piston in a shaft of light. Kate swayed and nearly dropped in a dead faint out of its path, when Thor stepped forward and caught it with a grunt.

The jolt of it sent a single heavy shudder down into the earth, and then the thing was resting quietly in Thor's grip. His arm quivered slightly and was still.

Kate felt quite dizzy. She didn't know exactly what it was that had just happened, but she felt pretty damn certain that it was the sort of experience that her mother would not have approved of on a first date.

"Is this all part of what we have to do to go to Asgard?" she said. "Or are you just fooling around?"

"We will go to Asgard . . . now," he said.

At that moment he raised his hand as if to pluck an apple, but instead of plucking he made a tiny, sharp turning movement. The effect was as if he had twisted the entire world through a billionth part of a billionth part of a degree. Everything shifted, was for a moment minutely out of focus, and then snapped back again as a suddenly different world.

This world was a much darker one and colder still.

A bitter, putrid wind blew sharply, and made every breath gag in the throat. The ground beneath their feet was no longer the soft muddy grass of the hill, but a foul-smelling, oozing slush. Darkness lay over all the horizon with a few small exceptional fires dotted here and there in the distance, and one great blaze of light about a mile and a half away to the southeast.

Here, great fantastical towers stabbed at the night; huge pinnacles and turrets flickered in the firelight that surged from a thousand windows. It was an edifice that mocked reason, ridiculed reality and jeered wildly at the night.

"My father's palace," said Thor, "the Great Hall of Valhalla, where we must go."

It was just on the tip of Kate's tongue to say that something about the place was oddly familiar when the sound of horses' hooves pounding through the mud came to them on the wind. At a distance, between where they stood and the Great Hall of Valhalla, a small number of flickering torches could be seen jolting toward them.

Thor once more studied the head of his hammer with interest, brushed it with his forefinger and rubbed it with his thumb. Then slowly he looked up, again he twisted around once, then twice and a third time, and then hurled the missile into the sky. This time, however, he continued to hold onto its shaft with his right hand, while with his left he held Kate's waist in his grasp.

25

◆

Cigarettes clearly intended to make themselves a major problem for Dirk tonight.

For most of the day, except for when he'd woken up, and except for again shortly after he'd woken up, and except for when he had just encountered the revolving head of Geoffrey Anstey, which was understandable, and also except for when he'd been in the pub with Kate, he had had absolutely no cigarettes at all.

Not one. They were out of his life, foresworn utterly.

He didn't need them. He could do without them. They merely nagged at him like mad and made his life a living hell, but he decided he could handle that.

Now, however, just when he had suddenly decided, coolly, rationally, as a clear, straightforward decision rather than merely a feeble surrender to craving, that he would, after all, have a cigarette, could he find one? He could not.

The pubs, by this stage of the night, were well closed. The late night corner shop obviously meant something different by "late night" than Dirk did, and though Dirk was certain that he could convince the proprietor of the rightness of his case through sheer linguistic and syllogistic bravado, the wretched man wasn't there to undergo it.

A mile away there was a twenty-four-hour filling station, but it turned out just to have sustained an armed robbery. The plate glass was shattered and crazed around a tiny hole, police were swarming over the place. The attendant was apparently not badly injured, but he was still losing blood from a wound in his arm, having hysterics and being treated for shock, and no one would sell Dirk any cigarettes. They simply weren't in the mood.

"You could buy cigarettes in the blitz," protested Dirk. "People took a pride in it. Even with the bombs falling and the whole city ablaze you could still get served. Some poor fellow, just lost two daughters and a leg, would still say 'Plain or filter-tipped?' if you asked him."

"I expect you would, too," muttered a white-faced young policeman.

"It was the spirit of the age," said Dirk.

"Bug off," said the policeman.

And that, thought Dirk to himself, was the spirit of

this. He retreated, miffed, and decided to prowl the streets with his hands in his pockets for a while.

Camden Passage. Antique clocks. Antique clothes. No cigarettes.

Upper Street. Antique buildings being ripped apart. No sign of cigarette shops being put up in their place.

Chapel Market, desolate at night. Wet litter wildly flapping. Cardboard boxes, egg boxes, paper bags and cigarette packets—empty ones.

Pentonville Road. Grim concrete monoliths, eying the new spaces in Upper Street where they hoped to spawn their horrid progeny.

King's Cross station. They must have cigarettes, for heaven's sake. Dirk hurried on down toward it.

The old frontage to the station reared up above the area, a great yellow brick wall with a clock tower and two huge arches fronting the two great train sheds behind. In front of this lay the one-story modern concourse already far shabbier than the building, a hundred years its senior, which it obscured and generally messed up. Dirk imagined that when the designs for the modern concourse had been drawn up the architects had explained that it entered into an exciting and challenging dialogue with the older building.

King's Cross is an area where terrible things happen to people, to buildings, to cars, to trains, usually while you wait, and if you weren't careful you could easily end up involved in a piece of exciting and challenging dialogue yourself. You could have a cheap car radio fitted while you waited, and if you turned your back for a couple of minutes, it would be removed while you waited as well. Other things you could have removed while you waited were your wallet, your stomach lining, your mind and your will to live. The muggers and pushers and pimps and hamburger salesmen, in no particular order, could arrange all these things for you.

But could they arrange a packet of cigarettes? thought Dirk, with a mounting sense of tension. He crossed York Way, declined a couple of surprising offers on the grounds that they did not involve cigarettes in any immediately obvious way, hurried past the closed bookshop and in through the main concourse doors, away from the life of the street and into the safer domain of British Rail.

He looked around him.

Here things seemed rather strange and he wondered why, but he only wondered this very briefly because he was also wondering if there was anywhere open selling cigarettes, and there wasn't.

He sagged forlornly. It seemed to him that he had been playing catch-up with the world all day. The morning had started in about as disastrous a way as it was possible for a morning to start, and he had never managed to get a proper grip on it since. He felt like somebody trying to ride a bolting horse, with one foot in a stirrup and the other one still bounding along hopefully on the ground behind. And now even as simple a thing as a cigarette was proving to be beyond his ability to get hold of.

He sighed and found himself a seat, or at least room, on a bench.

This was not an immediately easy thing to do. The station was more crowded than he had expected to find it at —what was it? he looked up at the clock—one o'clock in the morning. What in the name of God was he doing at King's Cross station at one o'clock in the morning, with no cigarette and no home that he could reasonably expect to get into without being hacked to death by a homicidal bird?

He decided to feel sorry for himself. That would pass the time. He looked around, and after a while the impulse to feel sorry for himself gradually subsided as he began to take in his surroundings.

What was strange about it was seeing such an immediately familiar place looking so unfamiliar. There was the ticket office, still open for ticket sales, but looking somber and beleaguered and wishing it was closed.

There was the W. H. Smith, closed for the night. No one would be needing any further newspapers or magazines tonight, except for purposes of accommodation, and old ones would do just as well for sleeping under.

The pimps and hookers, drug pushers and hamburger salesmen were all outside in the streets and in the hamburger bars. If you wanted quick sex or a dirty fix or, God help you, a hamburger, that was where you went to get it.

Here were the people that nobody wanted anything from at all. This was where they gathered for shelter until they were periodically shooed out. There was something people wanted from them, in fact—their absence. That was in hot demand, but not easily supplied. Everybody has to be somewhere.

Dirk looked from one to another of the men and women shuffling round or sitting hunched in seats or struggling to try to sleep across benches that were specifically designed to prevent them from doing exactly that.

"Got a fag, mate?"

"What? No, I'm sorry. No, I haven't got one," replied Dirk, awkwardly patting his coat pockets in embarrassment, as if to suggest the making of a search which he knew would be fruitless. He was startled to be summoned out of his reverie like this.

"Here you are, then." The old man offered him a beat-up one from a beat-up packet.

"What? Oh. Oh—thanks. Thank you." Momentarily taken aback by the offer, Dirk nevertheless accepted the cigarette gratefully, and took a light from the tip of the cigarette the old man was smoking himself.

"What you come here for then?" asked the old man—not challenging, just curious.

Dirk tried to look at him without making it seem as if he was looking him up and down. The man was wildly bereft of teeth, had startled and matted hair, and his old clothes were well mulched down around him, but the eyes which sagged out of his face were fairly calm. He wasn't expecting anything worse than he could deal with to happen to him.

"Well, just this, in fact," said Dirk, twiddling the cigarette. "Thanks. Couldn't find one anywhere."

"Oh ah," said the old man.

"Got this mad bird at home," said Dirk. "Kept attacking me."

"Oh ah," said the man, nodding resignedly.

"I mean an actual bird," said Dirk. "An eagle."

"Oh ah."

"With great wings."

"Oh ah."

"Got hold of me with one of its talons through the letter box."

"Oh ah."

Dirk wondered if it was worth pursuing the conversation much further. He lapsed into silence and looked around.

"You're lucky it didn't slash at you with its beak as well," said the old man after a while. "An eagle will do that when roused."

"It did!" said Dirk. "It did! Look, right here on my nose. That was through the letter box as well. You'd scarcely believe it! Talk about grip! Talk about reach! Look at what it did to my hand!"

He held it out for sympathy. The old man gave it an appraising look.

"Oh ah," he said at last, and retreated into his own thoughts.

Dirk drew his injured hand back.

"Know a lot about eagles, then, do you?"

The man didn't answer, but seemed instead to retreat still further.

"Lot of people here tonight," Dirk ventured again, after a while.

The man shrugged. He took a long drag on his cigarette, half-closing his eyes against the smoke.

"Is it always like this? I mean, are there always so many people here at night?"

The man merely looked down, slowly releasing the smoke from his mouth and nostrils.

Yet again, Dirk looked around. A man a few feet away, not so old-looking as Dirk's companion, but wildly deranged in his demeanor, had sat nodding hectically over a bottle of cooking brandy all this time. He slowly stopped his nodding, with difficulty screwed a cap on the bottle, and slipped it into the pocket of his ragged old coat. An old fat woman who had been fitfully browsing through the bulging black bin liner of her possessions began to twist the top of it together and fold it.

"You'd almost think that something was about to happen," said Dirk.

"Oh ah," said his companion. He put his hands on his knees, bent forward and raised himself painfully to his feet. Though he was bent and slow, and though his clothes were dirt-ridden and tattered, there was some little power and authority there in his bearing.

The air which he unsettled as he stood, which flowed out from the folds of his skin and clothes, was richly pungent even to Dirk's numbed nostrils. It was a smell that never stopped coming at you—just as Dirk thought it must have peaked, so it struck on upward with renewed frenzy till Dirk thought that his very brain would vaporize.

He tried not to choke, indeed, he tried to smile courteously without allowing his eyes to run, as the man turned to him and said, "Infuse some blossom of the bitter orange. Add some sprinklings of sage while it is still warm. This is very good for eagle wounds. There are those who will add apricot and almond oil and even, the heavens defend us, sedra. But then there are always those that will overdo things. And sometimes we have need of them. Oh ah."

With that he turned away once more and joined the growing stream of pathetic, hunched and abused bodies that were heading for the front exit from the station. In all about two, maybe three, dozen were leaving. Each seemed to be leaving separately, each for his or her entirely independent reasons, and not following too fast the one upon the other, and yet it was not hard to tell, for anyone who cared to watch these people that no one cared to watch or see, that they were leaving together and in a stream.

Dirk carefully nursed his cigarette for a minute or so and watched them intently as one by one they left. Once he was certain that there were no more to go, and that the last two or three of them were at the door, he dropped the cigarette and ground it out with his heel. Then he noticed that the old man had left behind his crumpled cigarette packet. Dirk looked inside and saw that there were still two bedraggled cigarettes left. He pocketed it, stood up, and quietly followed at a distance that he thought was properly respectful.

Outside on the Euston Road the night air was grumbling and unsettled. He loitered idly by the doorway, watching which way they went—to the west. He took one of the cigarettes out and lit it and then idled off westward himself, around the taxi rank and toward Saint Pancras Street.

On the west side of Saint Pancras Street, just a few yards north of the Euston Road, a flight of steps leads up to the forecourt of the old Midland Grand Hotel, the huge, dark Gothic fantasy of a building which stands, empty and desolate, across the front of Saint Pancras railway station.

Over the top of the steps, picked out in gold letters on wrought ironwork, stands the name of the station. Taking his time, Dirk followed the last of the band of old tramps and derelicts up these steps, which emerged just to the side of a small, squat, brick building which was used as a car park. To the right, the great dark hulk of the old hotel spread off into the night, its roof line a vast assortment of wild turrets, gnarled spires and pinnacles which seemed to prod at and goad the night sky.

High in the dim darkness, silent stone figures stood guard behind long shields, grouped around pilasters behind wrought-iron railings. Carved dragons crouched gaping at the sky as Dirk Gently, in his flapping leather coat, approached the great iron portals which led to the hotel, and to the great vaulted train shed of Saint Pancras station. Stone figures of winged dogs crouched down from the top of pillars.

Here, in the bridged area between the hotel entrance

and the station booking hall, was parked a large un-marked gray Mercedes van. A quick glance at the front of it was enough to tell Dirk that it was the same one which had nearly forced him off the road several hours earlier in the Cotswolds.

Dirk walked into the booking hall, a large space with great paneled walls along which were spaced fat marble columns in the form of torch holders.

At this time of night the ticket office was closed—trains do not run all night from Saint Pancras—and beyond it the vast chamber of the station itself, the great Victorian train shed, was shrouded in darkness and shadow.

Dirk stood quietly secluded in the entrance to the book-ing hall and watched as the old tramps and bag ladies, who had entered the station by the main entrance from the forecourt, mingled together in the dimness. There were now many more than two dozen of them, perhaps as many as a hundred, and there seemed to be about them an air of repressed excitement and tension.

As they moved about, it seemed to Dirk after a while that, though he had been surprised at how many of them there had been when he first arrived, there seemed now to be fewer and fewer of them. He peered into the gloom trying to make out what was happening. He detached himself from his seclusion in the entrance to the booking hall and entered the main vault, but kept himself never-theless as close to the side wall as possible as he ventured in toward them.

There were definitely fewer still of them now, a mere handful left. He had a distinct sense of people slipping away into the shadows and not reemerging from them.

He frowned at them.

The shadows were deep but they weren't that deep. He began to hurry forward, and quickly threw all caution aside to reach the small remaining group. But by the time he reached the center of the concourse where they had been gathered there were none remaining at all, and he was left whirling around in confusion in the middle of the great, dark, empty railway station.

26

◆

The only thing which prevented Kate from screaming was the sheer pressure of air rushing into her lungs as she hurtled into the sky.

When, a few seconds later, the blinding acceleration eased a little, she found she was gulping and choking, her eyes were stinging and streaming to the extent that she could hardly see, and there was hardly a muscle in her body which wasn't gibbering with shock as waves of air pummeled past her, tearing at her hair and clothes and making her knees, knuckles and teeth batter at each other.

She had to struggle with herself to suppress her urge to struggle. On the one hand she absolutely certainly did not want to be let go of. Insofar as she had any understanding at all of what was happening to her she knew that she did not want to be let go of. On the other hand the physical shock of it was facing some stiff competition from her sheer affronted rage at being suddenly hauled into the sky without warning. The result of this was that she struggled rather feebly and was angry at herself for doing so. She ended up clinging to Thor's arm in the most abject and undignified way.

The night was dark, and the blessing of this, she supposed, was that she could not see the ground. The lights she had seen dotted here and there in the distance now swung sickeningly away beneath her, but her instincts would not identify them as representing ground. Already the flickering beacons which shone from the insanely turreted building she had glimpsed seconds before this outrage occurred were swaying away behind her now at an increasing distance.

They were still ascending.

She could not struggle, she could not speak. She could probably, if she tried, bite the stupid brute's arm, but she contented herself with the idea of this rather than the actual deed.

The air was bad and rasped in her lungs. Her nose and eyes were streaming, and this made it impossible for her to look forward. When she did try it, just once, she caught a momentary blurred glimpse of the head of the hammer streaking out through the dark air ahead of them, of Thor's arm grasping its stunted handle and being pulled forward by it. His other arm was gripped around her waist. The strength of him defied her imagination but did not make her any the less angry.

She got the feeling that they were now skimming along just beneath the clouds. Every now and then they would be buffeted by damp clamminess, and breathing would become yet harder and more noxious. The wet air tasted bitter and deadly cold, and her streaming wet hair lashed and slammed about her face.

She decided that the cold was definitely going to kill her, and after a while was convinced that she was beginning to lose consciousness. In fact she realized she was actually trying to lose consciousness but she couldn't. Time slipped into a grayness though, and she was less aware of how much of it was passing.

At last she began to sense that they were slowing and that they were beginning to curve back downward. This precipitated fresh waves of nausea and disorientation in her, and she felt that her stomach was being slowly turned through a mangle.

The air was, if anything, getting worse. It smelled worse, tasted more acrid and seemed to be getting a great deal more turbulent. They were definitely slowing now, and the going was becoming more and more difficult. The hammer was clearly pointing downward now, and finding its way along rather than surging ahead.

Down still farther they went, battling through the thickening clouds that swirled around them till it seemed that they must now reach all the way down to the ground.

Their speed had dropped to the point where Kate felt able to look ahead now, though the acridity of the air was such that she was only able to manage a very brief glance. In the moment that she glanced, Thor released the hammer. She couldn't believe it. He released it only for a fraction of a second, just to change his grip on the thing, so that they were now hanging from the shaft as it flew slowly forward, rather than being pulled along by it. As he redistributed his weight into this new posture he hoisted Kate firmly upward as if pulling up a sock. Down they went, and down farther and farther.

There was now a roaring, crashing sound borne in on them by the wind from up ahead, and suddenly Thor was running, leaping over rocky, sandy scrubland, dancing through the knotted tussocks, and finally pounding and drumming his feet to a halt.

They stood still at last, swaying, but the ground on which they stood was solid.

Kate bent over to catch her breath. She then pulled herself up to her full height and was about to deliver a full account of her feelings concerning these events at the top of her voice, when she suddenly got an alarming sense of where she was standing.

Though the night was dark, the wind whipping at her and the pungent smell of it told her that some kind of sea was very close by. The sound of wild crashing breakers told her that in fact it was more or less beneath her, that they were standing very near to the edge of a cliff. She gripped the arm of the insufferable god who had brought her here and hoped, vainly, that it hurt him.

As her reeling senses began gradually to calm down she noticed that there was a dim light spreading away before her, and after a while she realized that this was coming off the sea.

The whole sea was glowing like an infection. It was rearing itself up in the night, lunging and thrashing in a turmoil of itself and then smashing itself to pieces in a frenzy of pain against the rocks of the coast. Sea and sky seethed at each other in a poisonous fury.

Kate watched it speechlessly, and then became aware of Thor standing at her shoulder.

"I met you at an airport," he said, his voice breaking up in the wind. "I was trying to get home to Norway by plane." He pointed out to sea. "I wanted you to see why I couldn't come this way."

"Where are we? What is this?" asked Kate fearfully.

"In your world, this is the North Sea," said Thor and turned away inland again, walking heavily and dragging his hammer behind him.

Kate pulled her wet coat close around her and hurried after him.

"Well, why didn't you just fly home the way we just did, but in, well, in our world?"

The rage in her had subsided into vague worries about vocabulary.

"I tried," responded Thor, still walking away.

"Well, what happened?"

"I don't want to talk about it."

"What on earth's the point of that?"

"I'm not going to discuss it."

Kate shuddered in exasperation. "Is this godlike behavior?" she shouted. "It bothers you so you won't talk about it?"

"Thor! Thor! Is it you?"

This last was a thin voice trailing over the wind. Kate peered into the wind. Through the darkness a lantern was bobbing toward them from behind a low rise.

"Is that you, Thor?" A little old lady came into view, holding a lantern above her head, hobbling enthusiastically. "I thought that must be your hammer I saw. Welcome!" she chirruped. "Oh, but you come in dismal times. I was just putting the pot on and thinking of having a cup of something and then perhaps killing myself, but then I said to myself, just wait a couple of days longer, Tsuliwa . . . Tsuwila . . . Swuli . . . Tsuliwaënsis—I can never pronounce my own name properly when I'm talking to myself, and it drives me hopping mad, as I'm sure you can imagine, such a bright boy as I've always maintained, never mind what those others say, so I said to myself, Tsuliwaënsis, see if anyone comes along, and if they don't, well, then might be a good time to think about killing myself. And look! Now here you are! Oh, but you are welcome, welcome! And I see you've brought a little friend. Are you going to introduce me? Hello, my dear, hello! My name's Tsuliwaënsis and I won't be at all offended if you stutter."

"I . . . I'm, er, Kate," said Kate, totally flummoxed.

"Yes, well I'm sure that will be all right," said the old woman sharply. "Anyway, come along if you're coming. If you're going to hang around out here all night I may as well just get straight on with killing myself now and let you get your own tea when you're quite ready. Come along!"

She hurried on ahead, and in a very few yards they reached a terrible kind of ramshackle structure of wood and mud which looked as if it had become unaccountably stuck while halfway through collapsing. Kate glanced at Thor, hoping to read some kind of reaction from him to give her a bearing on the situation, but he was occupied with his own thoughts and was clearly not about to share them. There seemed to her to be a difference in the way he moved, though. In the brief experience she had of him he seemed constantly to be struggling with some internal and constrained anger, and this, she felt, had lifted. Not gone away, just lifted. He stood aside to allow her to enter Tsuliwaënsis's shack, and brusquely gestured her to go in. He followed, ducking absurdly, a few seconds later, having paused for a moment outside to survey what little could be seen of the surrounding landscape.

Inside was tiny. A few boards with straw for a bed, a simmering pot hung over a fire, and a box tucked away in the corner for sitting on.

"And this is the knife I was thinking of using, you see," said Tsuliwaënsis, fussing around. "Just been sharpening it up nicely, you see. It comes up very nice if you get a nice sweeping action with the stone, and I was thinking here would be a good place, you see? Here on the wall, I can stick the handle in this crack so it's held nice and firm, and then just go *fling!* And fling myself at it. *Fling!* You see? I wonder, should it be a little lower, what do you think, my dear? Know about these things, do you?"

Kate explained that she did not, and managed to sound reasonably calm about it.

"Tsuliwaënsis," said Thor, "we have come not to stay but to . . . Tsuli—please put the knife down."

Tsuliwaënsis was standing looking up at them quite chirpily, but she was also holding the knife, with its great heavy sweeping blade poised over her own left wrist.

"Don't mind me, dears," she said, "I'm quite comfortable. I can just pop off any time I'm ready. Happy to. These times are not to live in. Oh, no. You go off and be happy. I won't disturb your happiness with the sound of me screaming. I'll hardly make a sound with the knife as you go." She stood quivering and challenging.

Carefully, almost gently, Thor reached out and drew the knife away and out of her shaking hand. The old woman seemed to crumple as it went, and all the performance faded out of her. She sat back in a heap on her box. Thor squatted down in front of her, slowly drew her to him and hugged her. She gradually seemed to come back to life and eventually pushed him away, telling him not to be so stupid, and then made a bit of a fuss of smoothing out her hopelessly ragged and dirty black dress.

When once she had composed herself properly she turned her attention to Kate and looked her up and down.

"You're a mortal, dear, aren't you?" she said at last.

"Well . . . yes," said Kate.

"I can tell it from your fancy dress. Oh, yes. Well, now you see what the world looks like from the other side, don't you, dear? What do you think then?"

Kate explained that she did not yet know what to think. Thor sat himself down on the floor and leaned his big head back against the wall, half-closing his eyes. Kate had the sense that he was preparing himself for something.

"It used to be things were not so different," continued the old woman. "Used to be lovely here, you know, all lovely. Bit of give and take between us. Terrible rows, of course, terrible fights, but really it was all lovely. Now?" She let out a long and tired sigh, and brushed a bit of nothing much off the wall.

"Oh, things are bad," she said, "things are very bad. You see things get affected by things. Our world affects your world, your world affects our world. Sometimes it is hard to know exactly what that effect is. Very often it is hard to like it, either. Most of them, these days, are difficult and bad. But our worlds are so nearly the same in so many ways. Where in your world you have a building there will be a structure here as well. Maybe it will be a small muddy hillock, or a beehive, or an abode like this one. Maybe it will be something a little grander, but it will be something. You all right, Thor, dear?"

The Thunder God closed his eyes and nodded. His elbows lay easily across his knees. The ragged strips of

Kate's nightgown bound about his left forearm were limp and wet. He idly pushed them off.

"And where there is something which is not dealt with properly in your world," the old lady prattled on, "as like as not it will emerge in ours. Nothing disappears. No guilty secret. No unspoken thought. It may be a new and mighty god in our world, or it may be just a gnat, but it will be here. I might add that these days it is more often a gnat than a new and mighty god. Oh, there are so many more gnats and fewer immortal gods than once there were."

"How can there be fewer immortals?" asked Kate. "I don't want to be pedantic about it, but—"

"Well, there's being immortal, dear, and then again there's being immortal. I mean, if I could just get this knife properly secured and then work up a really good fling, we'd soon see who was immortal and who wasn't."

"Tsuli . . ." admonished Thor, but didn't open his eyes to do it.

"One by one we're going, though. We are, Thor. You're one of the few that care. There's few enough now that haven't succumbed to alcoholism or the onx."

"What is that? Some kind of disease?" asked Kate. She was beginning to feel cross again. Having been dragged unwillingly from her flat and hurled across the whole of East Anglia on the end of a hammer, she was irritated at being abandoned to a conversation with an insanely suicidal old woman while Thor just sat and looked content with himself, leaving her to make an effort she was not in a mood to make.

"It's an affliction, dear, which only gods get. It really means that you can't take being a god any more, which is why only gods get it, you see."

"I see."

"In the final stages of it you simply lie on the ground and after a while a tree grows out of your head and then it's all over. You rejoin the earth, seep into its bowels, flow through its vital arteries, and eventually emerge as a great pure torrent of water, and as like as not get a load of chemical waste dumped into you. It's a grim business being a god nowadays, even a dead god.

"Well," she said, patting her knees. Her eyes hovered on Thor, who had opened his eyes but was only using them to stare at his own knuckles and fingertips. "Well, I hear you have an appointment tonight, Thor."

"Hmm," grunted Thor, without moving.

"I hear you've called together the Great Hall for the Challenging Hour, is that right?"

"Hmm," said Thor.

"The Challenging Hour, hmm? Well, I know that things have not been too good between you and your father for a long time. Hmm?"

Thor wasn't going to be drawn. He said nothing.

"I thought it was quite dreadful about Wales," continued Tsuliwaënsis. "Don't know why you stood for it. Of course I realize that he's your father and the All-Father, which makes it difficult. But, Odin, Odin—I've known him for so long. You know that he made a deal once to sacrifice one of his own eyes in exchange for wisdom? Of course you do, dear, you're his son, aren't you? Well, what I've always said is he should stand up and make a fuss about that particular deal, demand his eye back. Do you know what I mean by that, Thor? And that horrible Toe Rag. There's someone to be careful of, Thor, very careful indeed. Well, I expect I shall hear all about it in the morning, won't I?"

Thor slid his back up the wall and stood up. He clasped

the old woman warmly by the hands and smiled a tight smile, but said nothing. With a slight nod he gestured to Kate that they were leaving. Since leaving was what she most wanted in all the world to do, she resisted the temptation to say "Oh yeah?" and kick up a fuss about being treated like this. Meekly she bade a polite farewell to the old woman and made her way out into the murky night. Thor followed her.

She folded her arms and said, "Well? Where now? What other great social events have you got in store for me this evening?"

Thor prowled around a little, examining the ground. He pulled out his hammer and weighed it appreciatively in his hands. He peered out into the night and swung the hammer idly a couple of times. He swung himself round a couple of times, again not hard. He loosed the hammer, which bounded off into the night and split open a casually situated rock a couple of dozen yards away and then bounded back. He caught it easily, tossed it up into the air and caught it easily again.

Then he turned to her and looked her in the eye for the first time.

"Would you like to see something?" he asked.

27

♦

A gust of wind blew through the huge vaults of the empty station and nearly provoked in Dirk a great howl of frustration at the trail that had so suddenly gone cold on him. The cold moonlight draped itself through the long ranges of glass panels that extended the length of the Saint Pancras station roof.

It fell on empty rails, and illuminated them. It fell on the train-departures board, it fell on the sign which explained that today was a Blue Saver Day and illuminated them both.

Framed in the archway formed by the far end of the vaulted roof were the fantastical forms of five great gasometers, the supporting superstructures of which seemed in their adumbrations to be tangled impossibly with each other, like the hoops of an illusionist's conjuring trick. The moonlight illuminated these as well, but Dirk it did not illuminate.

He had watched upward of a hundred people or so simply vanish into thin air in a way that was completely impossible. That in itself did not give him a problem. The impossible did not bother him unduly. If it could not possibly be done, then obviously it had been done impossibly. The question was how?

He paced the area of the station which they had all vanished from and scanned everything that could be seen from every vantage point within it, looking for any clue, any anomaly, anything that might let him pass into whatever it was he had just seen a hundred people pass into as if it was nothing. He had the sense of a major party taking place in the near vicinity, to which he had not been invited. In desperation he started to spin around with his arms outstretched, then decided this was completely futile and lit a cigarette instead.

He noticed that as he had pulled out the packet, a piece of paper had fluttered from his pocket, which, once the cigarette was burning well, he stooped to retrieve.

It was nothing exciting, just the bill he had picked up from the stroppy nurse in the café. "Outrageous," he thought about each of the items in turn as he scanned down them, and was about to screw the paper up and throw it away when a thought struck him about the general layout of the document.

The items charged were listed down the left-hand side, and the actual charges down the right.

On his own bills, when he issued them, when he had a client, which was rare at the moment, and the ones he did have seemed unable to stay alive long enough to receive his bills and be outraged by them, he usually went to a little trouble about the items charged. He constructed essays, little paragraphs to describe them. He liked the client to feel that he or she was getting his or her money's worth in this respect at least.

In short, the bills he issued corresponded in layout almost exactly to the wad of papers with indecipherable runic scripts which he had been unable to make head or tail of a couple of hours previously. Was that helpful? He didn't know. If the wad was not a contract, but a bill, what might it be the bill for? What services had been performed? They must certainly have been intricate services. Or at least, intricately described services. Which professions might that apply to? It was at least something to think about. He screwed up the café bill and moved off to throw it into a bin.

As it happened, this was a fortuitous move.

It meant that he was away from the central open space of the station, and near a wall against which he could press himself inconspicuously, when he suddenly heard the sound of two pairs of feet crossing the forecourt outside.

In a few seconds they entered the main part of the station, by which time Dirk was well out of sight round the angle of a wall.

Being well out of sight worked less well for him in another respect, which was that for a while he was unable to see the owners of the feet. By the time he caught a glimpse of them, they had reached exactly the same area where a few minutes previously a small horde of people had, quietly and without fuss, vanished.

He was surprised by the red spectacles of the woman and the quietly tailored Italian suit of the man, and also the speed with which they themselves then immediately vanished.

Dirk stood speechless. The same two damn people who had been the bane of his life for the entire day (he allowed himself this slight exaggeration on the grounds of extreme provocation) had now flagrantly and deliberately disappeared in front of his eyes.

Once he was quite certain that they had absolutely definitely vanished and were not merely hiding behind each other, he ventured out once more into the mysterious space.

It was bafflingly ordinary. Ordinary tarmacadam, ordinary air, ordinary everything. And yet a quantity of people that would have kept the Bermuda triangle industry happy for an entire decade had just vanished in it within the space of five minutes.

He was deeply aggravated.

He was so deeply aggravated that he thought he would share the sense of aggravation by phoning someone up and aggravating them—as it would be almost certain to do at twenty past one in the morning.

This wasn't an entirely arbitrary thought—he was still anxious concerning the safety of the American girl, Kate Schechter, and had not been at all reassured to have been answered by her machine when last he had called. By now she should surely be at home and in bed asleep, and would be reassuringly livid to be woken by a meddling phone call at this time.

He found a couple of coins and a working telephone and dialed her number. He got her answering machine again.

It said that she had just popped out for the night to Asgard. She wasn't certain which parts of Asgard they were going to but they would probably swing by Valhalla later, if the evening was up to it. If he cared to leave a message she would deal with it in the morning if she was still alive and in the mood. There were some beeps, which rang on in Dirk's ear for seconds after he heard them.

"Oh," he said, realizing that the machine was currently busy taping him, "good heavens. Well, I thought the arrangement was that you were going to call me before doing anything impossible."

He put the phone down, his head spinning angrily. Valhalla, eh? Was that where everybody was going to tonight except him? He had a good mind to go home, go to bed and wake up in the grocery business.

Valhalla.

He looked about him once again, with the name Valhalla ringing in his ears. There was no doubt, he felt, that a space this size would make a good feasting hall for gods and dead heroes, and that the empty Midland Grand Hotel would be almost worth moving the shebang from Norway for.

He wondered if it made any difference knowing what it was you were walking into.

Nervously, tentatively, he walked across and through the space in question. Nothing happened. Oh well. He turned and stood surveying it for a moment or two while he took a couple of slow drags on the cigarette he had got from the tramp. The space didn't look any different.

He walked back through it again, this time a little less tentatively, with slow positive steps. Once again, nothing happened, but then just as he was moving out of it, at the end he half fancied that he half heard a half moment of some kind of raucous sound, like a burst of white noise on a twisted radio dial. He turned once more and headed back into the space, moving his head carefully around trying to pick up the slightest sound. For a while he didn't catch it, then suddenly there was a snatch of it that burst around him and was gone. A movement and another snatch. He moved very, very slowly and carefully. With the most slight and gentle movements, trying to catch at the sound, he moved his head around what seemed like a billionth part of a billionth part of a degree, slipped behind a molecule and was gone.

He had instantly to duck to avoid a great eagle swooping out of the vast space at him.

28

♦

It was another eagle, a different eagle. The next one was a different eagle too, and the next. The air seemed to be thick with eagles, and it was obviously impossible to enter Valhalla without getting swooped on by at least half a dozen of them. Even eagles were being swooped on by eagles.

Dirk threw his arms up over his head to fend off the wild, beating flurries, turned, tripped and fell down behind a huge table onto a floor of heavy, damp, earthy straw. His hat rolled under the table. He scrambled after it, stuffed it back firmly on his head, and slowly peered up over the table.

The hall was dark, but alive with great bonfires.

Noise and woodsmoke filled the air, and the smells of roasting pigs, roasting sheep, roasting boar, and sweat and reeking wine and singed eagle wings.

The table he was crouched behind was one of countless slabs of oak on trestles that stretched in every direction, laden with steaming hunks of dead animals, huge breads, great iron beakers slopping with wine, and candles like wax anthills. Massive sweaty figures seethed around them, on them, eating, drinking, fighting over the food, fighting in the food, fighting with the food.

A yard or so from Dirk, a warrior was standing on top of a table fighting a pig which had been roasting for six hours, and he was clearly losing, but losing with vim and spirit and being cheered on by other warriors who were dousing him down with wine from a trough.

The roof—as much of it as could be made out at this distance, and by the dark and flickering light of the bon-fires—was made of lashed-together shields.

Dirk clutched his hat, kept his head down and ran, trying to make his way toward the side of the hall. As he ran, feeling himself to be virtually invisible by reason of being completely sober and, by his own lights, normally dressed, he seemed to pass examples of every form of bodily function imaginable other than actual teeth-cleaning.

The smell, like that of the tramp in King's Cross station, who must surely be here participating, was one that never stopped coming at you. It grew and grew until it seemed that your head had to become bigger and bigger to accommodate it. The din of sword on sword, sword on shield, sword on flesh, flesh on flesh, was one that made the eardrums reel and quiver and want to cry. He was pummeled, tripped, elbowed, shoved and drenched with wine as he scurried and pushed through the wild throng, but he arrived at last at a side wall—massive slabs of wood and stone faced with sheets of stinking cowhide.

Panting, he stopped for a moment, looked back and surveyed the scene with amazement.

It was Valhalla.

Of that there could be absolutely no question. This was not something that could be mocked up by a catering company. And the whole seething, wild mass of carousing gods and warriors with their shields and fires and boars, and with their caroused-at ladies, did seem to fill a space that must be something approaching the size of Saint Pancras station. The sheer heat that rose off it all seemed as if it should suffocate the flocks of deranged eagles which thrashed through the air above them.

And maybe it was doing so. He was by no means certain that a flock of enraged eagles which thought that they might be suffocating would behave significantly differently from many of the eagles he was currently watching.

There was something he had been putting off wondering while he had fought his way through the mass, but the time had come to wonder it now.

What, he wondered, about the Draycotts?

What could the Draycotts possibly be doing here? And where, in such a melee, could the Draycotts possibly be?

He narrowed his eyes and peered into the heaving throng, trying to see if he could locate anywhere a pair of red designer spectacles or a quiet Italian suit mingling out there with the clanging breastplates and the sweaty leathers, knowing that the attempt was futile but feeling that it should be made.

No, he decided, he couldn't see them. Not, he felt, their

kind of party. Further reflections along these lines were cut short by a heavy, short-handled ax which hurtled through the air and buried itself with an astounding thud in the wall about three inches from his left ear and for a moment blotted out all thought.

When he recovered from the shock of it, and let his breath out, he thought that it was probably not something that had been thrown at him with malicious intent, but was merely warriorly high spirits. Nevertheless, he was not in a partying mood and decided to move on. He edged his way along the wall in the direction which, had this actually been Saint Pancras station rather than the hall of Valhalla, would have led to the ticket office. He didn't know what he would find there, but he reckoned that it must be different from this, which would be good.

It seemed to him that things were generally quieter here, out on the periphery.

The biggest and best of the good times seemed to be concentrated more strongly toward the middle of the hall, whereas the tables he was passing now seemed to be peopled with those who looked as if they had reached that season in their immortal lives when they preferred to contemplate the times when they used to wrestle dead pigs, and to pass appreciative comments to each other about the finer points of dead pig wrestling technique, than actually to wrestle with one again themselves just at the moment.

He overheard one remark to his companion that it was the left-handed three-fingered flat grip on the opponent's sternum that was all-important at the crucial moment of finally not quite falling over in a complete stupor, to which his companion responded with a benign "Oh ah."

Dirk stopped, looked and backtracked.

Sitting hunched in a thoughtful posture over his iron plate, and clad in heavily stained and matted furs and buckles which were, if anything, more rank and stinking than the ensemble Dirk had last encountered him in, was Dirk's companion from the concourse at King's Cross station.

Dirk wondered how to approach him. A quick backslap and a "Hey! Good party. Lot of energy," was one strategy, but Dirk didn't think it was the right one.

While he was wondering, an eagle suddenly swooped down from out of the air and, with a lot of beating and thrashing, landed on the table in front of the old man, folded its wings and advanced on him, demanding to be fed. Easily, the old man pulled a bit of meat off a bone and held it up to the great bird, which pecked it sharply but accurately out of his fingers.

Dirk thought that this was the key to a friendly approach. He leaned over the table and picked up a small hunk of meat and offered it in turn to the bird. The bird attacked him and went for his neck, forcing him to try and beat the savage creature off with his hat, but the introduction was made.

"Oh ah," said the man, shooed the eagle away, and shifted a couple of inches along the bench. Though it was not a fulsome invitation, it was at least an invitation. Dirk clambered over the bench and sat down.

"Thank you," said Dirk, puffing.

"Oh ah."

"If you remember, we—"

At that moment the most tremendous reverberating thump sounded out across Valhalla. It was the sound of a drum being beaten, but it sounded like a drum of immense proportions, as it had to be to make itself heard over the tumult of noise with which the hall was filled. The drum sounded three times, in slow and massive beats, like the heartbeat of the hall itself.

Dirk looked up to see where the sound might have come from. He noticed for the first time that at the south end of the hall, to which he had been heading, a great balcony or bridge extended across most of its width. There were some figures up there, dimly visible through the heat haze and the eagles, but Dirk had a sense that whoever was up there presided over whoever was down here.

Odin, thought Dirk. Odin the All-Father must be up on the balcony.

The sound of the revels died down quickly, though it was several seconds before the reverberations of the noise finally fell away.

When all was quiet, but expectant, a great voice rang out from the balcony and through the hall.

The voice said, "The time of the Challenging Hour is nearly at an end. The Challenging Hour has been called by the great God Thor. For the third time of asking, where is Thor?"

A murmuring throughout the hall suggested that nobody knew where Thor was and why he had not come to make his challenge.

The voice said, "This is a very grave affront to the dignity of the All-Father. If there is no challenge before the expiration of the hour, the penalty for Thor shall be correspondingly grave."

The drum beat again three times, and the consternation in the hall increased. Where was Thor?

"He's with some girl," said a voice above the rest, and there were loud shouts of laughter, and a return to the hubbub of before.

"Yes," said Dirk quietly, "I expect he probably is."

"Oh ah."

Dirk had supposed that he was talking to himself and was surprised to have elicited a response from the man, though not particularly surprised at the response that had been elicited.

"Thor called this meeting tonight?" Dirk asked him.

"Oh ah."

"Bit rude not to turn up."

"Oh ah."

"I expect everyone's a bit upset."

"Not as long as there's enough pigs to go round."

"Pigs?"

"Oh ah."

Dirk didn't immediately know how to go on from here.

"Oh ah," he said, resignedly.

"It's only Thor as really cares, you see," said the old man. "Keeps on issuing his challenge, then not being able to prove it. Can't argue. Gets all confused and angry, does something stupid, can't sort it out and gets made to do a penance. Everybody else just turns up for the pigs."

"Oh ah." Dirk was learning a whole new conversational technique and was astonished at how successful it was. He regarded the man with a newfound respect.

"Do you know how many stones there are in Wales?" asked the man suddenly.

"Oh ah," said Dirk warily. He didn't know this joke.

"Nor do I. He won't tell anybody. Says count 'em yourself and goes off in a sulk."

"Oh ah." He didn't think it was a very good joke.

"So this time he hasn't even turned up. Can't say I blame him. But I'm sorry, because I think he might be right."

"Oh ah."

The man lapsed into silence.

Dirk waited.

"Oh ah," he said again, hopefully.

Nothing.

"So, er," said Dirk, going for a cautious prompt, "you think he might be right, eh?"

"Oh ah."

"So. Old Thor might be right, eh? That's the story," said Dirk.

"Oh ah."

"In what way," said Dirk, running out of patience at last, "do you think he might be right?"

"Oh, every way."

"Oh ah," said Dirk, defeated.

"It's no secret that the gods have fallen on hard times," said the old man grimly. "That's clear for all to see, even for the ones who only care about the pigs, which is most of 'em. And when you feel you're not needed any more it can be hard to think beyond the next pig, even if you used to have the whole world there with you. Everyone just accepts it as inevitable. Everyone except Thor, that is. And now he's given up. Hasn't even bothered to turn up and break a pig with us. Given up his challenge. Oh ah."

"Oh ah," said Dirk.

"Oh ah."

"So, er, Thor's challenge then," said Dirk tentatively.

"Oh ah."

"What was it?"

"Oh ah."

Dirk lost his patience entirely and rounded on the man.

"What was Thor's challenge to Odin?" he insisted angrily.

The man looked round at him in slow surprise, looked him up and down with his big sagging eyes.

"You're a mortal, aren't you?"

"Yes," said Dirk testily, "I'm a mortal. Of course I'm a mortal. What has being a mortal got to do with it?"

"How did you get here?"

"I followed you." He pulled the screwed-up, empty cigarette packet out of his pocket and put it on the table. "Thanks," he said, "I owe you."

It was a pretty feeble type of apology, he thought, but it was the best he could manage.

"Oh ah." The man looked away.

"What was Thor's challenge to Odin?" said Dirk, trying hard to keep the impatience out of his voice this time.

"What does it matter to you?" the old immortal said bitterly. "You're a mortal. Why should you care? You've got what you want out of it, you and your kind, for what little it's now worth."

"Got what we want out of what?"

"The deal," said the old immortal. "The contract that Thor claims Odin has entered into."

"Contract?" said Dirk. "What contract?"

The man's face filled with an expression of slow anger. The bonfires of Valhalla danced deeply in his eyes as he looked at Dirk.

"The sale," he said darkly, "of an immortal soul."

"What?" said Dirk. He had already considered this idea and discounted it. "You mean a man has sold his soul to him? What man? It doesn't make sense."

"No," said the man, "that wouldn't make sense at all. I said an immortal soul. Thor says that Odin has sold his soul to Man."

Dirk stared at him with horror and then slowly raised his eyes to the balcony. Something was happening there. The great drum beat out again, and the hall of Valhalla began to hush itself once more. But a second or third drumbeat failed to come. Something unexpected seemed to have occurred, and the figures on the balcony were moving in some confusion. The Challenging Hour was just expiring, but a challenge of some kind seemed to have arrived.

Dirk beat his palms to his forehead and swayed where he sat as all kinds of realizations finally dawned on him.

"Not to Man," he said, "but to *a* man, and *a* woman. A lawyer and an advertiser. I said it was all her fault the moment I saw her. I didn't realize I might actually be right." He rounded on his companion urgently. "I have to get up there," he said, "for God's sake, help me."

29

◆

"O . . . ddddiiiiiiinnnnnn!!!!!"

Thor let out a bellow of rage which made the sky shake. The heavy clouds let out a surprised grunt of thunder at the sheer volume of air that moved beneath them. Kate started back, white with fear and shock, with her ears ringing.

"Toe *Rag*!!!!!!"

He hurled his hammer to the ground right at his very feet with both hands. He hurled it this short distance with such astounding force that it hit and rebounded into the air up to about a hundred feet.

"Ggggrrrraaaaaaaaah!!!!!!" With an immense explosion of air from his lungs he hurled himself up into the air after it, caught it just as it was beginning to drop, and hurled it straight back down at the ground again, catching it again as it bounded back up, twisting violently around in midair and hurling it with all the force he could muster out to sea before falling to the ground himself on his back, and pounding the earth with his ankles, elbows and fists in an incredible tattoo of rage.

The hammer shot out over the sea on a very low trajectory. The head went down into the water and planed through it at a constant depth of about six inches. A sharp ripple opened slowly but easily across its surface, extending eventually to about a mile as the hammer sliced its way through it like a surgeon's knife. The inner walls of the ripple deepened smoothly in its wake, falling away from the sheer force of the hammer, till a vast valley had opened in the face of the sea. The walls of the valley wobbled and swayed uncertainly, then folded up and crashed together in crazed and foaming tumult. The hammer lifted its head and swung up high into the air. Thor leaped to his feet and watched it, still pounding his feet on the ground like a boxer, but like a boxer who was perhaps about to precipitate a major earthquake. When the hammer reached the top of its trajectory, Thor hurled his fist downward like a conductor, and the hammer hurtled down into the crashing mass of sea.

That seemed to calm the sea for a moment in the same way that a smack in the face will calm a hysteric. The moment passed. An immense column of water erupted out of the smack, and seconds later the hammer exploded upward out of its center, pulling another huge column of water up from the middle of the first one.

The hammer somersaulted at the top of its rise, turned, spun, and rushed back to its owner like a wildly over-excited puppy. Thor caught at it, but instead of stopping it he allowed it to carry him backward, and together they tumbled back through the rocks for about a hundred yards and scuffled to a halt in some soft earth.

Instantly Thor was back on his feet again. He turned round and round, bounding from one leg to the other with strides of nearly ten feet, swinging the hammer around him at arm's length. When he released it again it raced out to sea once more, but this time it tore around the surface in a giant semicircle, causing the sea to rear up around its circumference to form for a moment a gigantic amphitheater of water. When it fell forward it crashed like a tidal wave, ran forward and threw itself, enraged, against the short wall of the cliff.

The hammer returned to Thor, who threw it off again instantly in a great overarm. It flew into a rock, hitting off a fat angry spark. It bounded off farther and hit a spark off another rock, and another. Thor threw himself forward onto his knees, and with each rock the hammer hit he pounded the ground with his fist to make the rock rise to meet the hammer. Spark after spark erupted from the rocks. The hammer hit each successive one harder and harder, until one spark provoked a warning lick of lightning from the clouds.

And then the sky began to move, slowly, like a great angry animal uncoiling in its lair. The pounding sparks flew faster and heavier from the hammer, more lightning licks arced down to meet them from the sky, and the whole earth was beginning to tremble in something very like fearful excitement.

Thor hauled his elbows up above his head and then thrust them hard down with another ringing bellow at the sky.

"O . . . ddddiiiiiiinnnnnn!!!!!"

The sky seemed about to crack open.

"Toe Raaaaagggggggg!!!!!!!!"

Thor threw himself into the ground, heaving aside about two skipsful of rocky earth. He shook with expanding rage. With a deep groan, the whole of the side of the cliff began slowly to lean forward into the sea as he pushed and shook. In a few seconds more it tumbled heavily into the seething torment beneath it as Thor clambered back, seized a rock the size of a grand piano and held it above his head.

Everything seemed still for a fleeting moment.

Thor hurled the rock into the sea.

He regained his hammer.

"O . . . !" he bellowed.

" . . . Dddddddddinnnnnnnnnn!!!!!!!!!!"

His hammer cracked down.

A torrent of water erupted from the ground, and the sky exploded. Lightning flickered down like a white wall of light for miles along the coast in either direction. Thunder roared like colliding worlds and the clouds vomited rain that shattered the ground. Thor stood exulting in the torrent.

A few minutes later the violence abated. A strong and steady rain continued to fall. The clouds were cleansing themselves and the weak rays of the early morning light began to find their way through the thinning cover.

Thor trudged back up from where he had been standing, slapping and washing the mud from his hands. He caught at his hammer when it flew to him.

He found Kate standing watching him, shivering with astonishment, fear and fury.

"What was *that* all about?" she yelled at him.

"I just needed to be able to lose my temper properly," he said. When this didn't seem to satisfy her he added, "A god can show off once in a while, can't he?"

The huddled figure of Tsuliwaënsis came hurrying out through the rain toward them.

"You're a noisy boy, Thor," she scolded. "A noisy boy."

But Thor was gone. When they looked, they guessed that he must be the tiny speck hurtling northward through the clearing sky.

30

◆

Cynthia Draycott peered over the balcony at the scene below them with distaste. Valhalla was back in full swing.

"I hate this," she said. "I don't want this going on in my life."

"You don't have to, my darling," said Clive Draycott quietly from behind her, with his hands on her shoulders. "It's all going to be taken care of right now, and it's going to work out just fine. Couldn't be better, in fact. It's just what we wanted. You know, you look fantastic in those glasses. They really suit you. I mean really. They're *very* chic."

"Clive, it was meant to have been taken care of originally. The whole point was that we weren't to be troubled, we could just do it, deal with it, and forget about it. That was the whole point. I've put up with enough shit in my life. I just wanted it to be good, one hundred percent. I don't want all this."

"Exactly. And that's why this is so perfect for us. So perfect. Clear breach of contract. We get everything we wanted now, and we're released from all obligations. Perfecto. We come out of it smelling of roses, and we have a life that is just one hundred percent good. One hundred percent. And clean. Just exactly as you wanted it. Really, it couldn't be better for us. Trust me."

Cynthia Draycott hugged herself irritably.

"So what about this new . . . person? Something else we have to deal with."

"It'll be so easy. *So* easy. Listen, this is nothing. We either cut him in to it, or we cut him *right* out. It'll be taken care of before we leave here. We'll buy him something. A new coat. Maybe we'll have to buy him a new house. Know what that'll cost us?" He gave a charming laugh. "It's nothing. You won't ever even need to think about it. You won't ever even need to think about not thinking about it. It's . . . that . . . easy. OK?"

"Hm."

"OK. I'll be right back."

He turned and headed back into the antechamber of the hall of the All-Father, smiling all the way.

"So, Mr.—" he made a show of looking at the card again —"Gently. You want to act for these people, do you?"

"These immortal gods," said Dirk.

"OK, gods," said Draycott. "That's fine. Perhaps you'll

do a better job than the manic little hustler I had to deal with first time out. You know, he's really quite a little character, our Mr. Rag, Mr. *Rag*. You know, that guy was really quite amazing. He did everything he could, tried every oldest trick in the book to freak me out, and give me the runaround. You know how I deal with people like that? Simple. I ignore it. I just . . . ignore it. If he wants to play around and threaten and screech, and shovel in five hundred and seventeen subclauses that he thinks he's going to catch me out on, that's OK. He's just taking up time, but so what? I've got time. I've got plenty of time for people like Mr. Rag. Because you know what the really crazy thing is? You know what's *really* crazy? The guy cannot draw up an actual contract to save his life. Really. To save . . . his . . . life. And I tell you something, that's fine by me. He can thrash around and spit all he likes—when he gets tired I just reel him in. Listen. I draw up contracts in the record business. These guys are just minnows by comparison. They're primitive savages. You've met them. You've dealt with them. They're primitive savages. Well, aren't they? Like the Red Indians. They don't even know what they've got. You know, these people are lucky they didn't meet some real shark. I mean it. You know what America cost? You know what the whole United States of America actually *cost?* You don't, and neither do I. And shall I tell you why? The sum is so negligible that someone could tell us what it was and two minutes later we would have forgotten. It would have gone clean out of our minds.

"Now, compared with that, let me tell you, I am *providing*. I am *really* providing. A private suite in the Woodshead Hospital? Lavish attention, food, sensational quantities of linen. *Sensational*. You could practically buy the United States of America at today's prices for what that's all costing. But you know what? I said, if he wants the linen, let him have the linen. Just let him have it. It's fine. The guy's earned it. He can have all the linen . . . he . . . wants. Just don't fuck with me is all.

"Now let me tell you, this guy has a nice life. A *nice* life. And I think that's what we all want, isn't it? A nice life. This guy certainly did. And he didn't know how to have it. None of these guys did. They're just kind of helpless in the modern world. It's kind of tough for them and I'm just trying to help out. Let me tell you how naive they are, and I mean *naive*.

"My wife, Cynthia, you've met her, and let me tell you, she is the best. I tell you, my relationship with Cynthia is *so good*—"

"I don't want to hear about your relationship with your wife."

"OK. That's fine. That's absolutely fine. I just think maybe it's worth you getting to know a few things. But whatever you want is fine. OK. Cynthia's in advertising. You know that. She is a senior partner in a major agency. Major. They did some big campaign, really big, a few years back in which some actor is playing a god in this commercial. And he's endorsing something, I don't know, a soft drink, you know, tooth rot for kids.

"And Odin at this time is just a down-and-out. He's living on the streets. He simply can't get anything together because he's just not adapted for this world. All that power, but he doesn't know how to make it work for him here, today. Now here's the crazy part.

"Odin sees this commercial on the television and he thinks to himself, 'Hey, I could do that, I'm a god.' He thinks maybe he could get paid for being in a commercial. And you know what that would be. Pays even less than the United States of America cost, you follow me? Think about it. Odin, the chief and fount of all the power of all of the Norse gods, *thinks he might be able to get paid for being in a television commercial to sell soft drinks.*

"And this guy, this *god,* literally goes out and tries to find someone who'll let him in a TV commercial. *Pathetically* naive. But also greedy—let's not forget greedy.

"Anyway, he happens to come to Cynthia's attention. She's just a lowly account executive at the time, doesn't pay any attention, thinks he's just a wacko, but then she gets kind of fascinated by how odd he is, and I get to see him. And you know what? It dawns on us he's for real. The guy is for real. A real actual god with the whole panoply of divine powers. And not only a god, but like, the main one. The one all the others depend on for their power. And he wants to be in a commercial. Let's just say the word again, shall we? A *commercial.*

"The idea was dumbfounding. Didn't the guy know what he had? Didn't he realize what his power could get him?

"Apparently not. I have to tell you, this was the most astounding moment in our lives. A . . . stoun . . . ding. Let me tell you, Cynthia and I have always known that we were, well, special people, and that something special would happen to us, and here it was. Something special.

"But look. We're not greedy. We don't want all that power, all that wealth. And I mean, we're looking at the world here. The whole . . . fucking . . . world. We could own the world if we wanted to. But who wants to own the world? Think of the trouble. We don't even want huge wealth, all those lawyers and accountants to deal with, and let me tell you, *I'm* a lawyer. OK, so you can hire people to look after your lawyers and accountants for you, but who are those people going to be? Just more lawyers and accountants. And you know, we don't even want the responsibility for it all. It's too much.

"So then I have this idea. It's like you buy a big property, and then you sell off what you don't want. That way you get what you want, and a lot of other people get what they want, only they get it through you, and they feel a little obligated to you, and they remember who they got it through because they sign a piece of paper which says how obligated they feel to you. And money flows back to pay for our Mr. Odin's very, very, very expensive private medical care.

"So we don't have much, Mr. Gently. One or two modestly nice houses. One or two modestly nice cars. We have a very nice life. Very, very nice indeed. We don't need much because anything we need is always made available to us, it's taken care of. All we demanded, and it was a very reasonable demand in the circumstances, was that we didn't want to know any more about it. We take our modest requirements and we bow out. We want nothing more than absolute peace and absolute quiet, and a nice life because Cynthia's sometimes a little nervous. OK.

"And then what happens this morning? Right on our own doorstep. Pow. It's disgusting. I mean it is really a disgusting little number. And you know how it happened?

"Here's how it happened. It's our friend Mr. Rag again, and he's tried to be a clever tricky little voodoo lawyer. It's so pathetic. He has fun trying to waste my time with all his little tricks and games and runarounds, and then he tries to faze me by presenting me with a bill for his time. That's nothing. It's work creation. All lawyers do it. OK. So I say, I'll take your bill. I'll take it, I don't care what it is. You give me your bill and I'll see it's taken care of. It's OK. So he gives it to me.

"It's only later I see it's got this tricky kind of subtotal thing in it. So what? He's trying to be clever. He's given me a hot potato. Listen, the record business is full of hot potatoes. You just get them taken care of. There are always people happy to take care of things for you when they want to make their way up the ladder. If they're worthy of their place on the ladder, well, they'll get it taken care of in return. You get a hot potato, you pass it on. I passed it on. Listen, there were a lot of people who are *very* happy to get things taken care of for me. Hey, you know? It was really funny seeing how far and how fast that particular potato got passed on. That told me a lot about who was bright and who was not. But then it lands up in my back garden, and that's a penalty-clause job, I'm afraid. The Woodshead stuff is a *very* expensive little number, and I think your clients may have blown it on that particular score. We have the whip hand here. We can just cancel this whole thing. Believe me, I have everything I could *possibly* want now.

"But listen, Mr. Gently. I think you understand my position. We've been pretty frank with each other and I've felt good about that. There are certain sensitivities involved, of course, and I'm also in a position to be able to make a lot of things happen. So perhaps we can come to any one of a number of possible accommodations. Anything you want, Mr. Gently, it can be made to happen."

"Just to see you dead, Mr. Draycott," said Dirk Gently, "just to see you dead."

"Well, fuck you, too."

Dirk Gently turned and left the room and went to tell his new client that he thought they might have a problem.

31

◆

A little while later a dark-blue BMW pulled quietly away from the otherwise deserted forecourt of Saint Pancras station and moved off up the quiet streets.

Somewhat dejected, Dirk Gently put on his hat and left his newly acquired and newly relinquished client, who said that he wished to be alone now and maybe turn into a rat or something like some other people he could mention.

He closed the great doors behind him and walked slowly out on to the balcony overlooking the great vaulted hall of gods and heroes, Valhalla. He arrived just as the last few stragglers of the revels were fading away, presumably to emerge at the same moment in the great vaulted train shed of Saint Pancras station. He stayed staring for a while at the empty hall, in which the bonfires now were just fading embers.

It then took the very slightest flicker of his head for him to perform the same transition himself, and he found himself standing in a gusty and disheveled corridor of the empty Midland Grand Hotel. Out in the great dark concourse of Saint Pancras station he saw again the last stragglers from Valhalla shuffling away and out into the cold streets of London to find benches that were designed not to be slept on, and to try to sleep on them.

He sighed and tried to find his way out of the derelict hotel, a task that proved more difficult than he anticipated, as immense and as dark and as labyrinthine as it was. He found at last the great winding Gothic staircase which led all the way down to the huge arches of the entrance lobby, decorated with carvings of dragons and griffins and heavy ornamental ironwork. The main front entrance was locked, as it had been for years, and eventually Dirk found his way down a side corridor to an exit manned by a great sweaty splodge of a man who guarded it at night. He demanded to know how Dirk had gained entrance to the hotel and refused to be satisfied by any of his explanations. In the end he had simply to allow Dirk to leave, since there was little else he could do.

Dirk crossed from this entrance to the entrance into the station booking hall, and then into the station itself. For a while he simply stood there looking around, and then he left via the main station entrance and descended the steps which led down onto the Saint Pancras Road. As he emerged onto the street he was so surprised not to be instantly swooped upon by a passing eagle that he tripped and stumbled and was run over by the first of the early morning's motorcycle couriers.

32

◆

With a huge crash, Thor surged through the wall at the far end of the great hall of Valhalla and stood ready to proclaim to the assembled gods and heroes that he had finally managed to break through to Norway and had found a copy of the contract Odin had signed buried deep in the side of a mountain, but he couldn't, because they'd all gone and there was no one there.

"There's no one here," he said to Kate, releasing her from his huge grip. "They've all gone."

He slumped in disappointment.

"Wh—" said Kate.

"We'll try the old man's chambers," said Thor, and hurled his hammer up to the balcony with themselves in tow.

He stalked through the great chambers, ignoring Kate's pleas, protests and general abuse.

He wasn't there.

"He's here somewhere," said Thor angrily, trailing his hammer behind him.

"Wh—"

"We'll go through the world divide," he said, and took hold of Kate again. They flicked themselves through.

They were in a large bedroom suite in the hotel.

Litter and scraps of rotting carpet covered the floors, the windows were grimy with years of neglect. Pigeon droppings were everywhere, and the peeling paintwork made it look as if several small families of starfish had exploded on the walls.

There was an abandoned trolleybed in the middle of the floor in which an old man lay in beautifully laundered linen, weeping from his one remaining eye.

"I found the contract, you bastard," raged Thor, waving it at him. "I found the deal you did. You *sold* all our power to . . . to a lawyer and a . . . an advertiser and, and all sorts of other people. You stole our power! You couldn't steal all of mine because I'm too strong, but you kept me bewildered and confused, and made bad things happen every time I got angry. You prevented me getting back home to Norway by every method you could, because you knew I'd find *this!* You and that poison dwarf Toe Rag. You've been abusing and humiliating me for years, and—"

"Yes, yes, we know all that," said Odin.

"Well . . . good!"

"Thor—" said Kate.

"Well, I've shaken all that off now!" shouted Thor.

"Yes, I see—"

"I went somewhere I could get good and angry in peace, when I knew you'd be otherwise occupied and expecting me to be here, and I had a hell of a good shout and blew things up a bit, and I'm all right now! And I'm going to tear this up for a start!"

He ripped right through the contract, threw the pieces in the air and incinerated them with a look.

"Thor—" said Kate.

"And I'm going to put right all the things you made happen so I'd be afraid of getting angry. The poor girl at the airline check-in desk that got turned into a drink machine. Woof! Wham! She's back! The jet fighter that tried to shoot me down when I was flying to Norway! Woof! Wham! It's back! See, I'm back in control of myself!"

"My table lamp," said Kate quietly.

"And Kate's table lamp! It shall be a small kitten no more! Woof! Wham! Thor speaks and it is so! What was that noise?"

A ruddy glow was spreading across the London skyline.

"Thor, I think there's something wrong with your father."

"I should bloody well hope so. Oh. What's wrong? Father? Are you all right?"

"I have been so very, very foolish and unwise," wept Odin. "I have been so wicked and evil, and—"

"Yes, well, that's what I think, too," said Thor and sat on the end of the bed. "So what are we going to do?"

"I don't think I could live without my linen, and my

Sister Bailey, and . . . it's been so, so, so long, and I'm so, so old. Toe Rag said I should kill you, but I . . . I would rather have killed myself. Oh, Thor . . . "

"Oh," said Thor. "I see. Well. I don't know what to do now. Blast. Blast everything."

"Thor—"

"Yes, yes, what is it?"

"Thor, it's very simple what you do about your father and the Woodshead," said Kate.

"Oh, yes? What then?"

"I'll tell you on one condition."

"Oh, really? And what's that?"

"That you tell me how many stones there are in Wales."

"What!" exclaimed Thor in outrage. "Away from me! That's years of my life you're talking about!"

Kate shrugged.

"No!" said Thor. "Anything but that! Anyway," he added sullenly, "I told you."

"No you didn't."

"Yes I did. I said I lost count somewhere in Mid-Glamorgan. Well, I was hardly going to start again, was I? Think, girl, think!"

33

◆

Beating a path through the difficult territory to the northeast of Valhalla—a network of paths that seemed to lead only to other paths and then back to the first paths again for another try—went two figures, one a big, stupid, violent creature with green eyes and a scythe which hung from its belt and often seriously impeded its progress, the other a small, crazed creature who clung onto the back of the bigger one, maniacally urging him on while actually impeding his progress still further.

They attained at last a long, low, smelly building into

which they hurried, shouting for horses. The old stable master came forward, recognized them and, having heard already of their disgrace, was at first disinclined to help them on their way. The scythe flashed through the air and the stable master's head started upward in surprise· while his body took an affronted step backward, swayed uncertainly, and then, for lack of any further instructions to the contrary, keeled over backward in its own time. His head bounded into the hay.

His assailants hurriedly lashed up two horses to a cart and clattered away out of the stable yard and along the broader thoroughfare which led upward to the north.

They made rapid progress up the road for a mile, Toe Rag urging the horses on frantically with a long and cruel whip. After a few minutes, however, the horses began to slow down and to look about them uneasily. Toe Rag lashed them all the harder, but they became more anxious still, then suddenly lost all control and reared in terror, turning over the cart and tipping its occupants out on the ground, from which they instantly sprang up in a rage.

Toe Rag screamed at the terrified horses and then, out of the corner of his eye, caught sight of what had so disturbed them.

It wasn't so terrifying. It was just a large white metal box, upturned on a pile of rubbish by the roadside and rattling itself.

The horses were rearing and trying to bolt away from the big white rattling thing, but they were impossibly entangled in their traces. They were only working themselves up into a thrashing lather of panic. Toe Rag quickly realized that there would be no calming them until the box was dealt with.

"Whatever it is," he screeched at the green-eyed creature, "kill it!"

Green-eye unhooked his scythe from his belt once more and clambered up the pile of rubbish to where the box was rattling. He kicked it and it only rattled the more. He got his foot behind it and with a heavy thrust shoved it away down the heap. The big white box slithered a foot or so then turned over and toppled to the ground. It rested there for a moment and then a door, finally freed, flew open. The horses screamed in fear.

Toe Rag and his green-eyed thug approached the thing with worried curiosity, then staggered back in horror as a great and powerful new god erupted from its innards.

34

◆

The following afternoon, at a comfortable distance from all these events, set at a comfortable distance from a well-proportioned window through which the afternoon light was streaming, lay an elderly one-eyed man in a white bed. A newspaper sat like a half-collapsed tent on the floor, where it had been hurled two minutes before.

The man was awake but not glad to be. His exquisitely frail hands lay slightly curled on the pure white linen sheets and quivered very faintly.

His name was variously given as Mr. Odwin, or Wodin,

or Odin. He was—is—a god, and furthermore he was a confused and startled god.

He was confused and startled because of the report he had just been reading on the front page of the newspaper, which was that another god had been cutting loose and making a nuisance of himself. It didn't say so in so many words, of course, it merely described what had happened last night when a missing jet fighter aircraft had mysteriously erupted under full power from out of a house in North London into which it could not conceivably have been thought to have fitted. It had instantly lost its wings and gone into a screaming dive and crashed and exploded in a main road. The pilot had managed to eject during the few seconds he had had in the air, and had landed, shaken, bruised, but otherwise unharmed, and babbling about strange men with hammers flying over the North Sea.

Luckily, because of the time at which the inexplicable disaster had occurred, the roads were almost deserted, and apart from massive damage to property, the only fatalities to have occurred were the as yet unidentified occupants of a car which was thought to have been possibly a BMW and possibly blue, though because of the rather extreme nature of the accident it was rather hard to tell.

He was very, very tired and did not want to think about it, did not want to think about last night, did not want to think of anything other than linen sheets and how wonderful it was when Sister Bailey patted them down around him as she had just now, just five minutes ago, and again just ten minutes before that.

The American girl, Kate something, came into his room. He wished she would just let him sleep. She was going on about something being all fixed up. She congratulated him on having extremely high blood pressure, high cholesterol levels and a very dicky heart, as a consequence of which the hospital would be very glad to accept him as a lifelong patient in return for his entire estate. They didn't even care to know what his estate was worth, because it would clearly be sufficient to cover a stay as brief as his was likely to be.

She seemed to expect him to be pleased, so he nodded amiably, thanked her vaguely, and drifted, drifted happily off to sleep.

35

◆

The same afternoon Dirk Gently awoke, also in the hospital, suffering from mild concussion, scrapes and bruises and a broken leg. He had had the greatest difficulty in explaining, on admittance, that most of his injuries had been caused by a small boy and an eagle, and that really, being run over by a motorcycle courier was a relatively restful experience since it mostly involved lying down a lot and not being swooped on every two minutes.

He was kept under sedation—in other words, he slept —for most of the morning, suffering terrible dreams in which Toe Rag and a green-eyed, scythe-bearing giant made their escape to the northeast from Valhalla, where they were unexpectedly accosted and consumed by a newly created, immense Guilt God which had finally escaped from what looked suspiciously like an upturned refrigerator on a skip.

He was relieved to be woken at last from this by a cheery "Oh, it's you, is it? You nicked my book."

He opened his eyes and was greeted by the sight of Sally Mills, the girl he had been violently accosted by the previous day in the café, for no better reason than that he had, prior to nicking her book, nicked her coffee.

"Well, I'm glad to see you took my advice and came in to have your nose properly attended to," she said as she fussed around him. "Pretty roundabout way you seem to have taken, but you're here, and that's the main thing. You caught up with the girl you were interested in, did you? Oddly enough, you're in the very bed that she was in. If you see her again, perhaps you could give her this pizza which she arranged to have delivered before checking herself out. It's all cold now, but the courier did insist that she was very adamant it should be delivered.

"I don't mind you nicking the book, really, though. I don't know why I buy them really, they're not very good, only everyone always does, don't they? Somebody told me there's a rumor he had entered into a pact with the devil or something. I think that's nonsense, though I did hear another story about him which I much preferred. Apparently he's always having these mysterious deliveries of chickens to his hotel rooms, and no one dares to ask why or even guess what it is he wants them for, because nobody ever sees a single scrap of them again. Well, I met somebody who knows exactly what he wants them for. The somebody I met once had the job of secretly smuggling the chickens straight back out of his rooms again. What Howard Bell gets out of it is a reputation for being a very strange and demonic man, and everybody buys his books. Nice work if you can get it is what I say. Anyway, I expect you don't want to have me nattering to you all afternoon, and even if you do I've got better things to do. Sister says you'll probably be discharged this evening so you can go to your own home and sleep in your own bed, which I'm sure you'll much prefer. Anyway, hope you feel better, here's a couple of newspapers."

Dirk took the papers, glad to be left alone at last.

He first turned to see what The Great Zaganza had to say about his day. The Great Zaganza said, "You are very fat and stupid and persistently wear a ridiculous hat which you should be ashamed of."

He grunted slightly to himself about this, and turned to the horoscope in the other paper.

It said, "Today is a day to enjoy home comforts."

Yes, he thought, he would be glad to get back home. He was still strangely relieved about getting rid of his old fridge and looked forward to enjoying a new phase of fridge ownership with the spanking new model currently sitting in his kitchen at home.

There was the eagle to think about, but he would worry about that later, when he got home.

He turned to the front page to see if there was any interesting news.